COSMOPOLITAN

PHANTOM QUEEN BOOK 2 - A TEMPLE VERSE SERIES

SHAYNE SILVERS

CAMERON O'CONNELL

 ARGENTO
PUBLISHING

Shayne Silvers & Cameron O'Connell

Cosmopolitan

The Phantom Queen Diaries Book 2

A TempleVerse Series

ISBN 13: 978-1-947709-13-3

© 2018, Shayne Silvers / Argento Publishing, LLC

info@shaynesilvers.com

CONTENTS

SHAYNE AND CAMERON

Shayne Silvers, here.

Cameron O'Connell is one helluva writer, and he's worked tirelessly to merge a story into the Temple Verse that would provide a different and unique *voice*, but a complementary *tone* to my other novels. *SOME* people might say I'm hard to work with. But certainly, Cameron would never...

Hey! Pipe down over there, author monkey! Get back to your writing cave and finish the next Phantom Queen Novel!

Ahem. Now, where was I?

This is book 2 in the Phantom Queen Diaries. This series ties into the existing Temple Verse with Nate Temple and Callie Penrose. This series could also be read independently if one so chose. Then again, you, the reader, will get SO much more out of my existing books (and this series) by reading them all in tandem.

But that's not up to us. It's up to you, the reader.

What do you think? Should Quinn MacKenna be allowed to go drinking with Callie? To throw eggs at Chateau Falco while Nate's skipping about in Fae? To let this fiery, foul-mouthed, Boston redhead come play with the monsters from Missouri?

You tell us...

DON'T FORGET!

VIP's get early access to all sorts of book goodies, including signed copies, private giveaways, and advance notice of future projects. AND A FREE NOVELLA! Click the image or join here:
www.shaynesilvers.com/l/219800

FOLLOW and LIKE:

Shayne's FACEBOOK PAGE:
www.shaynesilvers.com/l/38602
Cameron's FACEBOOK PAGE:
www.shaynesilvers.com/l/209065

We respond to all messages, so don't hesitate to drop either of us a line. Not interacting with readers is the biggest travesty that most authors can make. Let us fix that.

CHAPTER 1

The blubbery lip of the brutish, hulking bridge troll in front of me quivered in frustration. He gnashed his teeth together, staring me down with jaundiced eyes. I wondered, idly, how many people he'd eaten. How many bones had he splintered and mangled over the centuries with those elephantine tusks? My opponent fidgeted, and I could sense he was about to make his move; it was there, in his tensed shoulders, half as wide as I was tall, and his twitching hands, each large enough to palm a beach ball. I waited, pinned to my chair by his beady-eyed gaze, holding my breath. Almost a month's preparation boiled down to what would happen in the next few minutes, and I couldn't afford a single distraction. The gargantuan, green-skinned monster slumped forward, snorting through his pierced snout—the rusty septum ring as large as a bracelet—and rested his elbows on the table until it creaked from the strain.

"Fold," he said, in a plodding, gravelly voice that would have done Andre the Giant justice.

I threw my hands up. "Ye can't fold, ye idgit. You're the big blind!"

Paul, the aforementioned bridge troll, studied the cards in his hand once more before nodding. "Fold." He flipped them over and slid them across the table towards the dealer. Christoff, the owner of the bar and host of this little get together, glanced at me before collecting Paul's cards and insisting everyone else return theirs. I rolled my eyes and tossed my hand on the table, face-up—pocket Aces. Paul didn't even seem to notice, but the other members of our impromptu, bi-monthly poker night certainly did; Christoff shrugged at me apologetically; the other two—our newcomers, Othello and Hemingway—barely managed to stifle their laughter.

Othello was a charming Russian hacker who'd rescued me from a debacle several weeks back that had nearly put me in the hospital. We'd been in touch regularly over that span, exchanging information and gossip in equal parts, and she was fast becoming one of my very few friends, despite the fact that she was rarely around; she and her cohort of friends spent the vast majority of their time in the Midwest, oscillating between St. Louis and Kansas City.

Both cities had experienced more than their fair share of supernatural snafus in the last several years, most of which could be classified as Biblical in proportion; some of her stories made rivers of blood and locust plagues seem dull and mild by comparison. At this rate, I wasn't interested in a Midwest layover, let alone a vacation.

I had enough drama in my life already.

Not that leaving Boston was on my agenda, anyway. Sure, Titletown came with its fair share of baggage, especially for those of us who'd grown up in some of the rougher neighborhoods. But there was something about it I loved—a brutal, vicious history which had bled into its foundations, many of which still stood. I could sense that same hard edge in myself, sometimes —that urge to provoke, to hit and get hit. I don't know if that made me crazy, but it sure as hell made me a Boston native.

Thing is, you had to be a wee bit batshit to do what I did for a living; peddling magical artifacts sounds like an entertaining gig, I'm sure, but if you think selling drugs or guns on the black market is dangerous, you've never met a hungry Bandersnatch or pissed off a Jabberwock.

I've stared down creatures out of storybooks and squared off against nightmares, and I had the scars to prove it.

Which is why, as a black magic arms dealer, I knew it paid to have people you could rely on in a pinch; you never knew when you'd end up over your head or up to your neck and need to call in favors. Maybe that's why I'd invited Othello to tag along tonight; I figured she and Christoff would get along, plus we were a man down, what with Ryan returning to Fae at the behest of the King of the Faeries.

That's right, I still believe in faeries. I do, I do.

On the other hand, I doubt I would have invited Hemingway if not for Othello's insistence. The guy creeped me out. He'd aged significantly since I first met him, although he still appeared younger than the rest of us by more than a couple of years; I didn't have the gall to tease Othello about her jailbait boyfriend—I was pretty sure she'd retaliate by stealing my identity and leaving me penniless on the street. At least he looked legal now, as opposed to the prepubescent kid I'd met a few weeks before. Lately, Hemingway reminded me a lot of Matt Dillon in *The Outsiders*, both in appearance and temperament—he came off jaded, acting like nothing in the world could surprise him. What really bothered me about him were his eyes, though—it was like he was always staring at ghosts, until he looked right at you, and then he made you feel like *you* were the ghost.

I motioned for Christoff to deal again. The older man smiled and graciously followed through, expertly tossing cards before each of us. He and Othello chattered back and forth in Russian, flicking their eyes between me and the troll. Hemingway seemed to be following the conversation with little difficulty; he even sniggered at one point. I glowered at them all as I checked my cards. The five of spades and the seven of clubs. I sighed inwardly, then put in the big blind—a blue chip that was supposed to represent money but, in this case, represented information. Othello, who sat to my right, put in the small blind after a moment's hesitation.

Turns out she'd played before, but not with chips.

I'll let you figure out what she'd used instead.

The troll peered at his cards and grinned, his pale purple gums on display. Not much of a poker face, but—as you probably noticed—Paul rarely set himself up to fail. Fortunately for me, the game was rigged so that no matter who won, I got what I wanted. Which is the only kind of game I would play, really. Paul matched my big blind with a blue chip of his own, and the others followed suit.

"Burn and turn," I told Christoff. Christoff turned the first card face down and set it aside, then turned the next three face-up: the ace of hearts, the five of clubs, and the five of diamonds. I stifled my smug expression and studied my opponents, but—other than Paul, whose broad smile had grown into something leering and grotesque—there was no telling what anyone had; Hemingway might as well have been a still-life, and Othello's cherubic grin could have meant anything, or nothing.

Ordinarily, we'd have taken turns betting, but Paul didn't seem inclined to wait. He swatted his pile of chips, spilling them forward into the center of the table, and bellowed, "All in!" Hemingway's eyebrows rose at the outburst, then he casually slid his cards over to Christoff.

Othello studied her own chips before mimicking her boyfriend's nonchalant expression. "I'll call."

Paul seemed to deflate somewhat, but his grin hadn't faded.

"Me too," I said, drawing his unwelcome attention.

The bridge troll grunted. Apparently, he hadn't expected us both to go in with him—and anything that confused Paul made him mad. I'd met plenty of men like him, but none who could yank trees out of the ground and use them as whiffle bats; the bastard still owed me for what he'd done to my poor car. Not that he had any money to speak of—Bridge Tolls in the modern era were strictly a federal form of extortion.

Paul's residence notwithstanding, he lived on the goodwill of the Faerie Chancery, a shadowy organization that represented the interests of the various Faelings who had settled in Boston over the last few centuries. I knew very little about them, although I suspected they were behind a great many of the deals I'd made in the past. Paul's relationship to the Chancery was, in fact, the primary reason I'd invited him to join us for poker night.

All part of the plan.

"Alright, Christoff, turn the rest," I insisted.

He did, burning the first, turning the second, and then repeating the process. I stared down at the cards as if they mattered, flicking my gaze from the ace of hearts to the five of clubs, five of diamonds, four of hearts, and five of hearts. But, really, I was biding my time before the big reveal; I'd lucked into a four-of-a-kind—the third-best hand in poker—early on. Paul, growing impatient, tossed his cards down on the table with a self-satisfied chortle.

He'd had pocket aces.

I grinned and turned my cards for him to see. Christoff adjusted the cards he'd turned so three suits of fives sat higher than the rest. "The full house is trumped by four-of-a-kind," he declared. I could sense Paul's confusion; he never had been very good at counting past two. A moment later, I could make out the faint crunch of the wooden table splintering beneath his grubby, waffle-sized hands as he realized he'd lost. Christoff growled in warning, which seemed to register, somehow. Paul shot Christoff an apologetic look, released the table, and began picking up the splintered wood, popping the slivers into his mouth like M&Ms. He chewed with his mouth open, snorted, and folded his arms over his extraordinarily wide chest.

"No fair," he grumbled.

"Ye can never be too sure what the cards have in store for ye, Paul, me friend," I chastised. "Ye should know that by now."

"She's right, you know," Othello quipped, holding a single card up for us to see, her grin wider than I had ever seen it.

"Oh, that's fuckin' garbage," I cursed, glaring at Christoff, who had the good grace to at least pretend he had nothing to do with the turning of the tables.

Othello slid the two and three of hearts across the table.

"The straight flush wins," Christoff declared, coughing into his hand to hide his amusement. I stared down at Othello's cards in disbelief, knowing that she'd gone all-in with absolutely nothing; she'd had no reason to think she'd win. And yet, she had.

Fucking Russians.

CHAPTER 2

*T*hankfully, winning or losing didn't impact my plan; whether I bought Paul a congratulatory drink or a conciliatory one, the end result would be the same. I pretended to be upset, pouting my lower lip, and turned to the bridge troll, who seemed to be debating whether he should toss the table in a fit of rage. I punched his arm, lightly—which was about as fun as punching a brick wall. "Hey, boyo. How about I treat ye to a drink? We losers can commiserate together."

Paul glanced down to where I'd grazed him, then blinked owlishly at me. "Drink?"

"Aye," I said. "I t'ink ye and I deserve it after that fleecin' we took." I glared at Christoff, who chuckled and rose.

"What can I get for you?" he asked, headed towards the bar.

"Get Paul a Finnish Sledgehammer," I called out. "And I'll take anythin'… except a Fifth Horseman!" I added, cringing.

I turned to the other members of the table only to find Hemingway and Othello staring at me with leery expressions. "What are ye lookin' at me like that, for?" I asked.

"Where did you hear that name?" Hemingway finally asked.

"What name? Fifth Horseman? It's a cocktail they served here a while back. A nasty fucker, to be sure. Worst hangover of me life."

It had been, too. Christoff's pop-up bar was always coming up with new

6

gimmicks and fancy cocktails. Back when Ryan—the Faeling bar manager and Faerie Chancery freelancer—had worked here, I'd visited regularly enough to appreciate the novelty drinks, not to mention the rotating bar décor. The latest makeover had transformed the pro-American "Stand for St. Louis" concept into the more seasonally appropriate "St. Paddy's Pub" model, courtesy of Christoff's new bar manager, who I'd yet to meet. I hadn't realized how many different shades of green there were in the color spectrum until I'd arrived.

Christoff's bar might as well have been decorated by a leprechaun.

Hemingway's eyes narrowed before he turned to Othello. "I didn't realize his reputation had extended this far."

"Me either. Of course, declaring himself 'King of St. Louis' isn't going to help matters," Othello replied.

Hemingway rolled his eyes. "It's easy to like the man, but I swear he makes my job harder. All of our jobs."

I raised an eyebrow. I hadn't realized Hemingway even had a job. Aside from posing as a detective when we'd first met, I hadn't seen him do anything remotely work-related. Maybe he worked for Othello? It would explain how they'd met, though I was willing to bet there was a juicier story there. I'd tried prying into the nature of her relationship with the guy once or twice, but she'd always been somewhat cagey, so I'd given up; if she wanted to fill me in one day, she would.

Othello slid her hand around the back of Hemingway's neck and played with his shaggy hair. "I'm sure it will all work out." Hemingway nodded, his eyes fluttering closed, distracted by Othello's touch. She shot me a quick wink. "Besides, how bad could it be?" she added.

Hemingway grunted. "Remember his war with the Greeks?"

Othello shuddered. "Of course."

"Pretty sure that'll seem like kids playing with sticks and stones by comparison."

"That bad?" she asked, disbelieving. "What can we do?"

"Sorry," Hemingway sighed. "I've already said too much. If I keep going, War will stop by and drag me off. And he hates the color green." Hemingway glanced at the walls dispassionately, as if the idea of an offensive color made no sense to him.

I left them to their morbid, but ultimately baffling, conversation—couples were like that, always talking in half-formed sentences that made sense to them and no one else. I headed over to the bar, where Paul was already working on his second Finnish Sledgehammer, a drink Christoff and I had invented for this very occasion. The plan was to get the bridge troll well and truly sloshed. In our experience, a drunk Paul was a chatty Paul, and I had plenty of questions I needed answered.

See, a few weeks ago the Chancery had delivered a letter to my door requesting my appearance at a hearing to discuss my role in the sudden uptick in supernatural activity in Boston. Unfortunately, the letter was vague on the details.

They could have been referring to when I had unleashed—literally—a skinwalker in a public park, or maybe the fallout from a renegade wizard bent on opening a gateway to an alternate universe, or perhaps my little altercation with the Academy's Justices—elite wizards who represented magical law enforcement in every city except Boston, where the Chancery ruled supreme.

Or, you know, all of the above.

Because all that had happened in like, a two-day span.

The problem was, I had no idea how much the Chancery knew, or what they intended to do with me once they found out. As a Freak—someone with supernatural abilities—living in Boston, I was technically playing in their backyard. While I generally understood the legal system Regulars— those average, everyday people who can't do excessively cool shit—used, the Fae were a different species altogether. The Chancery's members included beings who'd lived centuries, even millennia, and came from an alien world.

A girl had to wonder whether innocent until proven guilty even applied.

"Hello, Ruby," Paul said as I approached. He'd always called me Ruby, probably because he was too dense to remember my name, but also on account of my hair color—a bright, burnished amber. Most men commented on my height first and my hair second, but being six-feet-tall didn't amount to much next to Paul, who was at least four feet taller and twice as wide. Sometimes the nickname brought unpleasant flashbacks of driving my car into his midsection...but moving on is part of life, right? I pasted a smile on my face and took the drink Christoff poured me with a thankful nod. He and I exchanged a look, which told me all I needed to know about Paul's state of inebriation.

"So, Paul," I said, casually, "about this hearing..."

CHAPTER 3

*P*aul filled me in between gulps, feeding me everything he knew about the Chancery's legal system from a plaintiff's point-of-view. The bridge troll had plenty to say on the subject—he'd been in his fair share of trouble with the Chancery in the past; his explosive temper tantrums had landed him in hot water more than once. According to Paul, I wasn't in that much trouble, or they'd have already come and thrown me into a deep, dark hole until they felt like letting me out.

Because that's the sort of thing they did.

"Cold," he repeated, shivering. "Cold, dark hole. Open sky." He shuddered. Bridge trolls had a thing about open skies, you see—sort of like claustrophobia in reverse. Supposedly, his kind were raised from birth to believe that if they fell asleep without some sort of roof over their heads, they'd simply float away at night until they got swallowed by the morning sun.

It was a rather horrific bedtime story, but an effective deterrent in Paul's case. After each incident, the bridge troll had been forced to stay in that hole and—because he refused to sleep the entire time he was down there lest he fly away and die—he'd come away from his hearings both delirious and cowed. I kept my opinions to myself, but his story made me very wary of the Chancery's stance on cruel and unusual punishment.

The only other assurance he had for me was that, if I was in legal trouble, they'd have found me a lawyer. Since many of the Fae had trouble communicating effectively, the Chancery had mandated a lawyer be present —someone who could speak on the plaintiff's behalf. I seemed to recall Othello saying something similar when I first met her, but I'd been doped up on painkillers at the time, and most of what had happened during my brief stint among the Justices was a blur.

Come to think of it, Othello had mentioned having a friend in the Chancery, hadn't she? I left Paul in his cups, deciding to pick Othello's brain to find out what, if anything, she knew.

I found her on the other side of the room, studying a curiously ornate picture of St. Patrick tucked away in the corner of the larger bar. Hemingway was nowhere to be seen. I strolled up beside her. "Everythin' alright?" I asked.

Othello nodded, but her ever-present smile had dimmed to something sad and self-pitying. "It is difficult between us sometimes. There are things he can't tell me, and a great many things he shouldn't, but could. It's hard to know when to press and when not to. Harder still not to know if he holds back because he doesn't trust me, or because he doesn't trust himself."

"I'm not entirely sure I follow," I admitted, "but he seems to like ye. He looks at ye like ye actually exist, which is more than I can say for the rest of us."

Othello chuckled. "Like I actually exist...that's one way of saying it." She cocked her head at an angle to stare up at me. "Don't take it personally. I don't think he means to come off so..."

"Dickish?" I offered.

"Distant," she clarified, nudging me with her elbow. "You have to understand that, for him, getting to know people can be a bit of a drag."

"Well, except for ye, obviously," I quipped, winking.

"I'm not the only one who has caught his eye." Othello bumped me with her hip and wandered away from the painting.

I followed with a grimace on my face, sincerely hoping that wasn't a subtle threesome invitation. Granted, I liked Othello and had no intention of screwing up our budding friendship—I'd always been one of those girls who craved female friends but got along much better with boys—if she tried to rope me into a three way, though, our friendship would end faster than the Red Sox's playoff hopes after Damon signed with the Yankees.

Not that I was bitter or anything.

"Not in that way," Othello said, laughing at the expression on my face. "Hemingway's not really the type to stray. If anything, he's all about his commitments. What I mean is, there's something about you that seems to nag at him."

I decided not to mention that the feeling was mutual. "Well, ye can let him know that he's welcome to snoop around if he t'inks it'll help. I'm not hidin' anythin'. Not much, anyway."

Othello nodded. "Speaking of things you are or are not hiding…has the detective called yet?"

I groaned. She was talking of course, about Detective Jimmy Collins, a former friend and lover who'd tried to rescue me from that renegade wizard I mentioned earlier. He'd nearly died in the process, or—to be more accurate—he *had* died in the process. But had been brought back to life thanks to a rather elaborate ceremony involving the soul of a nine-tailed fox spirit and the intervention of a god. I'd love to say that isn't as crazy as it sounds…but I'd be lying.

I know, my life is a hot mess.

I'd expected Jimmy to touch base once he recovered from his injuries, but it'd been weeks now and he still hadn't reached out. Boston PD's manhunt for the wizard who had attacked us had hit a dead end early on, and now I had more contact with his partner—Maria Machado, a woman I staunchly disliked—than I did with him. She'd returned my gun, personally, with a subtle warning not to use it again without ample provocation. It had taken everything in me not to laugh in her adorable little face; if she knew how often I had cause to draw my gun, she might have come up with a better precondition.

I was wearing my gun tonight, secure at the small of my back in a compression holster that minimized its profile beneath my sweater. The bulge it created earned me weird looks sometimes, but I could handle weird looks if it meant the difference between life and death. I reached back to touch that gun now, sliding my fingers against the slight perforations that improved the grip—sort of like clutching a safety blanket for comfort.

"No," I said, lowering my hand. "Not a peep."

"Sorry, Quinn."

I shrugged. "What can I say? I have a t'ing for emotionally unavailable men with muscles."

Othello laughed. "I'm sure you aren't the only woman with that problem.

But I have a favor to ask, you know...since you don't have any commitments..."

I bumped her with my hip, a little harder than was necessary. "Very funny."

She giggled. "I'm serious. I have a job for you, if you're interested. It would require some travel, though."

"How much travel? And when?" I asked, a little surprised. Othello had never reached out to me in this capacity before. Ever since our initial encounter, we'd kept our careers and our friendship separate. Othello ran one of the largest tech industries in the world—a tech company which so happened to fund magical research, most of which was off-book and confidential in nature.

As a black magic arms dealer, my job was a bit haphazard in comparison; I worked freelance, taking on jobs that promised significant returns on my investment—be that money, goods, or favors. Othello—using her hacking skills to essentially dissect my life before we'd even met—knew precisely what I did for a living, and who I'd done business with. Which meant she had something specific, and probably illegal, in mind. Otherwise there were plenty of other people she could pay to do the job, on the up-and-up.

"To New York, that's all," she replied. "In the next few days. There's an item being brokered that I want. Well, not me, per se. But the person who I want it for won't dirty his hands unless it involves a book." Othello's wry expression betrayed her feelings on the subject. I wondered if it was her boss, the man who had set himself up as the "King of St. Louis."

Nate Temple.

I'd met the wizard once here in Boston, one of those freak coincidences that could be attributed to equal parts fate and utter cockup. He'd come off as a belligerent buffoon, but now I suspected he'd been putting on a show of sorts—a ridiculous mask meant to keep his real face hidden from the rest of the world.

Like Black Magic Batman.

Aside from that initial meeting and what little I'd gleaned from talking to Othello, all I knew was what I'd scrounged up on Google—newspaper articles which ranged anywhere from "Meet the Imbecilic Playboy Who Screwed St. Louis" to "Orphaned Billionaire Gives Back with School for Troubled Youth." I'd even run across rumormonger sites that had him listed as one of the world's foremost experts on the arcane and an advocate of German dungeon porn. Frankly, I was happy to avoid the man; he sounded like all sorts of drama, and I could safely say the only royalty I was interested in was the Crown that came in a purple velvet bag.

"I don't t'ink I can make that," I said, regretfully. "I've got me hearin' with the Faerie Chancery this week."

"A hearing?" Othello raised an eyebrow. "Hold on, I'll be back in a few minutes." She fetched her phone from the purse she'd left slung on the back of her chair. She attached a device to it that I didn't recognize, punched in a code, and put the phone to her ear. When she caught me looking, she waved me away. I rolled my eyes, but did as I was told; Othello hoarded her privacy like a dragon hoarded gold...before you start getting ideas, I should mention that I'd never met a dragon and knew nothing about their currency preferences. Personally, I was banking on meeting one who'd offer me half his heart and make me immortal.

This is why I can't watch nice things.

I wandered back to the bar to get another drink. Paul was already sitting on the floor, humming to himself in a discordant tune that reminded me a lot of overly aggressive punk music. I met Christoff on the opposite end.

"Did you find out what you wanted to know?" he asked.

"Aye. Or, at least, I found out as much as Paul could tell me. I really wish Ryan were here." Ryan and I had never been extremely close friends, but he'd been one of the few people I'd trusted in this city; his Chancery connections had come in handy more than once. And, although I wouldn't admit it to anyone but myself, I missed our brunches. Finding a good brunch partner was always a challenge.

"I wish this, too," Christoff said, mournfully in his stunted English.

"I'm sorry," I said. "I shouldn't have brought it up." I could tell Christoff was still pretty broken up about Ryan's abrupt departure. He and Ryan had run this bar together for as long as I'd known them, although I had no idea how long they'd actually known each other before that. Judging from the look on Christoff's face, I could tell Ryan's friendship had meant more to him than merely having a business partner.

"How did ye two meet, anyway?" I asked, my insatiable curiosity trumping propriety—nothing new there.

"He was first man I met when I come to this country. Very kind. He knew what I was right away. He knew solitary ways of bear, but became my friend anyway." He brandished a hand. Fur began to sprout over the back of his palm, spewing forth like a time lapse video of grass growing. Claws the size of steak knives emerged to rap against the bar top. Then, Christoff reached for his drink, and they were gone.

"When was this?" I asked.

Christoff stared at the ceiling in consideration. "I left Russia after first Chechen War. So, this must have been in, what, 1997?"

I did a little mental arithmetic and shook my head. "Well, that answers that question."

"Which question?"

"I wondered if Faelings age like us in the mortal world. I'd always meant to ask Ryan, but never got around to it."

Christoff huffed. "No, Ryan looked same always. Always popular with the women, too." He chuckled. "Not so popular with my wife. She was like you, always teasing him. But she only had eyes for me. And I for her." Christoff rose, puffing out his chest with pride. I wanted to tease him, but Christoff was right to be pleased with himself; I'd met his wife—a gorgeous brunette in her early forties with an easy smile and vicious frown. They had two kids together, and I'd never met a better, more protective father. There were times that I wished I'd had someone like Christoff in my life when I was a little girl; my dad had been long gone before I was even born.

"Excuse me," Hemingway interrupted, sliding in beside me at the bar. "May I speak to Miss MacKenna alone for a minute?"

Christoff's smile fell away, but he nodded good-naturedly. "Of course, be my guest. I will see to our green friend." Paul had given up on sitting and now lay sprawled out across the floor, snoring loud enough to shake the bar.

I took a bracing sip of my whiskey before turning to face Hemingway, who studied me with a raptorial gaze. I fought the urge to headbutt him, if only to get a reaction for once. There was something about him—and I couldn't quite put my finger on it—that made my skin crawl. "What are ye lookin' at?" I asked, finally.

"That's actually what I'm trying to figure out."

"Pardon?"

"What you are. I'm still working on it."

Definitely about to headbutt him.

"Ye do know it's rude to look at a woman and tell her ye aren't sure *what* she is, right?"

He waved that away. "Not what I meant. What I meant was, I'm not sure how to classify what you can do, or the aura you give off."

"Aura?"

Hemingway nodded. "Yes. Here, tell me what you feel when I do this." He raised his hand and eased it towards me, palm up. I could sense he was inches away from my anti-magic field—a magical dead zone that shielded me from the various flavors of Freak out there, though exactly how it functioned was still a bit of a mystery to me. I drew back; I'd always been super self-conscious about my personal space, but, in this case, it wasn't only my bubble I felt he'd be invading.

"Please," he insisted, "stay still."

I ground my teeth but did as he asked. When his hand finally settled against my field, the sensation I felt was surprisingly pleasant. Not pleasurable, mind you, but pleasant. The best way I could describe it was that it felt like stepping outside on a beautiful day right when the sun hits your face—I couldn't help but bask in that sensation. Then Hemingway thrust his arm forward a few more inches.

The temperature cranked up tremendously. It wasn't pain, exactly, but if you've ever stood directly under an oppressive sun on a beach of white hot sand, you'll know how I felt. "Easy there!" I hissed.

I must've closed my eyes because—when Hemingway groaned—they shot open. Hemingway was sweating, his eyes tight, face pained. I took a step back and his arm fell limply to his side. He shuddered, took a deep breath, and started shaking his arm awkwardly. "Feels like it fell asleep," he explained.

"Everything alright here?" Othello asked, approaching the two of us with that sultry walk of hers, the clip of her heels pounding against the hardwood. She didn't seem particularly pleased by what she saw.

"T'wasn't me fault," I insisted, hurriedly.

Othello glared at Hemingway, who rolled his eyes. "Thanks for throwing me under the bus there, Quinn," he grumbled.

"Ye called me a *what* not five minutes ago," I reminded him. "I have no sympathy for ye."

"Spill it," Othello insisted, folding her arms.

"I wanted to test out her...what did you call it? Her *anti-magic field.*"

"And?" Othello asked.

"It didn't work like I'd expected. If it were simply an anti-magic field, I should've met with some resistance. Or side effects should be visible." He held up his arm and studied it, but whatever he saw seemed to confirm his theory. "Instead, it felt like I was being pulled in. I had to fight to resist it, and it wasn't easy."

I crossed my arms, hugging myself a little. I wasn't sure what that meant, but the fact that my field had tried to draw Hemingway in, rather than keep him out, bothered me. I preferred to keep most people at a distance; the idea that certain Freaks might be compelled to reach out and touch me gave me the creeps. "I'm sorry," I told them both. "I wasn't tryin' to do anythin' like that."

"Of course not, Quinn," Othello said, soothingly.

"Not your fault," Hemingway added. "If anything, it's mine. You'd think I'd know better than to touch the fence with the 'Keep Out' sign on display, especially at my age, but sometimes I can't help myself." He grinned, revealing a surprisingly charming smile. "Sorry for pushing. Not many things surprise me, anymore, and excitement is hard to come by."

"Excuse me?" Othello asked in a cool tone, her eyebrow raised.

Hemingway's grin widened. "Which is why I started courting Othello, of course."

"Nice save," I remarked.

"Very," Othello replied. She flashed him a dark look that promised all sorts of naughty punishments, then smiled. "So, what do you make of Quinn's ability?"

Hemingway's grin faded, and he shook his head. "I have no idea. I've never heard of anything quite like it. There are items out there that can shield you from magic, but not to this extent. Plus, her field is erratic. It reacts differently depending on what's thrown at it. It may not even be stable."

Well, *that* didn't sound ominous or anything. "So, are ye sayin' I'm like a bomb about to go off?" I asked.

Hemingway shrugged, but I sensed he was holding something back. "I'm saying I don't know what you are." He held up his hands. "No offense." He reached out for Othello's hand, squeezed it, and smiled. "Anyway, I've got to run. I have to start looking into the damage Nate did before he came back from Hell to confront the dragons."

Right. Because *that* didn't scream "let me make up an excuse to leave."

"Oh, right," Othello said, nodding as if he hadn't just uttered the world's most absurd sentence, "I'd almost forgotten." She leaned in and kissed him on the cheek. "Be safe."

I sighed.

I really needed to make some normal friends.

CHAPTER 4

*O*thello helped me into my jacket. "Don't mind him, he gets gloomy sometimes. He wasn't trying to freak you out." She handed over my scarf. I was sure I looked ridiculous all bundled up like this with spring right around the corner, but the weather on the East Coast had been as bipolar as a lovesick teenager this year; it was only a few degrees below freezing outside, but factor in the wind chill and it was practically glacial.

"Don't ye worry about it," I said, folding the scarf around my throat and freeing my hair from beneath both it and the lip of my jacket. "Although I t'ink he could have gone with somethin' other than 'unstable' to describe me field," I added, sarcastically.

Othello folded her arms over her ample chest, smirking. "Yes, well, he isn't exactly a poet. That, and something about you is nagging at him, throwing him off. I've never seen him troubled before. Sad, perhaps, maybe even worried. But solving the mystery that is your power presents yet another problem, and he already has a lot on his plate."

"What *is* he?" I asked. "Last time I saw him, he was but a wee lad. He's aged somethin' like ten years in a few weeks. And the way he talks…" I drifted off, realizing I was putting Othello in a tough position. Most Freaks liked to keep their identities and abilities a secret—a Darwinian precaution, in my experience. Asking how he was in bed would have been less intrusive.

Not that I was curious or anything.

"Quinn—"

"No, I'm sorry. I shouldn't have asked ye that."

Othello smiled. "It's alright. I was only going to say that he will share his role with you one day. You may think it's for his own protection, but I don't. I believe, deep down, he likes being treated like...well, like the rest of us." Othello settled back onto a barstool and looked away. "The world can be an unwelcome place for those who are different. Even among Freaks, there are those who are treated poorly. Some are shunned, others feared. I do not know if he has noticed yet, but he has surrounded himself with those who can see beyond such things. I think that's why he and Nate have become so close. It helps that Nate's about as sacrilegious as they come." Othello turned back to me and raised an eyebrow. "Though, when you start cursing, sometimes I wonder about that."

I blushed. "Aye, sorry about that. I get carried away sometimes."

Othello giggled. "Not to worry. I can be plenty expressive, myself. I simply make sure to do it in my language, and to save it for the right times." She winked meaningfully at me, trying to lighten the mood.

I smiled and studied the street outside through the window, glad to see it wasn't snowing. My Uber would be here soon, and Othello's driver had been parked outside waiting this whole time. Paul was passed out on the floor—Christoff often let him sleep it off, then kicked him out before sunrise. I felt like I understood Hemingway a bit better, at least, thanks to Othello's explanation. After all, I routinely kept people at a distance, worried that they'd judge my lifestyle—that they'd find out about my past and what I'd done to survive. Who was I to judge Hemingway for wanting to keep his secrets?

"Anyway," Othello said, drawing my attention, "I don't think he meant to frighten you. He's merely worried. For you as much as anyone."

"He's not the only one," I said, studying my hands for a moment before putting my gloves on. They were large for a woman's, the fingers long and tapered, the palms sturdy. I had a good grip; I'd spent years learning martial arts, including grappling. I'd always trusted in my own ability, in what I could achieve with what I had. Finding out I might have some unknown, untapped resource within me bothered me more than I cared to admit. It felt wrong, alien even—like whatever it was, it didn't really belong to me.

"So, about New York..." Othello said, perhaps sensing a need to change the subject.

"Oh, right. What about it?"

"I spoke with my friend in the Chancery. She said she'd move your hearing to a later date. To be honest, she seemed surprised to hear you'd been summoned at all, so it may be a good time for you to go out of town."

"Why's that?" I asked, ignoring the icy shiver that suddenly danced down my spine.

"Because she can be…single-minded in her pursuits. If she finds out someone in the Chancery is gunning for you, things may heat up considerably."

"Oh. Good to know," I said, wryly. I wasn't looking forward to dealing with the fallout from postponing the hearing, but the idea that I had someone from the Chancery in my corner was a welcome one. Even Ryan hadn't been able to offer me much protection; he'd been pretty low on their totem pole, from what I gathered.

"So, where should I start lookin' for this t'ing?" I asked.

"Actually, I know where it is."

"Alright…" Locating the magical artifact, or charm, or what have you was usually step one in my process. Once I'd managed that, I'd find a way to make sure it fell into my possession. I could usually rely on legal means to do so, but not always. Not surprisingly, it was the not-always situations that earned me the biggest payoffs.

"First, I want you to convince the man who owns it not to sell it to any other interested parties."

"Aye…"

"Then I need you to find out what he wants for it."

"Ah."

"And then I need you to get whatever that is and make a trade."

I sighed. "You're not givin' me a lot to work with, ye know."

"I know. But from what I recall, you managed to steal an extremely valuable case with little more than an address and a vague description of a target, right? Surely this won't be too much for you." Othello's grin was predatory. The fact that the case in question had actually belonged to Othello and her company meant she was still a little salty about the whole affair. That, or she had no qualms about using this job to even the score between us. Either way, she was blackmailing me. Nicely.

This was why we were friends.

"I'll meet you in the city once you have the item," she said a moment later.

"What is it?" I asked, realizing she'd yet to fill me in on that little detail.

"A seed. Think of it as a genetics experiment with a lot of potential."

"A seed?" I asked. It was hard to imagine a seed being worth this much trouble, but then I'd seen clients lose their shit over less—my go-to horror story involved a rapper and a pair of Air Jordans signed by Hermes.

What can I say? Everyone has their kinks.

"Yes," Othello confirmed. "I actually don't know much more than that. There are rumors about what it can do, but I'm not sure if I can believe anything I'm hearing."

"So why do ye want it?"

"Because sometimes rumors pan out."

That made sense. Although it always seemed like a lot of trouble to go through on hearsay alone, some of my best deals had come about thanks to hunches I'd had and risks I'd taken. When artifacts with magical properties were involved, you often found yourself fumbling around blindly, hoping to stumble onto something valuable in the dark. "Alright, I'll buy that," I said. "Now the real question…why me?" I waggled my finger at her. "And don't ye lie to me. I'm sure ye could hire someone else, if ye were so inclined."

"You mean we could afford to," Othello said, nodding. "This is true. But the magical community, while quite large and diverse, doesn't have many neutral parties. Finding someone talented enough who is also unaffiliated would be tough on such short notice, not to mention time-consuming."

I considered that for a moment. She wasn't wrong. There were very few independents out there; magical organizations like the vampires' Sanguine Council, the Faerie Chancery, and the Wizard Academy dotted the landscape. For most Freaks, enlisting was a prerequisite to survival. I'd only managed to avoid conscription thus far because I was so hard to classify—no one could claim sole jurisdiction over me.

It had nothing to do with my sparkling personality, I'm sure.

"So ye need someone ye can rely on not to sell this t'ing out from under ye, is that it?" I asked.

"I need someone I can *trust*," Othello clarified. "If it were a problem money could solve, I would not involve you. This is about priorities. I know what makes you tick." She raised her hand to interrupt my smart-assed retort. "I know who and what you want to protect, Quinn. What drives you.

Between that, your background, and your ability, I doubt I could find anyone better suited."

I bristled somewhat. "Ye aren't suggestin' those under my protection are in any danger, I hope?"

Othello looked a little hurt. "No, that wasn't a threat. What I meant was that you have a good heart, but also that you are not afraid to get your hands dirty. You know how to get a job done with minimal collateral damage. What I'm asking for is discretion."

I sighed. When she put it like that, it made it really hard to say no—not that I had planned to after she'd gone to bat for me against the Academy last month and the Chancery less than an hour ago. Unfortunately, I had begun to suspect that Othello knew more than she was letting on. "So," I began, "what aren't ye tellin' me?"

Othello smirked. "What makes you think I'm keeping things from you?"

I rolled my eyes and pointed to her bulging cheeks. "Because I t'ink ye can't help it."

Othello's expression turned wry. "All I know is what I'm sending you after, if it actually exists, is considered priceless. Which, ironically, means there are some who would pay a great deal for it."

"So ye want me to get me hands on it before they do?"

Othello nodded.

"Do ye know who I should be lookin' out for?"

"I can only guess who the buyers are," she replied, "but, given its origins, I would caution you to be prepared for anything under the heavens. Or above them, for that matter. The broker who has the seed is one of those super reclusive types with almost no digital footprint, but I'll forward everything I've been able to find so far."

CHAPTER 5

*T*he conversation hadn't gone on long after that, but it was Othello's description of the would-be buyers that I couldn't get out of my head. *Anything under, or above, the heavens.* I'd pressed her about that, but she'd put me off, pledging that she'd already told me everything she knew.

True to her word, she sent the information she'd compiled on the broker, which included a few grainy photos pulled from security cameras, a rough composite garnered from several dubious witnesses, and a confirmed location—a swanky hotel in Manhattan.

Good thing no one did swanky in Manhattan like a mouthy ginger from Southie with a chip on her shoulder.

The rest I could discover for myself.

*W*hile packing over the next couple days, I had contemplated how I'd approach the broker; in my experience, one's outfit could make or break a first impression. I could wear my most flattering dresses, play innocent, and set up an "accidental" encounter—a classic tactic used to con people for centuries. The problem was—despite how Hollywood depicted seduction gimmicks in Bond films—reality was often a lot less convenient. What if tall, leggy redheads weren't his type? What if he

23

was gay? What if he was one of those men who knew better than to let a random woman get close to him while he had a valuable artifact in his possession? What if he was gay *and* paranoid?

Besides, I hated dresses.

In the end, I decided I'd rely on my status and experience before relying on my gender. I'd spent a long time in Boston building a reputation for delivering goods that no one else could, and it was that reputation I'd use to develop a relationship with the broker. Don't get me wrong, there were badass Bond girls out there with some stellar backgrounds: nuclear physicists, assassins, smugglers, spies, and cold-blooded killers. I, however, didn't need James Bond to validate me.

I could save the day all on my own.

I found Dobby restocking shelves in the warehouse behind Christoff's bar. Dobby—a spriggan I'd named for his resemblance to the house-elf of Harry Potter fame—barely cleared waist-height when the lights were on, but, when the lights went out, he became a hulking shadow monster capable of dangling men in midair. Fortunately, the warehouse was well lit at the moment. I found him tottering precariously on a barstool, two bottles of Jameson tucked under one arm and counting in Gaelic, when I walked in.

"Oy, Dobby!" I called.

"A moment, my lady," Dobby replied. His voice, as usual, sent goosebumps up my spine. For a diminutive fellow, he had one of the sultriest, most masculine voices I'd ever heard. Sort of like Vin Diesel meets Barry White. In his shadow monster form, the voice took on a reverberative quality that made the very ground hum.

I sidled up next to him, studying his handiwork. In the weeks since Ryan's departure, Christoff had given his new ward the task of organizing the warehouse. The plan was originally drawn up to keep the spriggan's attention occupied—but it turned out the little guy displayed impressive attention to detail despite his occasional memory lapses; he'd had the place completely reorganized, stocked, and even cleaned after the first week. Now Christoff relied on him for all sorts of things, including taking inventory.

"Make sure ye have enough whiskey, alright? Otherwise ye would be the only reason I have to visit," I joked.

"On the contrary, the Bear Lord would miss you, my lady." Dobby noted, setting one of the bottles down inside a cabinet. "As he misses the young Fae barkeep."

"You're gettin' better with your English," I said, avoiding the subject of Ryan's departure.

"With your nonsense language? Yes. It is fascinating." Dobby replaced the second bottle and hopped down from the stool. "You see, I *miss* someone when I do not *hit* them," he said, pounding his fist against the palm of the other hand. "And yet, in your tongue, to miss someone might mean you wish you could see that person again." He shrugged, good-naturedly. "The Bear Lord visits and brings with him this gift of language. Sometimes he brings the language of the Slavs. They, too, have phrases that mean more than one thing."

"Oh?" I asked, wondering why Christoff had added Russian to Dobby's lessons. Who knew why Russians did anything they did?

I mean, meat jelly, people. C'mon.

Dobby nodded, sagely. "Oh yes. There's one that translates to 'hold your tail as a weapon' in your tongue, but which means to never give up in his. I suspect it has to do with the concept of retreat."

I grunted, marveling at how eloquent the spriggan had become in such a short time. I'd always considered myself intelligent despite my poor grades, but I'd never been very good at expressing myself when speaking. Part of it was the way I talked—my Irish accent had earned me a fair amount of teasing growing up. In a way, that had contributed to the poor grades; getting suspended for knocking the teeth out of my grade school bullies had regularly set me back.

Dobby gave the cabinet a once over before turning to face me, his comically large eyes brighter and more intelligent than they'd seemed when we'd first met. There was something shrewd in them, lurking beneath the surface. "Are you going somewhere, my lady?" Dobby asked.

"What makes ye t'ink that? And d'ye call every woman ye meet *lady*?" I asked, as an afterthought. It wasn't like I minded; every girl likes to be called a lady now and then. But, if I was being honest, I'd rather it come from someone my height.

And preferably my species.

"Because that's what you are," Dobby replied. "And I think that because you never come to see me on Tuesdays. The drink specials do not interest you, and you only visit when it is convenient."

I winced. I wanted to argue, but he was right. It wasn't Dobby I was avoiding, per se, but the responsibility Ryan had shackled me with when he left. As far as I was concerned, Dobby was an out-of-sight, out-of-mind problem; so long as Christoff didn't call with bad news, I could go about my day without giving him much thought. Visiting meant acknowledging that, at some point, Dobby might not want to stock shelves or take inventory. That, one day, he might want to use his newfound knowledge and substantial power to cause a ruckus in my city.

I had no idea how I'd stop him, if that happened.

He chuckled. "That was not a critique, my lady. I'm content with where I am, for now. I appreciate you putting me under your protection. I was merely explaining my reasoning."

I decided to move on, ignoring the "for now" portion of Dobby's response before I developed an ulcer. "I'm goin' to New York City."

"What for?"

"It's a job," I explained. "For Othello."

"Ah, yes. The woman you mentioned, but did not want me to meet."

"T'wasn't that I didn't want ye to meet," I insisted. "It's that I promised Ryan I'd keep you under the Chancery's radar. I trust her, but it might put her in a tough position, knowin' you're here. She has a friend in the Chancery. Someone relatively high up, I t'ink."

"The Chancery." Dobby nodded. "Yes, the young Fae mentioned them to me once or twice. He always seemed concerned about how they might react once I was discovered, but I reassured him that, so long as I was under your protection, they posed no threat to me."

I sincerely doubted that, but didn't feel like contradicting him. "Well, I still don't want ye gettin' into trouble, ye hear?" I said.

"Of course not, my lady."

"Good." I sighed. It worried me that Dobby thought I would be able to protect him if the Chancery came knocking. At this point, I wasn't entirely sure I'd be able to protect myself. That was the problem with the Fae: their magic was unpredictable. Ryan's illusions, his grammarie, had never blinded me to reality—but that didn't mean I was safe from the other Fae that lurked out there. A creature like Paul wouldn't have to hit me with magic to take me out—a tree would be more than adequate. "Well anyway," I said, "it's time for me to be goin'."

"Would you like me to come with you?" Dobby asked.

"Oh, well, I—"

Dobby held up the Ring of Gyges, an artifact I'd stolen from a vampire rock band at Ryan's request, which gave its wearer the ability to turn invisible. It was especially handy—no pun intended—in Dobby's case, since it meant he could slither around in his shadow monster form without panicking the masses. I realized he was suggesting I let him tag along, my very own invisible monster bodyguard. I shook my head. "No, I t'ink I can handle this one on me own."

Dobby nodded, then cocked his head a bit, as if listening to a frequency only he could hear. "Have you begun to use it, then, my lady?"

I arched an eyebrow. "Use what?"

"Your magic."

CHAPTER 6

I would have immediately demanded answers, but—before I could so much as blink—the sneaky little bastard slipped on the ring and disappeared faster than I could say "Bilbo Baggins."

"Oy!" I yelled. "Get back here!"

It was possible the spriggan was simply blowing smoke—his memory did tend to make him say weird things at inappropriate times. But, as perhaps the oldest Faeling I'd ever met, it made sense he might have encountered someone like me before—surely, I wasn't the first of my kind? I felt silly for not confronting him about it sooner. The next time I saw him, I vowed I'd make him talk, invisibility or not. I wasn't sure how one *could* coerce a spriggan, but where there's a will, there's a way.

If all else failed, I could always try shooting him.

"Ye better be ready to talk when I get back!" I belted.

I left the warehouse, returning home to finish packing; I had a few more fashion decisions to make before the flight in the morning. Fortunately, without my gun and gear I had plenty of room for clothes. Unfortunately, I felt naked without it.

Life's a bitch like that, sometimes.

. . .

*L*ater that evening, I headed over to my aunt Desdemona's house—our house, once. Dez wasn't really my aunt, but my mom's best friend. When my mother died giving birth to me, Dez had taken me in and raised me as her own. She'd been kidnapped only a few weeks ago, so lately I'd tried to make more of an effort to see her. Fortunately, she seemed to have moved past it in the last week or so.

I was glad to see her recovering so quickly, but that didn't mean I wasn't keeping an eye on her; sometimes trauma like that lingered, and I wasn't about to let her suffer alone. After all, it had been my fault she'd been taken in the first place.

"Hey, Dez!" I called as I came in, towing my luggage behind me. Dez had promised to give me a ride to the airport in the morning so I wouldn't have to bother with booking a hotel or calling an Uber. I hadn't wanted to inconvenience her, but staying with Christoff and his family hadn't seemed like an ideal situation, Othello had already flown back to St. Louis, and Jimmy hadn't returned my latest call.

I needed more friends.

"In the guest room, Quinn!" Dez called down from the second floor. I set my luggage aside and marched up the stairs, ignoring the slight twinge that plagued the knee I'd injured while taking on Academy Justices on behalf of a backstabbing skinwalker. I'd like to say that such occurrences were rare, but I had too many scars in too many places to make that stick. I'd considered letting a doctor give me a once over, but I was more than a little afraid she'd come back with a diagnosis that included grave looks and statements like "shouldn't be upright" or "requires immediate surgery."

I found Dez in her workshop, which she insisted on calling the guest room, even though overnight visitors were exceedingly rare. I was surprised to find it remarkably free of its usual clutter, a queen-sized air mattress blown up in the corner, smothered in decorative quilts. Dez smiled when I entered. "I know t'isn't your old bed, but I hope it'll do for tonight."

I hugged her. Dez was one of the very few people I felt comfortable enough to do that with; it was better to keep most people at arms-length, in my experience. "It's lovely, t'anks."

Dez pulled back from the hug and studied my face. "Ye seem tired. Everythin' alright?"

I considered giving her the skinny on my business trip to New York, but decided against it. I didn't want to worry her needlessly. Besides, if Othello's read on the situation was correct, I might not even be gone that long; I merely needed to find whatever it was the broker wanted in exchange for the seed and make a trade. Simple.

Yeah, right.

"Everythin' is fine, Dez. Just gettin' back into the swing of t'ings. Ye know how it is."

Dez flicked her eyes over my face once more before shrugging. "Suit yourself. If ye want to talk, ye know I'm here." She raised herself up on her toes and kissed my cheek lightly. "I'll let ye get settled in."

I waited until she left before collapsing on the air mattress with a gleeful whoop. I lay there for a few minutes, studying the walls. Dez had painted over them since I'd moved out, trading the soft shade of purple for a neutral beige. My posters were conspicuously absent; Jim Morrison's mugshot, Jimi Hendrix's afro, Freddie Mercury's mustache—all gone. I closed my eyes, remembering all the mornings I'd woken up and risen, bleary-eyed, and punched the play button on my stereo, blasting guitar riffs throughout the house.

Small wonder the posters were missing.

My phone rang. My eyes shot open and I fumbled for it, prying it free from my jacket to glance at the caller ID. It was an unknown number, but the area code was familiar. I went ahead and answered, ignoring that nagging voice in the back of my head that told me not to.

Telemarketer PTSD—it's a thing.

"This is Quinn MacKenna," I said.

"Hey, Quinn! It's Tanya. From the dojo."

"Oh, hello, Tanya." Tanya was a teenager, probably 16 or 17 years old, who trained with me at the Kenpo dojo across town. I hadn't been by since I hurt my knee, but my absence shouldn't have surprised anyone; I was known for popping in whenever I felt like it. The perks of being a third-degree black belt, I guess.

"I'm sorry to bother you, but Sensei mentioned you called to tell him you were going out-of-town. To New York City, right?"

"Aye," I drawled. "Why do ye ask?"

"Well, I—I was hoping...I mean, I wanted to know if you could do something for me while you're there?"

I could tell Tanya was exceptionally nervous, which was odd. She'd always seemed assertive, especially for her age. Maybe it was me. "Somethin' like?" I asked, trying to sound gentle.

Tanya took a deep breath. "It's my sister, Terry. She came by the dojo once or twice to pick me up, but I don't know if you two ever met."

"Aye, I remember." Tanya's sister was sort of hard to miss. The slightly older girl had one of those face and body combinations that made most women inexplicably catty—smooth, sun-kissed skin, a megawatt smile, and Victoria Secret Angel proportions.

"Oh, good. So, the thing is, Terry left two months ago. My, uh, well she and my mom had a fight. Terry decided she didn't want to go back for her second semester at college and that she wanted to move to New York City. Mom wasn't happy."

I chuckled. "Tanya, I can't go draggin' your sister home against her will."

"That's not what I'm asking," Tanya snapped. I heard her fight back a sniffle and felt the hairs on my neck stand up. Something wasn't right. "She wanted to try and make it out there, I get that," Tanya continued after taking a deep, calming breath. "Mom understood, too, even if she didn't like it. Terry got a place and things were okay. She and mom were talking again. Then two weeks ago she said she'd finally gotten a big break, and that she'd tell me more about it soon. Except she didn't. She disappeared." Tanya's voice cracked and I could tell she was on the verge of tears.

"So ye want me to check in on her while I'm there?" I asked, gingerly.

"No, we've already tried that. Mom flew down there a few days ago, but no one has heard from Terry in weeks. Money's tight, so Mom had to come home. There's a detective in charge of her case who might know more. Maybe you could talk to him? At least let us know if they're really looking? They won't tell us much, but I remember you said you knew a few policemen…" Tanya drifted off, then spoke again, softly. "Mom keeps saying Terry will pop up soon. I'm sure she's trying to make me feel better. I…I'd rather know the truth."

I paused for a moment before responding. "Listen, I'm not sure what I'll be able to do that isn't already bein' done by the police, but," I added, before she could break down on me, "I'll do everythin' I can to find out what they know. Ye have me number, so if anythin' changes—let's say she calls ye in the next few days—ye let me know, alright?"

"Oh, of course. Thank you! If you find her, can you do something for me?"

"Are ye sure ye want to keep pilin' on the favors?" I asked, teasing.

"Put her in a finger lock until she calls home."

I laughed. "See, it's times like these that I'm glad I'm an only child."

Tanya chuckled, but then her voice grew somber once more. "She and I aren't really into any of the same things, but she's always been there for me, especially after our dad died. She picked up the pieces for all of us, really."

"I'll do me best to find her," I reassured Tanya once again, praying that—when and if I found her sister—she'd be safe and sound, and breathing.

If I was being honest with myself, I'd never considered New York City an inherently dangerous place. I mean it had its shadier aspects, like any city —the thieving gangs who floated around Times Square looking for easy marks, the crazies who stalked the subways, the hipsters who ruined brunching. That didn't necessarily mean something awful had happened to Terry. Two weeks, after all, was a relatively short span of time. The fact that a detective was looking for her, however, didn't bode well. Good thing I had an ace-in-the-hole when it came to tracking down missing persons.

"Thanks, Miss MacKenna," Tanya said, again.

"It's Quinn," I corrected. "And don't mention it."

I'd called Othello immediately after getting off the phone with Tanya. She'd been surprised to hear from me so soon, but when I filled her in on the situation she'd been more than happy to help. I fed her Terry's full name and last known address, which I'd gotten from Tanya in a text, and Othello said she'd get back to me as soon as she found anything.

"See," Othello said, "I told you. Good heart."

"Aye, well don't go advertisin' that to me customers. I prefer 'em to t'ink otherwise," I replied.

"Oh, that's right! I'd forgotten. What do you charge? You'll have to send me an invoice for expenses and such."

I shook my head before realizing Othello couldn't see it. "Don't ye worry about that," I insisted. "Consider this me repayin' ye for the briefcase affair. Besides, you've seen me bank account. I'm not exactly hurtin' in the funds department."

It was true. While I didn't always give off the classiest vibe—I'd grown up on the fringes of Southie, after all—my tastes were expensive. Aside from the sexy AmEx Black card I used to routinely rack up outrageous bills

at Nordstrom and Saks, I didn't really flaunt my wealth; I used public trans-
portation, I sought out dive bars, and I hunted for bargains.

Truthfully—despite my spending habits—I had a lot more money than I
knew what to do with. I couldn't hold a candle next to Nate Temple and the
rest of the billionaires out there, mind you, but my invoices regularly hit six
figures. It was like Othello said: the more priceless the object, the more
people were willing to pay.

How much would you pay to breathe fire? To make others fall for you?
To cure a loved one? To fly?

Exactly.

"Nonsense," Othello insisted. "I was teasing you about the briefcase
before. How about gadgets? I've been doing some very interesting things
with nanobots recently."

"Nanobots?" I chuckled. "No, I t'ink I'm alright." But then a thought
occurred to me—one that should have done so much sooner. "Actually, I am
eager to get me hands on a wee bit of information."

"What is it?"

"I want to know how to cross into Fae."

Othello was silent on the other end of the line.

"Oy, did ye cut out?" I asked.

"No, I'm here."

The silence stretched. "Would ye be willin' to look into that for me
then?" I pressed.

"First, I want to know why you want to cross over. Then I need you to
tell me why you reached out to me," she said, tersely.

"For the same reason I called ye about Terry," I replied, confused by her
current attitude. "You're me best chance at findin' answers I can't find on
me own. Why?"

"Suspicious timing, that's all," Othello said, sounding somewhat
mollified. She sighed. "I don't know how to cross over, but I know
someone who does. If you return with the seed, he may be inclined to
help you. But he'll want to know your reasons, I can promise you
that. You won't be able to dodge him when he asks about your
intentions."

"I wasn't dodgin' ye, Othello. It's just...personal."

"I understand. We all have our secrets. Good luck tomorrow, and say
hello to your driver for me, when you get to the airport." She hung up. I

stared down at my phone, so excited I hardly registered Othello's clipped goodbye.

I might have found a way into Fae.

After years of searching, my desire to cross into the Fae realm had become a pipe dream of sorts—that extended vacation you always meant to take but never had the time or money for. I'd asked Ryan to find me a way in numerous times, but he'd always refused to help. I'd even briefly considered entertaining the lesbian overtures of a headless horsewoman named Cassandra—she'd casually slipped me her digits before opening a gateway to Fae—but I couldn't commit to kissing a floating head, no matter the gender.

I flopped back on the bed and did a little dance of excitement, ignoring the brief flash of guilt I felt for not telling Othello everything. I hadn't lied to her or anything—my reason for wanting to go *was* personal. It was also a bit embarrassing. Filling her in on my dad's absence in my life and my dream of discovering once and for all where I belonged felt too cliché—I could practically hear Disney's *Hercules* theme song playing in the background on a tiny violin.

To take my mind off it all, I mapped out the route from JFK to the precinct where Detective Ricci—the man in charge of Terry's case—worked. He might be able to give me an idea of where to start, depending on what they knew, if anything. Between Othello, myself, and the NYPD, I was confident we'd be able to give Tanya some answers—though perhaps unwelcome ones.

Despite all that, I went to sleep with a smile on my face.

CHAPTER 7

The flight into New York was uneventful. I strolled through John F. Kennedy Airport, trying not to bump into the several hundred other passengers herding towards the arrivals gate. I'd forgotten how congested New York City could be, but for some reason it bothered me less here than it might have anywhere else. While Boston was in my blood, I'd always had a special place in my heart for Manhattan. Here, everyone was weird—standing out from the crowd was the point. Here, no one batted an eye when I towered over them, or asked me to parrot their words in my "funny" accent. In fact, in New York, people rarely spoke to or looked at each other at all; eye contact and conversation were reserved for people you actually cared about.

Of course, that didn't mean I wanted to get stuck among the huddled masses any longer than I had to. I surveyed the throngs, angling and dipping wherever necessary, my suitcase trailing behind me. Once at the arrivals gate, I scanned the sidewalks for my driver, who I assumed would be holding a sign with my last name splayed across it.

I needn't have bothered.

"Miss MacKenna!" a familiar voice called from outside a set of automatic doors to my left, the Serbian accent so strong and the greeting so loud it turned a few heads besides mine.

I groaned.

"It is pleasure to see you again," Serge said, waving frantically, dressed in the standard uniform of a limousine driver: a black suit, tie, shoes, and cap. The swarthy, pudgy man looked remarkably better dressed than when I'd seen him last, when he'd asked for my protection after being on the run from both his employer and the Academy for several days.

Serge Milanovich was a skinwalker—a centuries-old witch who'd sacrificed his familiar for unearthly power. In his case, that power manifested itself in a mangy, beastly form that preferred using the royal 'we' to describe the various ways it intended to maim and desecrate you. It was very Dr. Jekyll, Mr. Hyde—if Jekyll were a manipulative, middle-aged Serbian man and Mr. Hyde a deranged monster intent on defiling everything it touched.

It would be fair to say Serge had become a prime contender for my least favorite person after he'd tried to kill me. Twice. He and I had tussled a few weeks back after I set him loose on an unsuspecting park full of civilians— yes, he was *that* skinwalker. Then, a few days later, I'd saved his miserable hide from a pair of Japanese Justices, only to have him lash out at all of us. We'd both ended up in Academy custody after that, at least until Othello showed up to take us away.

I'd never found out what happened to Serge after that; part of me hadn't really wanted to know. As Othello's employee and part-time bagman, Serge's lack of loyalty was disturbing—and punishable. I'd expected him to be in a dark hole somewhere, probably back in Siberia, where there were reportedly others like him imprisoned. But it seemed Othello was content to punish him by making him my driver.

Which was all kinds of rude.

"Serge," I said, "what are ye doin' here?" I rubbed the slight callous that I'd developed on my trigger finger. I hadn't realized how desperately I would miss my gun, or how soon.

"I am here as driver, for you. Othello asks me to take you where you wish."

"Did she now?" I quipped. "And how am I supposed to trust ye after everythin' you've done?"

Serge waved me to the side to make way for the various clusters of people hopping into taxis and boarding buses. He displayed his neck, pulling down the edges of his shirt collar to reveal a thin silver choker. "Othello said to not remove this time." Serge readjusted his suit a bit, grinning.

"And why do ye seem so pleased?" I asked, baffled. If someone ever put a collar on me it would be a guaranteed death sentence, and yet Serge looked like he was having the time of his life.

"Circumstances have changed. She is different, not what Serge expected. Nothing like our old master."

"Who's different? Othello?"

Serge nodded emphatically. "Yes."

Othello was his master? Who the hell ran the HR department at Grimm Tech, Christian Grey? "Who was your old master?"

"Rasputin," Serge said, then spat on the floor. Several passersby noticed and made faces. I didn't blame them. "The *kripl* left us to die in prison, not a word. Until at last Othello frees us and gives us job. At first, I think she is cruel, that we are to her like pawns. But no, she tests us. She gives us chance. She is first to do this in many, many years."

I sighed.

Leave it to Othello to earn the loyalty of the monsters.

Still, I knew better than to take Serge's word for it; he'd lied convincingly to my face more than once. If Othello wanted him to drive me around, fine, but I planned to keep my eye on him. "Alright," I said, "I need ye to take me to me hotel, and then we're headed to a police station."

"Police?" Serge asked, his eyes narrowing.

"What, are ye worried I'll turn ye in for what ye pulled in Boston?"

"Oh, no," Serge said, adjusting his black cap to scratch his head. "But what will we do with guns?"

"What guns?"

Serge chuckled. "Your guns. I buy you. Come, I show."

Huh.

Maybe Serge wasn't such a bad guy after all.

CHAPTER 8

Serge wasn't kidding about the guns. As he helped me with my suitcase, storing it in the trunk of the gleaming Lincoln Town Car, he let me briefly admire the duffel bag full of firearms he'd stored there. A quick inventory of what was visible included an MP5, an M4 assault rifle, two sawed-off shotguns, three different pistols of varying sizes, and an Uzi. A real, honest-to-God Uzi. I glanced around, making sure there were no prying eyes nearby—TSA would shit themselves if they knew Serge had this much firepower parked in their garage.

"We better not get pulled over," I muttered. If a cop decided to search the car and found this stash, not even one of GrimmTech's obscenely high-paid attorneys would be able to get us off.

"No, all are registered to you."

I wondered how good Serge's grasp of the English language really was, for a moment. Surely, he hadn't said that these guns were all registered to me? "Say that again," I demanded.

"Compliments of Othello. She says you want weapon, so Serge find."

"Ye bought all these in the last few days? How the hell did ye get 'em registered under me name?"

Serge chuckled and shut the trunk. "Buy, yes. Some were shipped. And registration is in computer, yes?"

I nodded, then rubbed the bridge of my nose. "Of course. She hacked the system." I realized Serge was holding the door open for me, so I climbed in back. It bothered me a little, having so many guns registered in my name. Ironically, as an arms dealer, I hadn't really dealt much in firearms. Most artifacts, by definition, lacked modern engineering, which included guns— although there were exceptions I always kept my eye out for. On the other hand, it felt good to know I was loaded for bear, not that I expected to need it.

"Why did ye buy so many, Serge?" I asked as he turned the engine over.

Serge used the rearview mirror to glance back at me. "My nose says is good idea."

"Your nose?"

"Yes. This city is full of smells. Some good, some not so good. Some very bad. Now we have better chances."

The skinwalker who'd faced down two Academy Justices felt we had better odds of survival with a duffel bag full of guns.

Great.

"I try to get bazooka, but is not easy," Serge said apologetically, mistaking my silence for disapproval.

I rubbed my temples. A fucking bazooka? "I t'ink we'll manage without. Let's go to the hotel," I said. "I'll decide what to do with these when we get there." I tried my best to downplay my enthusiasm; I could hardly wait to empty the duffel bag and play with all the new toys—regardless of how I felt about owning, or needing, them.

"And no speedin', ye hear?" I said, as an afterthought. It didn't matter if they *were* all registered to me, getting pulled over and caught with this stash would seriously suck; it looked like I was about to rob a bank. Hell, there was enough firepower back there to storm a military base.

And this was New York, not Texas.

J decided to skip rolling around on a bed full of guns because one, Darwinism, and two, I had other priorities; I dropped off the guns and headed to the police station unarmed. I hated to do it, but it'd seemed like the smarter option; most had metal detectors and I wasn't interested in being detained for several hours while they checked my concealed carry paperwork. Besides, if I wasn't safe surrounded by a building full of armed police officers, I doubted it would make much difference.

The precinct itself seemed more like a low-rise apartment building than a police station; windows lined the facing entrance, uniformly spaced, the façade drab and unappealing. Even without the address, I'd have been able to spot it from a mile away; a dozen police cruisers were parked outside. Jaywalkers snuck furtive glances at the precinct as they dipped between cars and cut across traffic.

The front desk was manned by a thin, elderly beat cop with a charming disposition. He sat behind a pane of smudged, bulletproof glass and asked me to sign in, assuring me Detective Ricci would be with me shortly. The lobby was somewhat dingy, the carpet a putrid shade of brown. The coffee was surprisingly good. I finished off two cups of it before Detective Ricci sauntered in nearly twenty minutes later.

Ricci was a heavyset guy, built like a powerlifter who'd traded in his dumbbells for donuts. With his last name, I'd thought he'd look Italian—olive-skinned with dark hair and dark eyes—but I was wrong; his hair was so blonde it blended seamlessly into his pasty white forehead, and his eyes were a murky blue-green. He and the cop at the front desk shared a few words, then he turned and waved me forward with a bland, mildly amused expression.

I rose and approached, delighting in the momentary widening of his eyes. Being tall could be a real pain in the ass—finding a big spoon who wouldn't inhale your hair when you slept, feeling like you were in a gynecologist's office every time you sat in your friend's Mini Cooper with your knees in your chest, squatting to turn door knobs with your arms full of groceries—but there were also some serious perks. Like intimidating men who viewed women as demure, dainty creatures. In that instance, my height became a not-so-subtle reminder that some of us could get whatever the hell we wanted off any shelf without their assistance.

I could open jars, too.

"Detective Ricci?" I asked, pleased to see his amused expression falter.

"That's me," Ricci said, planting his fists on his hips. "Are you the woman who called earlier? About the girl?"

I nodded. I'd called from the hotel, checking to make sure Ricci was in the precinct and would be willing to talk with me—sometimes cops were hesitant to discuss open cases with civilians. But the other detective I'd spoken to assured me he would be there and happy to fill me in, so I'd left a message on his voicemail letting him know to expect me. "Her ma and sister asked me to check in," I confirmed.

"Well, I'm not sure I can tell you anything I haven't already told them," Ricci said, flipping through a small notebook. "We've canvassed a few of the clubs in the area around her apartment, but nobody's seen her. Her neighbors said she moved out but didn't say where she was going. Of course, it's only been two weeks. It's possible she met a boy. Or maybe she's on a bender, lost her phone, and hasn't gotten around to calling her mom back." He shrugged apologetically. "It could be something as simple as that. We'll keep an eye out, but we're stretched pretty thin as it is." Ricci flipped through a manila folder and eyed her picture—an old volleyball photo her mother must have scrounged up. "Shame. She's a beautiful girl."

"Her bein' pretty is what makes it a shame?" I asked, suddenly itching to pick a fight. It wasn't that Ricci was wrong; he wasn't. For all we knew, Terry could have started a job or moved in with a boy or lost her phone—but I knew, instinctually, that Terry would never have kept Tanya out of the loop. That she would have found the time, found a way, to reach out. His jaded take on the situation was likely going to produce no real results. If Terry was going to be found, it wasn't going to be by someone who could so casually dismiss her disappearance.

"No, you're right, that was insensitive," Ricci said, sounding sincere. He sighed and shut the folder. "Look, I know it's hard to hear, but sometimes people just disappear. It doesn't always mean something horrible happened to them. I do hope she's okay. But I have to prioritize."

"Meanin' what? That'll it take findin' her body to convince ye to sort out what happened to her?"

Ricci's cheeks flushed in anger. "That's not what I'm saying." He paused, closed the folder, and took a deep, soothing breath. All the tension went out of his shoulders. I'll admit, if I hadn't been so ticked off by his attitude, I'd have asked him how he managed that little trick; I'd spent hours humping a yoga mat with less result.

"What I mean, is that," he continued, "the only way I can do my job and live with myself is if I tackle the cases I can actually solve. Finding out who's jacking cars in Brooklyn. Tracking down sex traffickers. Putting domestic abusers behind bars. A girl moves to New York City and forgets to call her family for a couple of weeks?" Ricci snorted. "It's a waste of man-hours."

"I hope ye can live with yourself if you're wrong," I retorted.

"Wouldn't be the first time, won't be the last," Ricci replied, sounding tired. "Have a good day, miss. We'll contact the family directly if we find anything."

He left.

The uniformed officer at the front desk hunched forward, tapping on the glass to get my attention. "Sorry for eavesdropping, miss, but I don't think you were being fair to Detective Ricci."

"Is that a cop solidarity t'ing? Sticking up for one of your own, even if he's a prick?" I asked, still miffed.

The old man chuckled. "No, he's definitely a prick. But he's got his silver lining. He's one of those detectives who likes playing the odds because it's safer than following hunches. He's a career guy, here to put in his time...but that's not all there is to him."

"Like what?" I asked, dubiously.

"Well," the old man sat back, "I remember there was this kid who kept getting pulled in a few years back. Dominican, a would-be gangster, always getting into fights or stealing things from convenience stores. It's tough with the young ones, especially since odds are it'll only get worse. Anyway, one day Ricci spots the kid on his way home and follows him. He goes up to the door, knocks, and meets the kid's mom. They talk. Ricci starts dropping by every week, checking in on the kid, making sure he's staying out of trouble—"

"How do ye know all this?" I asked.

The old man held a finger to his lips and winked. Had he been even a few years younger, I'd probably have decked him—but as it stood I'd probably have snapped his scrawny neck if it wasn't for the glass between us. "Except the kid doesn't stay out of trouble," the old codger continued. "He kills a guy. Says it was self-defense, and maybe it was, who knows? He gets time, either way. Ricci going out of his way to check in on the kid every week like he did? That's a decent thing to do. But I'll tell you a secret...every Wednesday he drives up to Altona to see that kid. He doesn't talk about it, but I file the time logs and note the gas mileage. The way I see it, it takes a decent person to try to help someone before they do something terrible. It takes a damn good one to help them after." He waved and flashed a smile. "Anyway, you have a nice day. Hope they find your girl."

. . .

I called Othello from the backseat.

"Hello, Quinn."

"Any news for me on Terry?"

"I'm tracking down a lead right now. Seems she had a few appointments with various talent-seeking types. Most were crossed off on her schedule, but there was a music producer she'd planned to meet the week she disappeared. A pretty big name, too. I can't tell if your girl kept the appointment, but the producer might be able to tell you more."

"Go ahead and send me the name and address, and I'll have *Serge* drop me by," I said, emphasizing the Serbian's name with a growl.

"Hello, Miss Othello!" Serge called from the front seat.

"Shut it, ye mangy bastard," I hissed, holding my hand over the base of the phone.

I had to wait for Othello to stop laughing before she responded, ignoring us both, "How's the hunt for the broker?"

"We're stopping by the hotel so I can change," I said, leaving out the reason I needed to change—namely that I wanted to see how many guns I could fit on my person without looking like Arnold Schwarzenegger in *Commando*. I considered thanking Othello for having Serge fetch the weaponry, but part of me was still stewing over her giggle-fit. "After that, I'll be headed to the hotel where he's stayin'. Ye sure ye have the right room number?"

"I'm sure," Othello said. "I have the name on the guest registry, too, but I doubt it will help much. It's obviously a fake."

"What is it?"

"Mr. McIntosh."

"Well, somebody enjoyed *Blank Check*."

"What?" Othello asked.

"It's a movie, about a—nevermind. It's not important."

"You Americans and your movies," Othello said. I could practically see the eye roll from her tone.

"I'll let ye know how it goes," I said. "Assumin' he's even home."

"Oh, right. Ask Serge for the thing."

"The what?"

"Just do it," she insisted, clearly amused.

Now it was my turn to roll my eyes. "Serge!" I yelled.

His shoulders tensed as he dodged an industrious cabbie lurching from one side of the street to the other. "Yes, Miss MacKenna?"

"Othello says to ask ye for the t'ing."

"Oh!" Serge reached into his jacket pocket, pulled out a thin plastic square the size of a credit card, and passed it back to me. I turned it over in my hand—it was surprisingly dense, but smooth.

A magnetic key to a hotel room door.

"If he's not home," Othello said, "feel free to let yourself in."

I was officially starting to feel a little spoiled.

CHAPTER 9

The lobby of the *Iroquois*—the relatively inexpensive, but luxurious, hotel in Manhattan Mr. McIntosh had chosen—had a stately grandeur to it that I admired. In a way, it reminded me of Dorchester in its prime, its Puritanical aesthetic reinforced by gleaming stone and polished wood.

The hotel Othello had put me up in was far more lavish by comparison. Stationed between Park and Madison Avenue, the five-star *Four Seasons* hotel had practically screamed bourgeoise. Between its ubiquitous wait staff and its old-money clientele, I'd decided to spend as little time there as possible; staying in places like that made it easy to forget the outside world existed.

Still, the room itself had been nice and spacious, though my duffel bag full of guns had looked remarkably out of place on their pristine bedspread. I wondered how that review would look: *Sorry, but your hotel décor doesn't really jibe with gunmetal black. Do better next time. Two stars.* Definitely posting that later.

Anonymously.

I cruised straight past the front desk and headed for the elevators, my phone pressed tight against one ear, speaking much louder than I needed to, "I don't care how much it costs. No, she can't do that, it's illegal in six states, including California. I don't care if he *is* a Senator..." The nearest employee, catching the tail end of my fake conversation, blushed and avoided eye contact.

I pretended not to notice.

Mr. McIntosh—or whatever his name really was—lived twelve stories up. Othello had accounted for the magnetic key I needed to make the elevator work, but that wouldn't help me if I got waylaid by a well-meaning attendant. The trick was to look confident, but—above all—preoccupied. Few people go out of their way to bother someone who looks busy—excluding the leering meatheads at the gym who insist on teaching you how to do something "right."

It worked.

The doors were inching closed when a man thrust a worn brown leather boot between them. The doors parted once more, and one of the most attractive men I'd ever seen stepped inside clutching a bag full of groceries to his chest. We exchanged glances—the awkward half-greeting between strangers on an elevator—and he smiled. "Could you hit floor 12 for me?"

I gawked for a moment but managed to rouse myself long enough to point at the button, which already glowed from when I'd pressed it a moment before. He chuckled and shifted the groceries. "Ah. Well thanks, anyway."

I turned away to hide my blush and subtly put as much space between us as I could, feigning interest in the elevator walls—which, unfortunately, were far blander than the hotel lobby. I was busy counting, slowly, to ten when he began humming a warbling tune that sounded remarkably like the trilling of a bird. It was lovely, but distracting. I struggled not to turn back around.

It wasn't so much that the guy was beautiful—although he was. I'd run into beautiful guys before. When you live in a major city, you're bound to share an elevator or two with some ridiculously attractive people; odds alone make that probable. Somehow, this was different. Have you ever seen someone who was so attractive you momentarily forgot your own name?

Yeah, that.

As we ascended, I tried to pin down what it was about him that'd triggered my malfunction—anything to excuse my brief, awkward relapse into a lovestruck, teenage girl. I snuck a sidelong glance and found myself staring again. Whatever it was I was attracted to, it was there in the slash of his cheekbones, the bristle of his five-o-clock shadow, and the cleft of his chin. It was even in the air; in the tight confines of the elevator, I could smell his cologne, a musky, woodsy scent that clung to the air like dust motes, infused with the aroma of his treated leather jacket and the faint odor of apples.

His lips unpursed to curve into a wide, crooked smile. He'd caught me looking back. "Sorry, I didn't realize I was humming. Habit."

I returned to my wall gazing. The elevator stopped, and he stepped off, strolling down the hallway. I waited until the last possible instant before doing the same, pausing until he turned the corner before cursing. "Of all the elevators in all the world, you had to step into mine..." I muttered, then sighed.

Mr. McIntosh.

The sketches hadn't done him justice at all.

CHAPTER 10

*H*e answered on the third knock. If he was surprised to see me, he didn't look it. Instead, he grinned, exposing a dimple in his left cheek. "The girl from the elevator. Did I drop something?" He glanced back into his apartment as if he'd know what it was by looking.

I shook my head and shoved my hands deeper into the pockets of my cream-colored trench coat, hoping he wouldn't notice that I'd balled them into fists to stop them from shaking. I seriously had no idea what was wrong with me. "No, I actually came up here to find ye," I said, my voice surprisingly firm. "We happened to get on the elevator at the same time, that's all."

"An Irish girl." His grin spread, then shrunk. "Wait, you were looking for *me?*"

"Aye." I cursed my wonky hormones and forced myself to make eye contact. Attractive he might have been, but I was a professional; I'd stared down creatures with lukewarm blood smeared all over their faces—I wasn't about to back down from looking a gorgeous man in the eyes while talking to him.

His irises were a pale shade of green speckled with brown flecks that glinted in the light. His pupils were dilated, which I'd read somewhere meant he was attracted to what he saw...or that the light in the hallway was dim.

Fuck.

"What for?" he asked.

I sighed, glancing down the corridor on either side to make sure I wouldn't be overheard. It was also a good excuse to break eye contact before I started drooling on myself like an idiot. "Ye have somethin' in your possession that I'm hopin' to trade ye for."

His grin fell away completely. The dimple flared back up, but this time in response to a sneer. "I can't believe they sent a girl." I bristled at that, but said nothing. Instead, we studied each other. I wondered—as I so often do when I encounter a man I'm attracted to—what he saw. What was he drawn to, or repulsed by? Did he see the gangly, frazzled creature I often did when I looked in the mirror?

I hoped not.

Now that I wasn't preoccupied with his face, I noticed he wore a slim-fitting thermal under a brown leather jacket, a series of necklaces draped at different intervals over a thin, broad chest. Dark denim jeans and the afore-mentioned brown leather boots completed the ensemble. We were about the same height, although the heels of my boots gave me a slight edge. He didn't seem to notice or care; the men who did inevitably puffed themselves up, raising incrementally on their toes to assert their dominance—which always reminded me of those yappy little dogs, determined to make up for their diminutive stature by hopping all over you in a bid for your attention.

"You're three days early," he said, grunting. "So, which of them sent you?"

"I'm not sure who ye mean," I replied. "I'm here on behalf of a corpora-tion willin' to make a deal for the seed. A middle-woman, so to speak. I'm hopin' you'll consider sellin' it to me, instead."

"A middle-woman..." He began to chuckle, then to laugh outright.

"What's so funny about that, then?" I asked, my hackles rising. I hated being teased, especially about my gender. Which meant he needed to watch his next words carefully, because—no matter how attractive he was—I was fully prepared to hit him with a right hook and destroy his handsome face.

God knows I'd done worse for less.

"I'm sorry. I can't tell if you're being serious or not." He opened the door wide and took a step back. "But you might as well come on in. Prying eyes and all that."

I figured he was kidding about the prying eyes, but once I stepped inside, he hazarded a look down either end of the deserted hallway to make sure no one was around. I wondered, briefly, what I'd gotten myself into—were the other buyers motivated enough to keep tabs on his hotel room? If they were, it meant they'd have no problem tailing me, as well. Or worse.

Fortunately, I already had an escape plan in place if need be—Serge was parked on a nearby side street, and I'd concealed two guns on my person, both within easy reach. You could never be too prepared, but I was confident I could run and gun my way out if I had to. It wouldn't be the first time I had to make a hasty exit after meeting a potential client. Considering my experience with clandestine meetings in hotel rooms up to this point, I figured the odds were fifty-fifty.

In contrast, this hotel room—as opposed to those I'd visited while delivering ill-gotten goods to various out-of-towners—was quaint and tidy. Mr. McIntosh, or whatever his name actually was, seemed to have made himself at home; the closet was full of clothes and the nightstand overloaded with books. Groceries were strewn out on the coffee table. He began sorting through them, putting the perishables in the fridge and the rest in a neat pile on the desk.

"So, what's your name, miss?" he asked.

"Quinn. Quinn MacKenna."

"Pretty name." He finished organizing the fridge and rose, turning to me with his hand extended. "It's a pleasure to meet you. I'm John."

"John McIntosh?" I asked, smirking.

He grunted, as if I'd surprised him. "No. John Chapman."

I reached out to shake his hand, and our fingers brushed.

That's when we both collapsed.

CHAPTER 11

I took stock of the plush carpet, curling my fingers into it as if I might claw my way to my feet. I stretched out my senses, wiggling my toes to make sure I wasn't paralyzed—not likely, I know, but the human body is a fragile thing, and that's the random shit you worry about after an accident. Once I knew my body was relatively unharmed, I felt for my anti-magic field.

I'd spent the past several weeks practicing this very thing—seeking out the aura of magic nullification that shielded me. I'd even managed to manipulate it, once or twice, expanding it outwards in a wave. I'd gotten the idea from my altercation with the wizard who'd kidnapped my aunt; in the aftermath of our fight, I'd discovered that my field had a tangible quality to it—that I could use it to nullify magic from a distance.

Which made it seem almost like magic.

The hardest part, unfortunately, was finding the field in the first place. It was as if my awareness of it had become so second nature that I'd forgotten it was even there. In a lot of ways, it reminded me of my skin. I mean, think about it: unless you get a sunburn or have an itch, you rarely stop to consider all the various sensations pressed up against you, right? My magic field was like that—a second skin.

I rolled over onto my side and began rubbing my fingers together. I wasn't sure why, but finding my field with my hands had proven easier than

51

anything else. Eventually, I could feel it, like a layer of lotion pressed between my fingers. The field was intact. Unharmed, even. Which meant Chapman hadn't been trying anything. Judging from the groans coming from a few feet away, I was guessing he'd taken as much of a blow as I had.

As I struggled to rise, I wondered if Hemingway were somehow responsible. Maybe his little experiment had set something in motion. What if it had become an open electrical circuit, ready to fry all comers—including me? As soon as I got back to Boston, I told myself, he and I would have a serious chat about the hazards of invading someone's personal space.

I managed to sit up, barely, my back propped up against a leg of Chapman's desk. The hand I'd intended to shake with trembled, and my heartrate had skyrocketed. It felt almost as if I'd sprinted up a flight of stairs; I was somewhere between nauseous and euphoric.

"What the fuck was that?" I asked, through gritted teeth. My tongue felt strange in my mouth, like I'd been given a dose of Novocaine, and the sound of my own voice made me wince—the lilting pitch of my accent ascending into dog whistle territory. My senses were going wild. Dirt. Everything smelled like damp dirt. I snuck a look at the base of my boots, wondering if I'd stepped in mud, but they were clean.

"You mean you didn't do that on purpose?" Chapman asked, groggily. "Well, whatever it was, it sucked." Chapman sat up, his breathing labored, and wiggled the fingers of his right hand. He seemed dazed, but suspicious. "Say, what are you, anyway?" he asked.

The next guy who asked me that was getting kidney punched, I swore to myself.

"What d'ye mean, 'what am I'?" I repeated. "What are ye?! And why does it smell like dirt? It even tastes like dirt." I ran my tongue across my teeth as if I could scrub it clean, then shuddered at the strange sensation that produced.

Chapman sniffed and crinkled his nose. "Really? Smells more like rot to me."

I glared at him.

"What?" He rose, a little unsteady, and flopped onto the nearby couch. "You're tellin' me ye have no idea what just happened?"

Chapman shook his head and shrugged, though the effort seemed to take a lot out of him. "Sorry, no. I'd offer to help you up, but I don't think moving is a good idea. Or touching."

"Ye never answered me question," I said, closing my eyes to stop the room from spinning. "What are ye?"

"More of a who, really," he said.

"Well, obviously. Who are ye, then?"

"We went over that already. You, Quinn. Me, John." He tried to sound chipper, but it came out flat coming from a downturned mouth. "Anyway, at least this means you're not a Regular. I'd have been worried, otherwise."

"How d'ye figure that?"

"Well, I've shaken plenty of hands before without ending up on the ground."

"No," I said, through clenched teeth as another wave of nausea came and went. "I mean why would ye have been worried if I were a Regular?"

"That's not important. The real question is, how did you even get up here?"

"What do ye mean?"

"I mean there's a ward around the whole building to keep out anyone or anything abnormal. I figured you had to be a Regular, and that's why they'd sent you. I didn't realize there were loopholes in my security."

"There aren't," I replied, opening my eyes to find the room was once again stationary. "Wards don't work on me." Wards were fancy magical barriers meant to serve as protection from all sorts of creatures out there— think of them like impenetrable walls, often designed to deter specific magical entities. To have one that worked on all manner of Freak was impressive. Unfortunately for him, I could walk through wards as if they were tissue paper.

"How is that possible?" Chapman asked.

"I'll start answerin' your questions when ye start takin' mine more seriously," I replied.

Chapman shrugged. "Suit yourself. You can keep your secrets, but you'll have to leave, either way."

"Excuse me?"

"It's nothing personal. Listen, just tell whoever it is you're working for that I've already sold the seed. And let them know that the buyer won't be outbid. I promise you have nothing to offer me that I need, or want."

I got to my feet, wobbling a little, looming over him. He didn't as much as look up at me, and he definitely didn't seem to have anything else to add. My hands tightened into fists by my sides, and I fought the frustrated urge to draw my gun and pistol-whip him until he gave me the seed. But it wouldn't work. I could read it all over his face—there was a quiet desperation there, an earnest desire that I leave him alone, that I couldn't comprehend. He wasn't lying. If anything, he was being brutally honest.

"Ye asked me what I am," I said, after a moment of silence. "I'm a woman who follows through. Ask around. Even in this city, there are plenty of people who'll tell ye that much." I fetched a business card from my coat pocket and set it on the desk. My name and phone number were on it. Well, not my actual phone number. But a number that would connect to me, eventually.

Thanks again, Othello.

"Not very good at taking no for an answer, I take it?" Chapman asked, his eyes haunted, tired.

I leaned in until my face hovered above his, forcing him to meet my eyes. "No ward will ever keep ye safe from me," I said. I winked, trying to brighten his mood like I would a child.

To my surprise, he laughed. "I'll be sure to keep the door unlocked."

I took a step back, turned, and headed for the door, treading as carefully as I could. "Don't worry," I called with a wave, "I have a key."

CHAPTER 12

I decided not to call Othello until I had results to share. Chapman claimed he'd already brokered a deal, but—thanks to his slip of the tongue—I knew I had three days before he parted with the seed. Which meant I had a couple days, at most, to find leverage. If this job had taught me anything, it was that there's always a way to get what you want, provided you knew where to apply pressure.

Finding that leverage, however, wasn't going to be easy; Chapman was an enigma wrapped in a fineass riddle. Aside from the fact that I found him unreasonably attractive, I had very little to go on: his name, his hotel preference, and the fact that—for some reason—our skin-to-skin contact resulted in seizures.

And not the sexy kind.

Lately, I'd been relying on Othello for times like these. Having her around was like having access to Google on steroids. But even she had her limitations, and she'd already given me everything on Chapman that she'd found. Having access to his real name might help, but John Chapman didn't strike me as a particularly uncommon name. What I needed, I decided, was to do a little old-fashioned sleuthing.

First, I had to get out of the car before I threw up. The nausea, which had faded once I left Chapman's hotel room, had bubbled back to the surface; the constant lurch that came with New York City traffic was enough to make anyone woozy. For once, I appreciated the chilly weather; the frigid air would do me good.

I had Serge drop me off a few streets down from Penn Station and told him I'd make my own way back. He didn't seem pleased about me cavorting about on my own, but I brushed that off; as much as I liked the convenience of having a driver, I'd managed to survive without one for years. Besides, New York deserved to be seen without glass in the way. Seen...and smelled.

I strolled past Madison Square Garden, dodging the numerous pedestrians milling about, the various urban scents mingling and brushing past: the acrid stench of pot, the clean, crisp scent of a man's aftershave, the savory odor of seared animal flesh from a gyro stand at the end of the block.

I picked up a few conversations as I went but understood very few; I heard the nasally exchange of French, the halting droll of Czech, the boisterous chittering of Mandarin. Funnily enough, what few English conversations I could make out were so smothered in New York flavor that they were more or less unintelligible, as well.

Admittedly, I hadn't always cared for New York. I mean, *Yankee* fans lived here. But I'd found that—the older I got—the more I valued what the Big Apple had to offer. It had something no other city, not even Boston, had —an edgy quality that pushed you to move faster, talk louder, and dress smarter.

In Boston, it paid to be tougher than the nails they'd use to seal your coffin. In New York City, it paid to own the nails, the wood, and the mortuary—a fiscal lesson I'd learned in my late teens. A few months out of high school, eager to start my "adult life" and get out of the rut that afflicts those of us who graduate high school without direction of any kind, I'd packed my meager belongings, said my goodbyes, and left Boston. I was a penniless, gangly girl who hated having her personal space invaded.

And I'd come to New York City.

That's right, people. I never said I was brilliant.

I ended up paying fifteen-hundred dollars a month to sleep in a closet. That's not a metaphor, either; I slept in a friend's walk-in on a cot that she must have bought at a Guantanamo Bay Clearout Sale. I'd done everything I could to pay rent each month—waited tables, worked catering events, sold pot—when it got to the point that I had to choose between having a place to live or having enough to eat, I'd left with my tail between my legs, begging Dez to take me back.

I'd returned a few times since with a progressively healthier bank account. Coincidentally, each time I came, I'd had a little more fun. Most of that could be attributed to shopping, but part of it was knowing—deep down—that I wouldn't have to worry about where I was going to sleep, or what I could afford to eat. Money's a funny thing. When you have it, you don't really think about it; when you don't, it's all you think about.

Frankly, I was glad to have checked off that part of my life—I had plenty of other shit to worry about. Shit like the homeless man with the smoke and sparks spewing from his eyes and mouth, waving at me, the dog beside him wagging her tail.

A brief look around told me that I'd worked my way into the heart of Penn Station without realizing it, my feet taking me to familiar places. The man with his face on fire sat against a large tiled mural in a large alcove that curved towards the subway platforms, a cardboard sign in front of him that read "Ninjas Killed My Family: Need Money for Kung-Fu Lessons." Everyone else, hurrying to catch their next train, passed by him without a second glance, even as sparks landed precariously close to their feet. The Ifrit—a breed of djinn rarely seen outside the Middle East—ignored them, but waved me over after flashing an expectant grin.

I adjusted, snaking my way to his side, and shoved a crisp hundred-dollar bill into his cup. His dog, a half-blind Saluki—an Arabian Greyhound, deep-chested and long-limbed with brindled fur—nudged me with its head until I reached down to scratch behind its ears.

"Talk to me, Karim," I said, my mind racing with sudden possibilities.

*K*arim was what you might call an informant. There were Freaks like him all over the city—information brokers willing to trade what they knew for a little incentive. Karim, like most of the Freaks living on the fringes of society, preferred cold hard cash. Easy to spend, hard to trace. He and I had met years ago, not long before I gave up on New York and headed back to Boston. I'd been riding the subway, headed downtown, when he'd stepped on—his eyes like liquid flame, his dreadlocks and beard made out of volcanic ash.

I'd almost peed myself.

He'd caught me staring as the train took off and approached a few stops later. At first, I'd planned to bolt, but there was something about Karim—his smooth, smoky tenor, maybe, or the chill vibe he gave off—that put me immediately at ease. Later I learned that only Freaks were capable of seeing through the illusion charm he wore—interwoven bracelets made of hemp that looped over each wrist. To everyone else, Karim appeared no different than so many of the homeless living in NYC—especially if those individuals were to channel the spirit of a Middle Eastern Bob Marley. It was a good disguise, especially in New York City; most people avoid looking too hard at the homeless. Karim used that anonymity to his advantage, keeping his eyes and ears open.

Stumbling upon him now was pure luck.

"Well hey there, *zeebaa*," Karim said, his accent gruff and reeking of Queens, with only a trace of its Persian origins. "Been a while."

"Aye, it has. And how have ye been?"

"Can't complain. You?"

"Livin' the dream," I quipped, shrugging. Karim's dog hunkered down, forcing me to drop to a knee to continue petting her. I winced and resolved to get some new boots while in town; these were one of my cutest pairs, but my feet were already starting to ache, and New York was not kind to shoes, or feet. Being a girl could be frustrating like that: the better you looked, the more pain you were probably in.

Karim chuckled. "I bet you are. So, you paid. Ask away." He patted various pockets, then produced a pack of rolling papers and a dime bag full of pot. "Hope you don't mind."

I didn't. As creatures of the Islamic underworld, Ifrits were traditionally hostile at best—I'd encountered a sultan's djinn-laden security team once and had experienced their unfortunate temperament firsthand. Karim's stoner tendencies mellowed him out considerably, so I certainly wasn't going to stop him. I watched him prepare a joint and continued petting his pup, catching that sweet spot behind her ear. "I need you to tell me everything you know about a broker here in town. A guy named John Chapman."

Karim grunted, spinning the thin sheet of paper with remarkable precision. "Whatcha wanna know 'bout the Nurseryman, for?"

"The who?"

Karim raised the joint, licked its edge, and pinned it closed with his thumbs. "The Nurseryman. Appleseed. Johnny Appleseed."

I pulled off my sunglasses so I could look Karim in the eye and see if he was fucking with me or not. "John Chapman is Johnny Appleseed," I said. "Ye have got to be kiddin' me."

"I ain't seen that dude in forever. Used to come 'round all the time. You know, for apple picking season up north. Pretty sure he started that trend."

"I just met him," I explained. "He has somethin' I need."

"Same ol' Quinn," Karim said with a chuckle, "always in a rush." He lit the joint with his tongue—a simple flick. He took a deep toke before exhaling the smoke. It mingled with the haze of hot air that constantly wafted off his body. "Sorry, I can't tell you much that you couldn't find out yourself. He was one of the originals. The American legends."

"Next you'll be tellin' me all about John Henry and Paul Bunyan," I scoffed.

"Ain't much worth telling. Bunyan wandered up to Canada, last I heard. Henry got into the jazz scene. You'll find him wherever that's kicking off these days."

I gave up on decorum and settled down next to Karim, half tempted to ask him to pass the roach. The idea that American legends were out there, still breathing long after the history books had set them aside, floored me. Of course, I shouldn't have been that surprised. According to Othello, there were legends popping up all over St. Louis—Achilles owned a bar there. That's right, *the* Achilles. In comparison, Johnny Appleseed seemed significantly less far-fetched. Of course, that also meant I'd been crushing on a long-dead folk hero.

My luck in a nutshell.

I sighed. "Anythin' else ye can tell me?"

Karim flicked the ash off his joint. "Well, I'd probably have told you this for free, but it looks like there's something big in the works. Word is there're big shots in town throwing their weight around. Most of my people have already gone to ground. Me and Jasmine here'll be headed that way, ourselves, before long."

"Somethin' big like what?" I asked.

Karim shook his head. "Gotta be pretty bad to shake up this town. You know New Yorkers—nothing fazes 'em. I caught a whiff of something the other day, though, which got me spooked. I was uptown for a change, and could've sworn I saw one of the Nephilim. I booked it out of there as fast as I could. One demon is as good as another to that bunch—they get confused easy and ask questions later."

I frowned. The Nephilim were half-human, half-angel servants of God. From what little I knew of them, they sounded a lot like a paramilitary organization—Heaven's militia. What with everything that had gone down at the Vatican recently, though, I hadn't expected them to pop up on US soil for a while. Not unless we'd had something to do with it. "Wonder what they're doin' here..." I muttered.

"I wouldn't stress about it, *zeebaa*. Wrap up whatever you've got going on with Appleseed and bounce."

"I would, but it's complicated. I have to make a trade, but I don't know what he wants."

Karim seemed to consider that. "I'll ask around, see if I can't find out. Maybe..." Karim paused. "Hey, this place look a little dead to you?" he asked.

I followed his eyes and realized he was right; over the course of our conversation, our little section of Penn Station had become deserted. Which made no sense. Barring construction or freak accidents, Penn Station was never this empty. It would take a miracle. The sound of boots clipping the concrete echoed down the corridor and a figure made out of pure light strolled towards us.

A miracle. Or, you know, an angel.

*T*he being stopped a few feet from us, the light it emitted almost oppressively bright. I put my sunglasses back on. "Hey, tone it down! I'm tryin' to see here," I yelled, mimicking Dustin Hoffman's accent in *Midnight Cowboy*. The light dimmed, then faded altogether, revealing a primly-dressed man in a tailored navy-blue suit. He had a khaki trench coat folded over one arm and an umbrella in his other hand.

"My apologies," he replied. "Side effect. Clearing out any part of this city for any length of time takes a little doing. I tried it on Times Square once and glowed in the dark for two years straight."

I exchanged a look with Karim, trying to determine if I'd just heard an angel make a joke. The Ifrit was grinning maniacally. It was hard to tell if he was stoned—what with his eyes being made from roiling flames and all—but then he giggled. "This is some good shit," he commented, admiring the joint.

Totally stoned.

The man's attention shifted to the Ifrit. He sighed. "An infernal. Does this mean you're with them?"

"With whom?" I asked.

"He thinks I'm a demon," Karim said, nudging me. "I mean, I *am* a demon. But he thinks I'm, you know, working with the Christian demons. Pitchforks and horns and shit. Corrupting souls." He took another hit and sighed.

"You're not, are ye?" I asked, raising an eyebrow.

"No way. Their benefits package sucks ass. Besides, they don't know the meaning of the word 'chill.' It's all Armageddon this and Armageddon that with those guys."

"It is closer than you'd think," the man interjected. "That's why I'm here, actually. I followed you from Mr. Chapman's hotel. I'd like to know what you offered him, and who you're working for."

"Why should I tell ye?" I asked, rising to my feet. This didn't seem like the sort of conversation to have sitting down. Besides, I wanted fast and easy access to the gun at my back, if necessary.

"Because we have already made a deal with Mr. Chapman, and it's my job to ensure the handoff goes smoothly."

"And who are ye?"

"I'm one of the Grigori. My name is Darrel."

Karim's snicker earned a glare from the man, but the Ifrit held up his hands in surrender. "Sorry, I couldn't help it. It's just too funny."

"His name?" I asked, smirking.

"No, you. You're the only person I know who has shit like this happen to them. I didn't even know the Watchers were around anymore, and you've got them watching *you*. If I bought into karma, I'd wonder what you did to deserve all the attention."

Sadly, I had to agree with Karim. It wasn't so much that I went out looking for trouble; I'd had plenty of deals end amicably, with little to no bloodshed. But for most, a bad day at work could be solved with a bubble bath and a bottle of wine. My bad days, on the other hand, necessitated an Emergency Kit and prescription-strength painkillers.

I studied the angel with the unfortunate name, weighing my options. My Biblical knowledge was limited, but after spending most of my formative years in Catholic school, I knew enough to get by. From what I could recall, the Grigori were angels tasked with monitoring mankind, which meant I'd done something to draw their attention. In a way, it was flattering. I mean, people prayed for angelic intercession every day, right? Guess that made me special.

Thing is, I was a little underwhelmed. Ever since I'd begun tangling with creatures fresh out of storybooks, I'd kept an eye out for angels. Who wouldn't after being raised in the Church? But they'd proven elusive; this was my first time actually meeting one. I guess I'd always pictured some gorgeous behemoth bathed in light with impossibly beautiful wings carved out of fire and glass. The reality—a smartly dressed, average-looking man of intermediate height—was disappointing. I guess it showed, too.

"Quit looking at me like that," Darrel the Angel said.

"Darrel, really?" I asked, leaning this way and that to look him over.

"What's wrong with Darrel?"

I shrugged. "Nothin'. Just wonderin' where ye keep your crossbow."

"Oh, hah hah." Darrel mocked, folding his arms over his chest. "It's not even spelled the same. And it's *Darrel*," he said, putting the emphasis on the second syllable.

"Whatever ye say, Reedus," I teased, surprised he'd even gotten the reference. "So, what are ye givin' Chapman for the seed?" I asked, hoping to catch him off guard.

"Something only Heaven can give. Quit stalling. Who are you working for, and how were you able to pass through the wards we put around the hotel?"

"Those were your wards?" I asked, surprised.

"Of course. Mr. Chapman requested a few days to…prepare. We agreed, but on the condition that he be monitored at all times. We intend to protect our investment. Which is why I'm here, talking to you." Darrel said the last as if he were talking to a child.

Karim turned his furnace-eyed stare to me. "You walked through wards drawn by angels?"

I shrugged.

"That's so rad, girl," he said, nudging me for the second time.

Darrel coughed impatiently. "Your employer?"

I wavered back and forth between telling him the truth. Othello hadn't strictly forbidden me from mentioning GrimmTech's interest in the seed, but then she hadn't mentioned angelic meddling, either…or maybe she had. I played back our conversation in my head and groaned.

"What?" Darrel asked.

"Prepositions," I responded, mournfully.

"Excuse me?"

"Under. Above." I sighed. "Nevermind. Listen, I appreciate the position you're in, but I canno' go around divulgin' information on a client. Bad for business, ye see."

The angel scowled. "I see. Well, it looks like we're at an impasse, then. You don't want to tell me who you work for, and I can't have you running around the city screwing things up. So, you'll have to leave."

"The hell I will," I said, scoffing.

"Oh, I wasn't asking. Don't worry, this won't be painful." Darrel reached for me, snatching at my forearm. Karim's dog lost her shit, her claws scrabbling across the ground as she barked and snarled. I jerked back, but he was surprisingly quick—inhumanly so. Karim tried to intervene, but Darrel flicked a hand at the Ifrit, sending him flying into the tiled mural, pinning him in place with what looked eerily like The Force. A few chips of the wall broke off and drifted to the floor in slow motion, as if gravity had momentarily given up.

Darrel's light returned, momentarily blinding me.

CHAPTER 13

*T*he light faded.

I blinked away tears and yanked my arm free of Darrel's grasp only to find he'd already released me. I looked around, not sure what to expect...but everything looked more or less the same—excluding the section of wall that had been shattered, and Karim, who had keeled over onto the ground, moaning.

I turned, fully prepared to take on an angel, but Darrel's expression was so bewildered that it would have felt like punching a baby. He spun in a slow circle. "I don't understand..."

"What were ye tryin' to do, ye bastard?" I shouted.

"Shhh, I'm thinking."

Oh, hell no.

Who the fuck did he think he was talking to?

I snatched him by his collar, drew back, and coldcocked him as hard as I could. I put the full force of my body behind the throw, twisting my torso, juking my ankle—my right hook was nothing to sniff at...unless I hit you with it, and then you'd be sniffing to keep the blood off your face. After what he'd done to Karim and his dismissive attitude towards me, I fully intended to break the angel's jaw.

But that didn't happen.

Darrel stared at my fist, which hovered a few inches from his face, in surprise. No matter how hard I tried to make up the difference, I couldn't force my knuckles any closer; it felt like when you try to shove two magnetic poles together, as if I'd slide off to the side before I ever managed to touch him. Out of curiosity, I reared back and fired two more shots at him—a jab with my left, followed by a straight. Again, I was stopped short. Darrel flinched with each attempt, however—which likely meant he wasn't the one responsible for blocking my attempts.

"That's enough," he said, flinging his hand at me like he had with Karim. Nothing happened. He glared at his hand like it was a dysfunctional appliance.

Karim, now sitting upright, started laughing wheezily. "You two look ridiculous. She's over here shadow-boxing, and you're putting on a light show." He rubbed the back of his neck. "You didn't have to chuck me at a wall, though. Dick."

"Why didn't we move? And how are you immune to my power?" Darrel demanded, ignoring Karim altogether.

I shrugged. "I could ask ye the same t'ing. How come I can't hit ye?"

"I've seen this sort of thing before," Karim said, struggling to his feet.

Darrel whirled. "Where?"

"Back home, a long time ago. It happens sometimes when different pantheons run into each other."

"What do ye mean, 'different pantheons'?" I asked.

Karim rolled his shoulders loose. "Let's just say there ain't no point in you two going at it. Ever seen oil and water? How they separate? It's kinda like that." He grinned. "Here, watch."

If I thought Karim had looked scary before, he appeared doubly so, now. His skin, already a burnished brown, darkened to a smooth, stony obsidian, and his hair burst fully into flame, flickering in a mane around his face like a corona. His teeth and nails grew long and sharp. His body lengthened and twitched until he stood a full three feet taller than me—his baggy clothes accommodated the transformation, shirt stretched wide to display a reproduction of Johnson Beaver's latest album cover: a teenage heartthrob tonguing a lollipop.

I shuddered.

When Karim finally made his move, it was with a speed and ferocity that

I'd witnessed only once before—when I'd watched a god battle a demon in an alternate dimension. Before I knew it, Karim had Darrel pressed up against a stone column in the middle of the spacious alcove by his suit jacket, though the angel seemed remarkably unfazed.

"This suit's expensive, you know," Darrel said, nonplussed.

"Hush," Karim said, his voice reverberating, laced with grit. "Pay attention." He set the angel down. Darrel rolled his eyes and brushed flecks of ash off his lapel, but didn't seem interested in retaliating.

Karim launched himself at me before I could ask what was going on. I flinched and took a step back, but found Karim's massive claw inches from my chest, stopped as surely as my fist had been from striking Darrel. "See," Karim said, the flames around his face sputtering as he reverted back to his usual self, "no dice."

"I've never seen anything like this," Darrel said, clearly put-out.

"It's not how t'ings usually work for me, either," I confirmed, eyeing Karim, wondering where he'd seen this sort of interaction before. While my anti-magic field kept me safe from various types of magic, it had never shielded me from physical violence. Granted, if I grappled with a werewolf or a vampire—beings whose physical strength far outclassed my own—their magically augmented strength disappeared, but a fight with a grown ass man or woman was still a fight. This was something else altogether. It reminded me, somewhat, of my first altercation with Hemingway; my field had expanded and physically pushed him back several feet, repelling him.

At this point, I decided that I really needed to have that chat with Othello's boyfriend; I couldn't afford for my field to go haywire any more than it already had. I mean, not getting teleported against my will or Force Pushed into a wall was all well and good, but what happened if my field hyperextended itself at the wrong time, or took me and someone else out like it had with Chapman, or—worst of all—stopped working altogether. I hadn't realized how much I relied on it to protect me, to even the playing field when the monsters came calling.

A fair fight, that's all I ever asked for.

Now I couldn't rely on that, all thanks to Hemingway and his wandering hand.

You know what I mean.

Karim pretended he hadn't heard me and sidled back over to his dog,

Jasmine, who hadn't moved once during the whole altercation. "I'll bet there are some of your kind upstairs who might know what I'm talking about," Karim said to Darrel, retrieving Jasmine's leash. "Ask around."

"What are ye not tellin' me, Karim?" I asked, taking a step forward.

Karim glanced back at me. There was the mischievous gleam I was used to, but also a tinge of pity. Which made no sense. "I always knew there was something different about you, *zeebaa*. Be cool." He led Jasmine and together they walked directly towards the mural, then disappeared, the edges of their bodies catching fire—like the lit corners of a street magician's flash paper, curling inward—until all that remained were sparks fluttering to the ground.

"What the fuck is that supposed to mean?" I shouted at the empty air he left behind, my hands clenched into fists. I was really getting tired of all the people out there who seemed to know more than I did about who, or what, I really was. First Hemingway, then Dobby, and now Karim. It pissed me off. I whirled to face Darrel. "Do ye know what he was talkin' about?"

Darrel opened his mouth, but a bell chimed overhead and interrupted whatever he'd been about to say. He sighed and picked his coat up off the ground; he must have dropped it when Karim struck. Darrel patted it down, then put it on.

"Hey, I asked ye a question!" I shouted.

"Sorry, I can't stay and chat. Staff meeting."

"What?"

"Bureaucracies," Darrel said, waving a hand. "You'll find them every-where. I won't bore you with the details." He checked his watch. "Listen, if anyone asks, I gave you a firm talking to and warned you to walk away from all this, alright?" He glanced up at me. "It really is in your best interest to stop reaching out to Mr. Chapman. We may not be able to deter you directly, but that doesn't mean you'll be safe if my superiors deem you—or whoever you represent—a threat."

I sneered. "I hope ye know that doesn't scare me."

"It should, but I can see that it doesn't." Darrel sighed, face looking trou-bled. "You mortals can be so baffling, sometimes."

Light pulsed and I raised my arm over my face to block it out. When I dropped it, Darrel was gone, and I was left alone in a subsection of Penn Station. The alcove swiftly filled up with people headed from one subway platform to the next. I huffed, but joined them, planning to make my way uptown to the hotel room. I needed a nap and—despite what I'd said to Darrel about not being afraid—a plan, should he follow through on his end.

Besides, I had a phone call to make.

Othello had some explaining to do.

CHAPTER 14

*O*thello didn't pick up. I left several voicemails, filling her in on my day, the sarcasm escalating with each attempt. Part of me wondered if she was screening my calls. After taking some time to cool down, I decided that was unfair. Sure, she might've known more about who would be after the seed than she'd let on, but it wasn't like angels went around advertising their acquisitions on the web.

I was betting the seed itself was responsible. Why else would angels go through so much trouble? I racked my brain, trying to think about what would make a seed so valuable, but came up with squat. A seed to what? Fortunately, I at least had an inkling of what Chapman—or Johnny Appleseed, assuming Karim had been telling the truth—wanted. I wasn't sure what Heaven was offering, or how I'd match it, but it was a start.

After my nap, I checked my e-mail and saw that Othello had sent the itinerary of the music producer Terry had been slotted to meet. The time stamp was for that morning, before I'd gone to see Chapman. "Better call me back," I muttered, perusing the producer's itinerary to decide where it would be best to intercept her. According to Othello's info, she would be in a studio for a couple more hours. I sighed. Security there would be tight. Being a Freak had its advantages—but against tasers and a host of muscle-bound bodyguards, I was pretty much powerless.

What I needed was to track her down in the open, somewhere public, somewhere she wouldn't feel threatened by a strange woman probing her with questions. Ordinarily, I'd have called, explained my situation, and set up a meeting. But a quick Google search had revealed the producer's celebrity status; without a badge, getting in to see her would take days, maybe even weeks. The fact that Terry had managed it in her brief time in New York was a little impressive, actually.

In the end, I found what I was looking for in Othello's notes—a few habit predictors that indicated where the producer liked to spend her free time, including a night club she regularly frequented. I checked my phone for the time. I had several hours to kill before New York City's nightlife kicked off. I called Serge's cell.

"Yes, Miss MacKenna?"

"Bring the car around, Serge."

"Okay. Where do we go?"

"We're in New York City. I'm going shoppin'."

*T*he nightclub, *The Three-Headed Chimera*, was underground, accessed by a stairwell and manned by both a bouncer and a stamper—the person responsible for taking your money and branding you at the door. I forked over a crisp twenty-dollar bill and sauntered in with Serge hot on my heels. He was so close, in fact, that he bumped into me when I froze a few feet into the club.

"Sorry, Miss MacKenna," he began, but I waved him off. I was too busy admiring the club's interior to care. Behind the bar and along the booths were staffers wearing togas—like authentic togas, not knotted bedsheets you'd find at a frat party. Mounted on walls and along the bar top sat various taxidermied creatures from legend, including the club's namesake, a chimera with a lion's front, a goat's middle, and a snake's end. Other highlights included a hydra, a harpy, and a griffin—the hybrid parts attached seamlessly to provide a glimpse into a Greek scholar's imagination.

Honestly, I was impressed by the concept.

Unfortunately, the music sucked. The DJ, a skinny, ballcap-wearing guy with more tattoos than blank skin, played a track from the 50s, a doo wop song that had never made it to the radio and never would, for good reason. I cringed, but decided to stick it out, making my way to a booth in the back that would offer me a good vantage point.

Frankly, I was surprised; I'd expected to find an acclaimed music producer in a more upscale setting. You know, a place you couldn't get into unless you were very beautiful, very rich, or both. Instead, we seemed to have stumbled onto one of those quirky bars with tasteless music where you can buy beer in a can.

After midnight came and went, my ears practically bleeding from the series of awful tracks—the DJ had opted for sappy ballads of the slit-my-wrists variety—I was fairly convinced that Othello's information had been faulty. Why this place, after all? I was about to call it a night when I spotted the music producer crossing the empty dance floor towards the DJ booth.

I jerked up, elbowed Serge, and nodded in her direction.

"That's her," I whispered.

Serge nodded, breathing through his mouth to avoid being over-whelmed by the stench of sweaty, unwashed bodies, spilled liquor, and public toilets. "She is pretty," Serge acknowledged, as if that was why we were here. I frowned at him, but he wasn't wrong.

The producer, who went by the name Austina, was a few inches over five feet tall, attractive, with smooth olive skin and dark features. She was flanked on either side by long-haired Samoan men, judging from the intricate tribal tattoos racing up their beefy arms. I watched as she curled her finger, drawing the DJ's attention. He stooped down and she whispered something in his ear. I saw his knees buckle a little and his hand shot out to grasp the railing that surrounded his equipment, almost like he'd been socked in the stomach.

Or, judging from the ecstatic expression on his face, had an orgasm.

The DJ returned to his tables and, within moments, had a brand-new track playing—a catchy tune this time, with a solid baseline. Dancers began filling the stage, gyrating to the music. He fiddled with his equipment and began working in a mash-up, the result twice as good.

I snapped my mouth shut before flies could get in.

The newly-gathered crowd parted for the producer with eerie precision, as if choreographed, and she and her bodyguards took over one of the few empty booths remaining. I frowned. That little move should have drawn all sorts of attention—no one sauntered through a crowd like that without being *somebody*. And yet, no one seemed to care, or even notice.

No one except me.

I considered how to approach her. Making a good first impression would be key. Maybe I'd wait until she went to the bathroom, get in line behind her, and strike up a conversation? No matter what, the fact that I'd come here specifically to question her would cause friction—but less so if she felt I wasn't a threat. I was still plotting when Austina scanned the bar and caught me staring in her direction.

She squinted, scowled, and then cocked her head to whisper something into her bodyguard's ear. The big man rose and strode forward, dodging the pawing of more than a few of the leather-clad women in the process. He materialized beside our table, his shadow blocking out the light from the single disco ball that twirled overhead. "My boss wants to know what you think you're doing here," he said.

I scowled back at him. "I t'ink I'm enjoyin' meself. What's it to her?"

Confusion and irritation warred across the man's face. "This club is off-limits to Freaks. Don't you know that?"

My eyebrows shot up. I leaned sideways until I could see past the big Samoan. Austina, whose animosity hadn't faded, glared at me. I settled back into my seat and tried to decide what to do next.

"You should go. Now." The Samoan folded his arms across his chest, and I marveled at his shirt's ability to withstand the muscles beneath it. Cotton abuse. I shook my head, wondering idly if the Samoan and the Rock were related. Cousins, probably.

But, like, first cousins.

"I didn't know this place was off-limits," I said, trying to deescalate the situation. "But I did come here to talk to your boss. I—"

The bodyguard held a hand up and pressed the other to his ear, where a small device was attached. I realized he had an ear piece, the wire dangling behind his thick neck. He listened intently, then nodded. "Understood." His attention turned back to me. "If you don't leave now, I'll be forced to escort you out. The boss isn't seeing anyone tonight. You made a mistake coming here."

I pinched the bridge of my nose. Great. Serge coughed, drawing my attention. He pointed to his neck and the silver collar that encircled it with a questioning expression, grinning. I elbowed him, much harder this time. "Not a chance."

The bodyguard's attention shifted to the smaller man beside me, assessing the threat. Had we all been Regulars, the mild-mannered Serbian likely wouldn't have set off alarm bells. But Freaks were different—our appearance had no bearing on our abilities. For all the bodyguard knew, Serge was a nuclear explosion waiting to happen. Which meant his boss must be one scary lady—why else would he be willing to take us on in public? Unfortunately for him, he was assessing the wrong person.

Remembering the sage advice of the warrior known as Patrick Swayze, I leaned back, cocked my leg under the table, and drove my heel into the bodyguard's knee, sending him crumpling to the floor—take the biggest guy in the world, shatter his knee, and he'll drop like a stone...thank you *Roadhouse*. The bodyguard howled in pain, rolling on the floor, eyes pinched shut.

"Somebody get help," I yelled over the roar of the music. "I t'ink he's hurt!"

A panicked crowd moved back as one while a few industrious patrons rushed to the bar to tell the staff that a man had collapsed on the dance floor. I figured that sort of thing happened from time to time, and that they'd have a plan to deal with the poor guy. I stepped over him and approached Austina's table. Her second bodyguard stood, fully prepared to manhandle me—and not in a good way—but a slender hand on his wrist halted him.

"Let me deal with this," Austina said, looking up at me. As I watched, her eyes flashed with a pale, golden light. "Well, mortal, you're here. Tell me what you want. Fame, fortune, inspiration? If you were hoping I'd help you, I can assure you that you've gone about things the wrong way."

I blinked a few times. "Actually, I'm here to ask about a girl."

The light in Austina's eyes faded to a warm shade of brown. "You what?"

So much for making a good first impression.

CHAPTER 15

$\mathcal{A}$ ustina's bodyguard had rejoined us at the table, an ice pack placed squarely over his swollen knee. I considered apologizing, but I doubted it would make much difference—it's not like saying sorry would bring down the swelling. Instead, I focused on Austina, who was preoccupied with ordering a drink from a waitress. Up close, she was even prettier than I'd thought; she had a classical beauty to her I couldn't quite describe except to say that if I could draw worth a damn, I'd be tempted to sketch her like one of my French girls.

"So," she said, facing me, "you say you came to ask me about a girl. Before we discuss that, though, I want to know how you found out about this place and somehow missed the memo that it's *Freaka non grata.*"

"If I said the internet, would ye believe me?" I asked.

Austina grunted. "If Pythagoras had known what his theorems would one day be used for, he'd be rolling over in his grave."

"The mathematician?" I asked, momentarily thrown by the reference.

"Of course. Every brilliant thing mankind has done can be traced back to the Greeks. Modern medicine? Greeks. Astronomy? Greeks. Maps? Greeks. Civilization?"

"Greeks?" I offered, sarcastically.

"Greeks," Austina affirmed, solemnly.

"Right..." I didn't feel compelled to argue. My sole experience with

Greek culture was limited to a guy I'd dated a few years back who'd turned out to be a bit of a misogynistic scumbag—not exactly a worthwhile sample size. "Anyway, that's how I knew you'd be here," I said. "But obviously there wasn't anythin' written there about Freaks, one way or the other."

The drinks arrived. Austina took hers and sipped on it for a moment, considering my response. She grunted, again. "Alright, let's say I believe you, and that you aren't yet another attractive, but ultimately talentless, mortal looking for stardom…ask your questions."

My brow furrowed, but I ignored her insinuation. "A friend of mine went missin' a little while back," I said, "and the last appointment she made was to see you. I was hopin' to at least find out whether or not ye met with her."

"Name?" Austina held out her hand. The bodyguard I hadn't maimed handed her a small tablet. She tapped it with a stylus a few times before looking up at me, expectantly.

"Oh, Terry Mutschler."

"Mutschler…No. I have a Terry Moore?"

I shrugged. "Could be?"

"Gorgeous, a little shorter than you? Big, blue eyes? A body to make Aphrodite jealous?"

"Sounds about right. Did ye meet with her, then?"

"I did. I remember her specifically because the girl had no range. No talent for writing lyrics. She fumbled through most of the chords on her guitar. Usually my people vet someone thoroughly before sending them my way. Saves me time. Occasionally I'll find a raw talent and sign them immediately—that's what I did with Johnson Beaver, you know—but that's rare. I complained to my assistant, but she said the girl had booked an appointment without references, which never happens." Austina shrugged.

"Were ye mean to her?" I asked, testily. I could only imagine Terry's reaction. A girl struggling to make it in the big city being told she was talentless by someone like Austina? Maybe that's what had driven her away. Shame alone might have kept her from calling home.

"Of course not," Austina retorted. "Just because I couldn't stand listening to her doesn't mean I'm blind. Girls that look like that can make a lot of money. She could be the next Heidi Klum, the next Gisele. I sent her to my sibling, Milana."

"Your sibling?"

Austina polished off her drink, then leaned in until our faces were almost touching. Gold poured from her pupils, flooding her irises and finally pooling in the sclera until her eyes were all the same shade of molten metal. "You don't know who I am, do you?"

"You're Austina—"

She barked a laugh. "That's *a* name, but not *my* name. The names my sisters and I choose are linked to our natures and vary depending on the era. Austina, as in Austin, Texas, the Live Music Capitol of the World. Milana, as in Milan, the Fashion Capitol of Fashion Capitols. Did you really not know?"

"Know what?" I asked, utterly baffled by the course of our conversation. It was almost as if she was offended I had no other agenda other than to find Terry. I wondered if this was how famous people ended up: always aching to be recognized and worshipped.

"Know that you sought one of the Muses."

"The what?"

"The Muses." Austina studied me and sighed, clearly exasperated. "The Nine Muses. Daughters of Zeus. *The* Zeus." She settled back and smiled, her eyes reflecting neon strobes. "Surely you've heard of him?"

I nodded, dumbly.

"Of course," Austina said, wryly. "Everyone's heard of *him*."

I took a second to compose myself. A daughter of Zeus. I was talking to a daughter of Zeus. A Muse. One of the nine goddesses responsible for pretty much every notably inspired act that had ever taken place. And yet, for the life of me, all I could think was that she looked nothing like the cartoon songstresses in *Hercules*.

I wisely kept that thought to myself.

She slipped a card onto the middle of the table, "Take this. Oh, and I don't ever want to see you here again, understood?" Before I could respond, she and her bodyguards became golden statues and melted before my eyes, leaving behind a puddle of liquid gold that pooled at our feet. A nearby waitress hurriedly mopped it up, oblivious to the precious metal staining her hands.

Talk about a flashy exit.

CHAPTER 16

*S*erge drove us back to the hotel, dodging the late-night traffic—mostly taxis and Ubers at this point in the evening. I thumbed the card Austina had given me, studying the card stock, running my fingers over the embossed letter M emblazoned on the front. Austina had assured me that she'd let her sister know I would be in touch, which would save me the trouble of having to stake out yet another Muse.

I still wasn't sure how I felt about the whole meeting a goddess thing. I mean, sure, I'd run into Sun Wukong the Monkey King—one of the gods of the Chinese pantheon—only a few weeks ago. But that had been in an alternate dimension, after going through a portal that wasn't supposed to exist. Looking back on it, the whole experience seemed so surreal that some days I wondered whether I'd made it all up—a lucid fever dream of some kind, maybe. But this? Meeting a goddess at a Manhattan nightclub? That had definitely happened. Hadn't it?

Ironically, I'd met an angel only a few hours earlier and hardly batted an eye. I think, deep down, that my Catholic indoctrination was to blame—angels and demons I could wrap my head around, but the idea that gods actually existed, gods that were worshipped before *the* God, directly contradicted everything I'd been taught growing up. Bizarrely, I found myself facing, not so much a crisis of faith, but a crisis of proof.

Othello's ringtone stopped me from dwelling on all things cosmic. It even made me grin a little.

"About time," I said, humming the *From Russia With Love* theme song under my breath.

"Sorry, board meetings. Have to occasionally reassure our investors that we won't sell the company to a competitor for no reason."

"Is that normal?"

Othello chuckled. "Define normal."

"Fair point," I replied. "So, guess who met a goddess a few minutes ago?"

"You? That's nice. Which one?"

"Which...Othello, a goddess. A real one. With gold eyes and everythin'."

"Well that's different. I've only run across a few gods working for Nate, but I don't recall any of them having eyes that glowed. But then again, it's easy to get distracted. I mean, Ganesh has the head of an elephant, and Shiva has like four arms."

I realized I was gaping. I closed my mouth and pursed my lips. "Well, fine, whatever. Way to ruin it for me."

Othello laughed at me, not bothering to soothe my injured pride.

"Anyway," I continued, spitefully, "did ye listen to me voicemails?"

"I did. And I'm sorry. One of the sources I pulled mentioned something about angel involvement, but it was one of many rumors I picked up. I was hoping you'd be able put in your bid before anyone else came sniffing around. The broker only came into town yesterday."

"Johnny Appleseed, ye mean," I clarified, my tone disapproving.

"Yes, about that," Othello said. "Did you call him 'sexy' in one of your voicemails?"

I grunted. "So?"

"Nothing," Othello said, giggling. "Nothing at all."

"Ye just wait 'til ye see him for yourself," I said, huffing.

"Sure, sure. Anyway, tell me more about this goddess you met."

I filled her in on Terry's meeting with Austina, as well as where Austina fell in the Greek pantheon. The news that I'd met a goddess hadn't surprised her, but the fact that she was Greek seemed to make her a little leery.

"Old wounds," Othello said, "that's all. The last Greek goddess we tangled with caused a lot of mayhem. We were lucky to walk away from it."

"What happened to her?"

Othello paused, as if unsure whether to tell me. I was seconds away from changing the subject when she sighed. "Nate killed her."

"He *what?*"

"It was a war. And one thing you'll learn about Nate, about all of us, really, is that we take care of our own. Anyone who hurts us pays." I sensed something lurking beneath her words, a past experience, perhaps. A painful memory.

The intensity in Othello's voice shocked me more than the sentiment. I decided not to pry; I had plenty of my own painful memories, after all. "I understand completely. No one fucks with me and mine and walks away." I pictured the mortified face of the wizard who'd kidnapped my aunt—the terrified expression he wore right before he was taken by the monster who would eventually kill him—and smiled. "No one."

"I know," Othello said, her tone brightening. "That's why we're friends."

We were still laughing when something big struck the car from the side, tearing into it. My phone flew out of my hand and landed on the floorboards. I screamed in shock, ducked away from the spray of glass and the sound of metal shredding, and clipped my head hard against the window.

There was a blinding flash of pain.

And then, for a moment, silence.

CHAPTER 17

The sound of Othello's tinny voice screeching nearby brought me out of my daze. My phone had survived somehow; I could see the pale blue glow on the floorboard only a foot away, but I couldn't reach it. My hands wouldn't move. Something wet was running down my face, threatening to drip into my eye. I blinked it away once. And again.

"Quinn! Quinn, are you alright?!"

The pain hit me all at once, like a wave breaking inside my body. I whimpered from the sensation but ground my teeth to stop from crying out; I'd been hurt before—I knew how to push pain aside. What I needed, first and foremost, was to get the hell out of the car before we got hit again, or the gas tank blew. Adrenaline poured through me and I managed to sit up, groggily. I fumbled in my attempts to reach my phone, but finally got it to my ear. "I'm here," I said.

"What happened?!"

I held the phone away from my ear. "Shout a little quieter, would ye?" I muttered. "Somethin' hit us."

"An accident? Hold on, I'll pull up the tracker and get an ambulance there right away. I'm sure there's traffic footage, too."

"Aye, ye do that. I'll be here." I wiped the liquid away from my face. My hand came away slick and sticky with blood. I glanced down at myself and realized it had run down my front, too, ruining my top. "Son of a bitch!" I cursed.

"What is it?" Othello asked, distracted, but concerned.

"Nothin', never ye mind."

"How's Serge?" Othello asked.

Oh, right. The driver. I studied the car's interior and noticed the passenger side looked completely wrong—the whole of it had been punched in, dented so severely that I couldn't distinguish the leather seats from the metal. Serge was slumped forward onto the airbag, unconscious. I reached around, dipped my bloody fingers under the collar around his throat, and felt for a pulse.

"He's fine," I said. "Well, as fine as can be expected, considerin' we got in an accident."

"Quinn, I don't think it was an accident."

"What do ye mean?" I shuffled until I could see out the window, trying to get a better look at who had hit us. Whoever it was, they would be lucky to have survived. Hell, we were lucky to have survived. As I sought out the other vehicle, I realized there was surprisingly little sound. Even this late, I'd expect to hear sirens and horns blaring and such; in New York, any traffic hiccup became a logistical nightmare, so road collisions were usually handled pretty quickly.

That's when I saw what had hit us.

"Quinn, wake up Serge! Now. You have to get out of there."

"Little late for that," I whispered.

The rear passenger side door, little more than a mangled sheet of metal at this point, was torn off its hinges and flung out onto the street. A creature— humanoid, but only just—thrust its face into the hole it'd created, cavernous sockets where the eyes should have been, a face carved from granite and glass. When it spoke, the pain in my head intensified, landing somewhere between chewing on aluminum foil and the worst migraine I'd ever had.

"Give us the seed."

I cursed and held my phone up directly to my mouth. "Othello, I am goin' to kill ye if I end up dyin' here over some Goddamned plant!"

The creature flinched.

"Hold on, I'll see what I can do," Othello replied, then hung up. I stared at my phone in disbelief, then groaned and shoved it into my jacket pocket.

The creature put two massive hands on either side of the hole it'd created and pried it wider. "Come out, give us the seed, and we will leave you to the care of your mortal doctors."

"I don't have the seed, ye daft rock," I said, glaring at him.

"We saw you leave the hotel. We know you met with one of the Grigori. You are the seed bearer."

I grimaced. "Please tell me that's not the term ye plan to go with. I'm not bearin' anyone's seed anytime soon."

The cragged face of the creature, coupled with the lack of eyes, made gauging its expression tricky, but I was beginning to sense impatience. "The name is unimportant, only the seed matters."

"Speakin' of names," I said, buying time, "what's yours? I can't go around callin' ye Rock Biter."

The creature took the hood of the car and slowly peeled it back, the shriek of metal like nails on a chalkboard. "I am Gomorrah."

I pinned my hands over my ears and shouted, "Like Gomorrah, Gomorrah? Sodom and Gomorrah, Gomorrah?"

"Yes. I was born in the ashes of that city and hold the souls of those who were punished."

"So are ye a demon, then?" I asked.

"I serve."

"Cause that's not vague," I muttered. With the roof nearly torn off, I could see Gomorrah's entire body: a mass of stone held together by sand and flame that glittered like glass in some places—he looked every bit the nightmare you'd expect. Once he'd made room for his massive torso, he hunched forward, reaching for me.

I squirmed away. "I told ye, I don't have the damn seed!"

"Then I will bring you back to the Marquis. He will not be pleased."

Gomorrah finally got his massive hands around my legs, but when he drew back, nothing happened. I'd slipped out of his grasp as smoothly as a wriggling fish. He tried again. Nothing.

I laughed, mostly delirious from blood loss and adrenaline at this point. It all made sense; it was like Karim had said: oil and water. Of course, that didn't solve my immediate problem. I still had a head wound to deal with, and the possibility that the car could explode had only risen thanks to Gomorrah's demon-handling of the door and roof. Then there was Serge.

Getting him out and dragging him to safety would be a bitch under any circumstance. I glanced over to make sure he was still alright.

Except Serge wasn't there.

The driver's seat was empty, the airbag hanging limp near the floorboard, slashed open. I must not have heard him get out over the sound of Gomorrah peeling the car apart like a tin can. I hoped he'd gone for help, although I was pretty sure the NYPD weren't equipped to take this thing down. Maybe SWAT would have an answer. That's when I heard it: a familiar howl echo from the other side of the car. I didn't need to look to know what I'd see: a bipedal, barrel-chested skinwalker, vaguely shaped like a werewolf, eyes glowing green.

Serge hadn't gone for help. Serge *was* the help.

CHAPTER 18

*G*omorrah looked up in time to catch a skinwalker with his face. Serge—the silver collar still wrapped around his throat—landed on top of the demon, claws extended. He swung down again and again, gouging into Gomorrah's upper body, sending stone chips and sparks flying. I realized the skinwalker was repeating something, a mantra, in that eerie, disembodied voice of his.

"Mine, mine, mine, mine..."

I blocked that out; I wasn't trying to dwell on what *that* meant. As much as I appreciated Serge's interference, I wasn't sure how long he could hold off the demon, which meant I needed to take advantage of the time I had. The hole Gomorrah had made was wide enough for me to climb through, but then I risked getting caught in the middle of their fight. What I needed was to get as far away as possible.

I turned, fiddling with the handle on the driver side. The door was stuck, probably pinned closed after the collision. I swung around and lay back, cocking both feet in the air. I kicked the door as hard as I could. Once. Twice. I could hear Serge's labored breathing and Gomorrah shifting on the ground, his rocky skin digging into the pavement.

I kicked a final time, throwing all my weight and what little energy I had left into it. I heard the metal groan and, when I tried the door this time, it gave with an ear-piercing squeal, opening wide enough for me to slip through. I scurried out and took off down the street, baffled by the lack of pedestrians. Where was everyone? I stopped and studied the intersection behind me. Serge was squaring off against Gomorrah, who'd finally clambered back to his feet. Aside from the two of them, there wasn't a single individual on the street. It reminded me of what Darrel had done at Penn Station, times a hundred. Had Gomorrah done that? "But how...?" I asked myself, my ears ringing.

"My doing," a voice whispered over my shoulder.

I spun around too quickly for my injured body to handle, stumbled, and went down onto one knee. A figure sat on the trunk of a car a few feet away —a reedy, older man, the skin of his face and neck covered in scars. He kicked his legs like a child on a roller coaster, rocking the car back and forth slightly. "The Marquis would like to have a word with you, if you please."

"Tell him to go fuck himself," I said, my voice hoarse from exhaustion. I felt for the gun at my back, resolving to give the bastard a few more scars if he came anywhere near me. My other gun, a smaller caliber pistol I'd kept in my pocket, must have fallen out in the car.

The man giggled, his laugh painfully high-pitched. "You tell him. We'll see how that goes."

I heard a yelp from behind me and turned in time to watch Serge take a backhand that launched him into the remains of our car. The gas tank, which had held up admirably up to this point, blew, and the resulting explosion drove me onto all fours, sending my gun skidding across the pavement.

The man's obnoxious laughing continued. "Ooh, fireworks."

I fought against the blackout I knew was coming. Suddenly, a pair of shoes appeared in my peripheral vision. No, not shoes...hooves? I fell over, wondering who'd let a horse in on this party.

Everything went dark.

CHAPTER 19

I woke to a nurse recording data on my chart, an EKG beeping, and a vase of fresh flowers sitting on the table beside my bed—an artfully arranged mound of blue-eyed-grass, my favorite flower since I was a little girl.

There was also a man leaning against the doorframe.

"Hello again," Chapman said.

"Johnny Appleseed, is it? So, was it ye?" I asked.

"Pardon?"

"On the horse."

Chapman's brow knotted. He and the nurse exchanged looks. She finished marking down my vitals and stepped out of the room, flashing him a knowing smile. "She's had a head injury, don't be surprised if she's a little...not herself," she advised before leaving.

I snorted. "Not like he knows me, anyway."

Chapman stepped into the room, noted the flowers, and took a seat in the corner of the room. He'd dressed for the cool weather in a dark green turtleneck, a jacket and hoodie secure in the crook of his arm now that he was indoors. He stared out the window, looking posed and impossibly handsome—like a cover model in a turtleneck campaign.

I didn't even want to think about how I looked. Scraped and bruised and potentially broken, my makeup hours old, eyes bloodshot. Whatever. I was honestly beyond caring.

"Um, are ye goin' to tell me why you're here?" I asked, irritably. "I'm guessin' ye have no idea what horse I'm talkin' about." There was a white knight joke in there somewhere, but I was too tired and in too much pain to make it. Looks like they'd avoided doping me up on morphine this time around.

Totally going to file a complaint.

"Darrel stopped by this morning," Chapman said. "He told me you were attacked by demons last night. They thought I'd passed the seed to you to give to him, which would have been clever, if it'd been true."

I groaned. So, that was why Gomorrah had targeted us. In all the confusion, I hadn't paid much attention to motive—survival had been my main priority. I realized the nurse had been wrong; my head throbbed and my body ached, but otherwise I felt like my usual, crabby self. "What the fuck does this seed even do?" I muttered.

Chapman cocked an eyebrow. "You mean you don't know?"

I ground my teeth. "My employer was a little coy with the details. To be fair, I'm pretty sure her information was spotty, at best."

"Well, you figured out who I am. Or what people call me, anyway."

I nodded. "I know who ye say ye are. I'm not sure I entirely believe it."

He chuckled. "You met an angel yesterday and got attacked by demons last night and you don't believe *I* exist?"

When he put it like that, it did sound a little ridiculous. "Shut up. I have a head injury. I'm not meself."

"Do you know what I was, then? My profession, I mean."

"A nurseryman," I said. "You took care of trees."

"I did, when I was mortal. Since then, I've been responsible for taking care of other things. Let's just say there are a lot of untended gardens out there, and I'm responsible for most of them."

"So, the seed?" I pressed.

Chapman huffed and stared out the window again, the overcast light from outside bathing one side of his face in a uniform shade of grey. "The seed is all that remains of a tree. I should say it's all that remains of *the* tree. The one that led us to where we are now, and what we've become."

"Which tree would that be?"

Chapman folded his hands in his lap and glanced back at me, his eyes hooded. "The Tree of Knowledge. From the Garden of Eden."

Oh. *That* tree.

CHAPTER 20

*C*hapman rose to leave, doggedly ignoring my follow-up questions.

"The less you know, the better," he claimed. "Get some rest. Recover. I'll make sure none of the Grigori bother you from now on."

"Aye, that's all well and good. But how do ye plan to keep me safe from the other side?" I asked, pointing out the flaw in his plan. They'd attacked me before with almost no guarantee I had the seed, so what would stop them from doing it again?

"I've agreed to meet with their representatives. They know I have the seed and have no intention of passing it off to anyone else."

"Why would ye do that?" I asked, baffled. His guilty expression said it all. "Wait, you're meetin' with demons to stop them from comin' after me a second time?"

Chapman sighed. "It wasn't ever supposed to come to this. I never wanted to jeopardize innocent people."

"What are they offerin' ye that's worth all this trouble?" I asked, for perhaps the fourth or fifth time. At this point, I wasn't even concerned about leverage. I genuinely wanted to know what could be so valuable he'd risk everything to get it.

"Something only they can," Chapman said, echoing Darrel's assertion from the day before. "Now, I've got to go." He approached my bedside and placed a hand on the rail. "Can I get you anything before I go?"

I stared up at him and briefly fantasized about doing things that, in my condition, could best be described as suicidal—and that's assuming we could even touch each other without ending up twitching on the floor. "No," I grumbled, finally, feeling as prickly as I ever had; it was like he'd offered me chocolate while I was on the strictest diet imaginable.

"Take care of yourself, Miss MacKenna."

"You too, Appleseed."

He headed out, pausing at the door for a moment. "You know, I always hated it when people called me that. I never wanted to be a legend. Just a good man."

"From what little I've seen," I said, haltingly, the unfamiliar taste of a compliment giving me pause, "ye seem a wee bit o' both."

"Thanks." Chapman smiled and ducked out of the room, leaving me to my troubled thoughts.

*T*he seed to the fucking Tree of Knowledge.

I could see now why Othello hadn't told me more; I'd probably have laughed in her face if she'd been upfront about what she'd sent me after. I mean, angels and demons were all well and good, but Adam and Eve? The Garden of Eden? The Tree of Knowledge? Those were all part of a creation myth, and I'd walked away from organized religion a long time ago. Hell, I'd switched schools my junior year because I couldn't wrap my head around people who took the Bible literally.

Guess I owed my Theology teacher an apology.

I lay in the hospital bed for maybe a minute before Othello strode through the door, hurrying to my side. She paused at the edge of my bed as if unsure how I would react, her eyes downcast. I was surprised to see her, but at least now I knew who'd brought the flowers—I wondered how many of my likes and dislikes Othello had tucked away in a file on her computer. Maybe I should outsource her on birthdays.

"Quinn, I am so sorry," Othello began. "I did not know—"

"How's Serge?" I interrupted. Othello's apology could wait. In fact, if I were being honest with myself, I didn't need one to begin with. Sure, she'd gotten me involved in one hell of a mess—no pun intended—but it wasn't like she'd done it on purpose. On the other hand, the last time I'd seen the Serbian was when he'd landed on our car. A car that had been blown to shit.

If Serge had gotten hurt trying to save me, *then* Othello would have something to apologize for.

"He's fine. Skinwalkers are more or less invulnerable to physical damage. You tried shooting him once, remember?"

I remembered. My bullets had hit the skinwalker center mass but hadn't left so much as a mark on him. In hindsight, I realized Serge's impregnability made him the perfect guy to have my back; magic couldn't touch me, and nothing but magic could touch him. We made one hell of a duo.

Too bad his alter ego was a deranged animal that liked to pee on things to assert its dominance.

"Right. That's good, then. Ye don't need to apologize, Othello. I know ye didn't intend for this to happen," I said, waving casually at the hospital bed. "And I know about the seed." I directed her to a nearby chair with a nod. Othello took a seat, looking nervous, probably trying to gauge my reaction to the news that she'd sent me after a priceless religious artifact that shouldn't even exist. I smiled to reassure her. "So, the nurse left before givin' me the damage report. Care to fill me in?"

Othello looked relieved to change the subject. "Concussion, a few lacerations, some bumps and bruises, but nothing broken. The doctors say it was a miracle that's all the damage you walked away with, but then they were looking for injuries consistent with a car accident, not a run in with a demon."

"So ye were able to track down what hit us?"

"I saw it on the camera, for an instant, before it took out the car. Then the footage stopped."

"So ye didn't see the other bastard? The scarred one?" I asked.

Othello frowned. "No, it wasn't a man. In fact, I didn't know what it was, originally, but I knew who to send."

"Are ye talkin' about the horse?"

Othello looked surprised. "You remember?"

"I remember seein' a horse, right before passin' out."

Othello fetched the chair from the other side of the room and took a seat beside my hospital bed. "That was Hemingway. He stepped in to save you. He couldn't interfere directly, but he hid you and Serge—bringing you here was my idea. He was against getting involved, at first. Stepping in is not something he's supposed to do. But when I showed him what attacked you, he seemed…well, angry. Very angry."

"It was too soon," Hemingway said from the doorway, mirroring Chapman's pose from earlier. A man I didn't recognize stood next to him, his back turned to us as if guarding the door.

"Too soon for what?" I asked, ignoring the stranger.

"For Gomorrah and the rest of the Unclean. That's the name of the creature who attacked you."

"Aye," I nodded. "The rock monster and I had a nice little chat before he tried to kidnap me. Although t'is the first I've ever heard about the 'Unclean,'" I admitted.

"They're practically indistinguishable from demons in most ways," Hemingway replied. "But they are able to act with more freedom. More autonomy. Think of them like mercenaries."

"The scarred fucker said they were servin' someone named the Marquis. Any idea who that is?" I asked.

Hemingway frowned. "There was no scarred man," he said.

I blinked rapidly. Had I imagined it? Dreamt it? No, I was sure of it. There had definitely been someone there. A hideously scarred man.

With a horrifying laugh.

Hemingway's companion grunted and spoke, still turned away, interrupting the silence. "Your Marquis could be anyone. They're all about titles down there. Duke this and Count that. But if he's controlling Gomorrah, my guess is it's one of the Fallen. Maybe even one of the Lieutenants."

Hemingway ran a hand through his hair, ruffling it a bit in frustration. "Things are escalating. They're interfering directly. Both sides. But why now?"

"They want the seed," I explained.

"The seed?" Hemingway asked, raising an eyebrow.

Othello dipped her head. "I asked Quinn to track down a rumor I heard. About a seed."

Hemingway's companion tensed, taking a sharp breath, drawing Hemingway's attention. They shared a look and a small exchange I couldn't quite make out.

"They can't have it," Hemingway said, his expression stern.

"Well, obviously not," I said. "I don't want the bastards that attacked us gettin' ahold of it, either, but"

"No," Hemingway interrupted. "Not the Fallen. Or not only the Fallen. Heaven cannot claim it, either."

"Why not?" Othello asked, saving me the trouble.

Hemingway folded his arms over his chest. "Think of the seed like a nuclear weapon. Right now, both sides are armed, but neither has the upper hand. Peace exists because neither is sure they could win. That—and there are a few level-headed people in charge serving both camps who are content to play the long game. The seed might upset that balance."

"What happens then?" Othello asked.

"Then my brothers and I go to work," Hemingway answered in an emotionless tone that brought chills to my spine.

Othello blanched.

The silence in the hospital room stretched until it practically hurt—like staring at a taut rubber band about to break. Finally, I couldn't take it anymore. I raised my hand. Hemingway's eyebrows shot up. "What?"

"Where can I get a horse that teleports?"

The figure behind Hemingway laughed, his voice raspy. "Don't you dare go recruiting another one." Then he walked off into the hall.

I took that as a no.

CHAPTER 21

*H*emingway stood vigil at the window. "I'm sorry, Quinn. I know you've been through hell—metaphorically speaking. But I need your help."

"With what?" I asked, fidgeting with my hospital gown. "And who was that guy?" The gown's material was thin and itchy; I couldn't wait to change into something that made me feel less like a victim.

"That was one of my brothers. He was checking up on me." Hemingway's face told me that he wasn't fond of being on any kind of leash. He sighed. "I need your help retrieving the seed. The only way this doesn't go to shit is if a third party, someone independent, takes possession."

I glanced at Othello, trying to get her read on the situation, but she seemed preoccupied; I could practically see the wheels spinning in her head as she planned her next move. I liked that about her—her ability to adapt and overcome.

"That's what I've been tryin' to do," I said, finally. "But Chapman won't trade for it. Apparently, the Grigori offered him somethin' we can't. I tried to get him to tell me, but he refused."

"Appleseed was here?" Hemingway asked, facing me.

"Ye just missed him," I replied. "Ye might have even seen him on your way in. About my height, a green turtleneck, brown hair, brown eyes. Young."

"Wait, *that* was Johnny Appleseed?" Othello exclaimed, tuning back into the conversation. "That hunky guy we passed in the lobby?"

Hemingway pursed his lips but seemed more amused than jealous. He ignored Othello's outburst. "I can only guess what they're offering him, but the Grigori are known for keeping an eye on mankind. They never get involved. In fact, for angels, they're surprisingly reasonable. If *they* are making a grab for power, things are worse than I thought."

"It gets worse," I said. "He's arranged a meetin' with the other side as well, tryin' to lure 'em away from yours truly."

Hemingway muttered a few obscenities under his breath. "Maybe you can use that to your advantage, somehow?" he asked, absentmindedly. "Pit one side against the other."

I shared a look with Othello. She could read the question on my face and shook her head, but I couldn't wait any longer. I had to know. "Who are ye?" I asked. "Ye saved me life, I know, and I appreciate that. But now you're askin' me to risk the life ye just saved to stop Heaven and Hell from goin' to war, so I t'ink the least ye can do is tell me who I'm doin' favors for."

Hemingway slipped his hands into his jacket pockets, his eyes cool and distant, his mouth turned down at the edges. Othello started to say something, but he shook his head. "No, she's right. Besides, I'm sure she'd figure it out on her own sooner or later."

He locked eyes with me and that eerie sensation—the one that made the hairs on the back of my neck prickle—returned. "A few people know me as Hemingway these days. Friends, mostly. But the rest of the world knows me, has known me, by another name." The lights flickered for an instant and I swore I could see a dark and foreboding figure in Hemingway's place. "I am Death, one of the four Horsemen of the Apocalypse." He smiled, but it was a sad, wistful thing. "And, contrary to what most believe, my brothers and I are in no rush to see that happen. We cannot stop it directly, but we can...nudge it further into the future, here and there, if we're careful."

I had to look away. I stared at my hands, at the abrasions and torn skin left behind after our tussle with Gomorrah and the scarred man. "So, what does that make me, then?" I asked, softly.

"What?" Hemingway asked.

"When ye tested me field, ye realized somethin' ye didn't want to share. Somethin' about what I am. My field hasn't been actin' the same since. Tell me what it was ye did, what ye felt, or I won't help ye."

"Quinn—" Othello began, gently.

"No," I glared at them both. "I'm tired of people I'm supposed to trust keepin' secrets. Even if they mean well. He owes me an explanation, and I intend to hear it. The world be damned."

Hemingway surprised me with a grin. "You remind me more and more of someone I know. I should say first that I don't know what, if anything, I did that affected your field. That wasn't my intention." He took a moment, considering his next words carefully. "But you're right, I did keep something from you. It's not so much about what you are, though, as what you aren't. Do you remember when we first met, when you saw me as a child? When I said I couldn't see your death?"

I nodded. It had seemed like an odd comment at the time, but in hindsight it made even less sense. Could Hemingway see people's deaths? I realized that his title probably came with a host of fringe benefits like that—although I'm not sure whether I'd consider that one a gift or a curse.

"I've been at this job a long, long time," Hemingway continued. "And there are special cases, sometimes. People destined to be brought back, or ghosts who linger. But I sensed you were different."

Hemingway paused, sighed, and sat back against the windowsill. "When I touched your field and it tried to draw me in, I realized that you couldn't possibly be human." This time when he met my gaze, I read the emotion in his eyes. I realized why he hadn't told me; he hadn't wanted to upset me.

Death had a conscience. Go figure.

"How is that possible?" Othello said.

"I don't know," Hemingway admitted. "It makes no sense to me, either. Everything about you, aside from your ability, screams human. You bleed, you age…you even smell like one."

"I what?" I asked, gaping.

"My horse has a good nose for these sorts of things."

I could have sworn I heard a horse's whinny peal from his coat pocket.

"I still don't understand, Quinn," Othello said, shaking her head. She sat forward, resting her hand on my arm. "I am sure there's an explanation."

"Aye, there may be," I replied. "When ye went diggin' up information on me, before we met," I began, "did ye ever find out anythin' about me father? Any mention of who he might be?"

Othello shook her head, brow furrowed. "No, but I also was not looking that far back. Why?"

"I know all about me ma from Dez's stories. But I don't know anythin' about him. Not even his name. All humans die, right?" I asked Hemingway, waiting for his affirmative before continuing. "Well, me ma died. Which means he's the one. He has to be." I clenched the crisp white linen bedsheets until my knuckles went white. "I've been lookin' for me da for as long as I can remember, but it always felt like I was lookin' in the wrong place." I glanced at Othello. "That's why I wanted to go to Fae. I t'ink he may be there, that he may be one of them. If I'm not human, maybe he can tell me what I am."

Othello squeezed my arm. "I understand."

"The Fae realm is a dangerous place," Hemingway said, digesting the possibility. "But you may find your answers there. I've never heard of a hybrid—half-mortal, half-Fae—but being Death doesn't come with omnipotence. I let Othello handle that side of things." He and Othello grinned at each other.

"Well then," I said, stretching. "I suppose it's time I get cleared to leave."

"Already?" Othello asked, concerned.

"Ye and I had a deal, didn't we? I get ye the seed, and you'll put me in touch with someone who'll take me to Fae. I get what I want and, bonus, I put a stop to Armageddon. Meanwhile Death," I said, grinning, "will owe me a favor."

Hemingway frowned, but nodded.

I was *so* getting a horse.

CHAPTER 22

Serge, smiling wide, met us at the car—an uncanny replica of the one that had been blown to smithereens the night before. For a guy who'd taken an airbag to the face, not to mention survived an explosion, he looked ridiculously chipper. Othello wheeled me towards him; hospital policy said someone had to do it, and Hemingway had left shortly after I'd been discharged, promising to return if and when he could.

For once, I was sorry to see him go.

"Miss MacKenna! It is good you are well," Serge said cheerfully, opening the car door.

"Aye, t'anks to ye," I admitted.

Serge blushed. "It is my pleasure to help woman in need."

"But," I said, catching a glimpse of the silver collar around his throat, "how'd ye shift with that on?"

"I modified it," Othello interjected. "I did not want anyone removing it the way you did. So instead I linked the collar to my phone."

"Ye did what?"

Othello smirked. "It took some tricky coding, but I think magic and science have a lot to learn from one another." She pulled out her phone—a slim black device which looked nothing like any model I'd ever seen—and showed me an app which read: Leash Law. "Once I knew you were in danger, I cancelled the spell on the collar remotely."

Serge caught my awed expression and chuckled.

"What are ye laughin' at? She's scary," I said. "Ye sure ye want to be takin' orders from her?"

Othello bumped me as I clambered into the back. "Hush, or I will put a collar on you, too."

"Don't threaten me with a good time," I muttered, grinning.

Serge waited until Othello had joined me in back before shutting the door. He pulled away from the curb of the hospital at a crawl. "So, where do we go?"

I fetched Milana's card from my pocket. It was stained pink from blood, but still legible. The rest of my belongings, sadly, hadn't survived the trip to the hospital; I'd had to send Othello to the gift shop downstairs to buy me clothes. She'd returned with a set of New York Jets-themed sweatpants and hoodie, both of which I would eventually have to burn and never speak of again.

"The hotel," I said. "I've got an errand to run before we take on the cosmos."

"We," Othello clarified. "We have an errand to run."

"Ye don't need to do that," I said. "Ye have a business to manage and board members to please."

"Perhaps. But you are my friend, and because of me, you were hurt. I won't risk that happening again. We'll stick together from now on."

There was no point arguing further. If Othello wanted to tag along to meet Milana, fine. Once that was done, and Terry had been found, I'd insist she leave. Having Othello nearby was reassuring; her detective skills alone made her as valuable as any Freak out there. But if Heaven and Hell came knocking on our door again, I wouldn't be able to protect her. She'd be a liability and could end up seriously hurt, or worse.

I couldn't let that happen.

That settled, I booked an appointment to meet with one of the nine Muses later that day. It could have waited, sure, but—truthfully—I was worried about our odds of making it out of this thing in one piece. Tanya and her mother deserved closure, one way or the other.

And I intended to give it to them.

CHAPTER 23

*M*ilana's agency, *GRK Model Management*, sat squarely in the middle of Greenwich Village—one of those quaint brick buildings with thick glass windows and ivy running up and down the sides that one sometimes sees in New York, but could never afford to buy. Othello and I lounged in the lobby downstairs. We'd sent Serge on ahead to stake out Chapman's hotel and report to us at regular intervals. That way, if Chapman made a move, we'd know it.

The lobby was cozy, with a large sectional taking over one corner of the room, which is where we'd been told to wait. Our appointment time had come and gone, but no one seemed to be in any hurry, so we took the opportunity to peruse the various fashion magazines on display, casually remarking on the shifting trends—sheer skirts, plaid raincoats, and socks with heels.

"Genius," Othello said. "Pure genius."

"We're takin' it back," I said. "One smart weather decision at a time. Ye watch, by next year the *ushanka* will be all the rage."

Othello snorted.

The woman at the front desk, lovely enough to be a model herself, if a bit short, waved to get our attention. "Milana will see you now." I scanned the room and she pointed up the staircase towards two individuals working their way down, arms linked, as if to clarify.

The first, a handsome, young, Asian man, laughed at something said by his companion—a tall, dark individual with a mound of luxurious hair drawn back into a loose bun, whose features were exceptionally androgynous. It was this person who met us at the base of the stairs with an implacable gaze and knowing smile.

"I'll be right with you, ladies," Milana said, huskily, giving the young Asian man a once-over before popping the top button of his shirt and swiping a hand through his hair. She stepped away, and suddenly I could see that he wasn't handsome, but beautiful; his skin flawless and smooth, his body trim and fit. He grinned and headed out the door, oblivious to Othello and I's leering gazes.

"The boy landed a scent campaign this morning," Milana explained as she waved him goodbye. "He's very excited."

"Which scent?" I asked, trying to be conversational as I pried my eyes away.

"It's Johnson Beaver's newest scent. Boy Toy, I think it's called." Milana caught my incredulous expression and smirked. "You should have seen what the Greeks did with the boys, if you think that's in poor taste."

"I didn't say anythin'," I replied.

"So, you're here about Terry," Milana said, ascending the stairs, clearly expecting us to follow.

"We are. We were hopin' ye could tell us whether or not ye met, and where ye last saw her. Her family is really worried."

"We'll talk more in my office," Milana said.

We trailed her up the stairs and I realized that Milana, in her grey pantsuit and boots, cut a rather robust figure—her shoulders broad and muscular enough to shame a female bodybuilder, her thighs thick and sweeping, with an ass that refused to jiggle. Between that, the throaty timbre of her voice, and her makeup-less face, she gave off a jarringly masculine vibe.

Milana's office was decorated in a modern style that looked like it could have come straight from IKEA's showroom floor—a mixture of chrome and glass encased in white with flashes of color here and there to break up the monotony. She strode over to her desk and took a seat, encouraging us to do the same with a wave of her hand.

"When was the last time you heard from Terry?" Milana asked.

Othello and I exchanged looks.

"She's a family friend," I explained. "I'm here on her sister's behalf. She hasn't been heard from in several weeks, from what I understand."

Milana steepled her fingers in front of her mouth and frowned, clearly displeased by something. "Terry came to see me about a week ago. My sister, who you met, saw her potential for what it was. I'll admit I was eager to sign her. So eager, in fact, that when she told me more about her situation, I immediately encouraged her to move into one of our model apartments in Brooklyn. It's hard for the girls who come from elsewhere, especially without the support of their families. Putting them up in one of our model apartments minimizes their risk and allows them time to go to castings and find work."

"It does not hurt your bottom line, either," Othello remarked, snidely. "You become their agent and their landlord. Ten percent off the top and you take the rent out of their paychecks."

Milana dipped her head in acknowledgment. "This industry is remarkably cutthroat. Yes, I double-dip, as it were. But it doesn't always pan out. Say a girl comes to the city hoping to become famous. She stays at our apartment for three months, books only a few jobs, and makes maybe a few hundred dollars. She decides she wants to go home. We do not force her to stay. More importantly, despite the fact that she owes us three month's rent, we eat the cost. There is no debt involved."

I crossed my legs and considered Milana's position. In a way, Othello was right; skimming the extra income was a mercenary practice. But Milana's arrangement meant the chances of eviction—of being mercilessly forced onto the street when unable to pay that month's rent—were significantly decreased. If I'd had that opportunity when I'd first come to New York, I'd have taken it in a heartbeat.

"So, did she move in?" I asked, returning to the subject at hand.

"She did. She was in the process of finding a job, last we spoke. I encourage my models to work on the side. Something flexible, preferably on weekends, like waiting tables. She was very excited. Thankful. It's nice, representing girls like her, girls who appreciate the opportunity for what it is."

"Which is what, exactly?" I asked, curious. I found Milana's take on things surprisingly refreshing. I'd expected someone more flamboyant and ridiculous—an eccentric consumed by fashion, somewhere between Lagerfeld and Quant. It was a welcome change from Austina's paranoia and obsession with status.

Milana paused to consider the question. "You could say that the attention is the most important thing. Many models crave it. Traveling to exotic locations and attending glamourous parties. Being known and catered to..." Milana waved these away as if dismissing them. "The truth, however, is that every social interaction is dictated by how one looks. Symmetry and aesthetics. This industry helps shape perception. It defies convention and stagnation. Our models become a part of that. Standards of beauty are established, and—as a result—society grinds on."

"Ye make it seem almost philosophical, what ye do," I said, smirking.

Milana grinned. "Do you know who invented philosophy?"

I sighed. "The Greeks?"

"Very good." Milana paused and gave me a once over, studying me like you might an anatomical drawing—intrigued by my individual parts, but without agenda. "Have you ever considered modeling, yourself? You have very unique features. And so tall," she noted.

I grinned. "Ye couldn't afford me. Besides, unless scars are in season, I don't t'ink I'm your girl."

Milana shrugged. "You have my card, if you reconsider. I think you'd be surprised what society likes or dislikes. Times change. Names change. Years ago, I would have been vilified for dressing as a man. Now such things are common, even encouraged."

"Unlike my sisters, I find beauty in function as well as form," Milana said, rising to pop the button of her suit jacket and peel it off, revealing a stylish V-necked tank top, a thick clavicle, and an expanse of smooth, rippling muscle. She slung the jacket over her chair. "Perhaps that's why I chose to represent the children of this age. They defy our outdated standards and our antiquated classifications...but I digress. I believe we were talking about the disappearances."

"Disappearances?" Othello asked. "As in, more than one?"

Milana sighed. "So it seems. Terry is one of a handful who have gone missing across several agencies. Most are unaware of the trend, but I pay attention to such things."

"Have ye reported it to the authorities?" I asked.

"Your mortal police? Of course not."

"Why not?"

"A few missing models around the legal drinking age in a city this size? I doubt I would be taken seriously. And besides, I find it's best to avoid their attention. Detectives are often too astute for their own good; they can't help themselves from poking around."

I grunted, thinking of Jimmy. When we'd first met, after nearly a decade apart, I'd gone out of my way to keep him in the dark and out of harm's way, but he'd refused to believe my half-truths and excuses. In the end, that obstinacy had almost gotten us both killed. Maybe Milana was right.

"Besides," Milana continued, "I have no idea what happened to them, only suspicions. Rumors. The sort that Regulars would find childish or crazy."

"What rumors?" I asked.

"From what I've been told, the vampires in this city have become restless. The Master here used to keep a low profile, but lately things have changed. His vampires have become bolder, even reckless. I believe the abductions are related. Official channels say that the Sanguine Council plans to send a representative to New York City to...evaluate things. But I fear it may be too late for Terry and the others."

"Can't ye step in?" I asked. "You're a goddess, after all."

Milana's smile was condescending at best. "I'm afraid you have things confused. We gods and goddesses are powerful. Immensely so, depending on the circumstances. But we are not free to act without consequence. Interfering is reserved for mortals, and mortals alone. The heroes you read about—Achilles, Hercules, Odysseus—were all mortals when they made their marks on the world. Exceptional, but mortal."

Othello muttered something under her breath.

"What?" I asked.

"I said 'Hercules was an exceptional asshole.' He nearly killed a friend of mine," Othello clarified.

Milana arced an eyebrow. "Your friend survived Hercules?"

"She killed him."

Milana's sharp intake of breath caught me by surprise. "A woman killed Hercules?"

Othello nodded, then grinned. "Achilles is a pretty good guy, though. Great calves."

Milana leaned forward onto the desk, more than a little shaken by Othello's admission. She studied Othello. "So, you must be one of those who fought against the Greeks when Athena called. One of Master Temple's people."

"I work in his IT Department," Othello quipped.

"My sisters and I were not called," Milana said, a brief flash of anger flitting over her face. "It seems I was not worthy to fight alongside my people."

"Against us?" Othello asked, her amused expression gone in an instant. "That would have been unwise."

I shot Othello a guarded look. While I agreed with the sentiment, I didn't really think pissing off a goddess in her office was the wisest move. Especially one we needed answers from.

Milana shook her head mournfully. "You misunderstand. Not to fight against anyone in particular, but to be given that chance. It's a dream of mine, to fight, to pit my strength against others…but I am a Muse, born to inspire, not to wage war."

Othello and I nodded as one. As women, we were constantly held to a different standard because of our gender, especially when it came to the limitations of our bodies. Milana's desire to push past those limitations struck me as perfectly legitimate. Frankly, I'd been fighting my whole life— schoolyard brawls that had eventually turned into real bouts against worthy opponents. The fierce joy I took out of those altercations was addictive; without them, I would be little more than a shell of myself.

Othello perked up as if struck by an idea. "Did you ever meet Asterion?"

"The Minotaur?" Milana said, surprised. "No, I haven't. Why?"

"He and Achilles have set up a sort of Fight Club for immortals and mortals, both. A place for them to test each other's strength without dying."

I gawked at Othello. She'd never told me that. Suddenly, St. Louis didn't sound so bad. I frowned a moment later. "Wait, isn't the first rule of Fight Club not to talk about Fight Club?" I asked.

Othello chuckled. "That's why I didn't tell you about it. That, and I figured you might fly there immediately, guns blazing. But Milana here is a goddess. And a Greek goddess at that. I don't see anyone refusing her entry."

I scowled at my Russian companion, but she ignored me. On the other hand, I could tell Milana was completely taken with the idea; Milana stared at Othello as if *she* were the mythical being in the room. "Can you really do that?" she asked.

"I can. And I will. Strengthening our ties to the magical community is part of my job. Nate has a lot of infuriating habits, but one of his best traits is his ability to bring people together. I'm sure he'd welcome you."

My scowl turned thoughtful. I pointed at Othello. "I t'ink ye just want free samples of designer clothes."

Now it was Othello's turn to glower at me.

"Whatever you want," Milana said. "Name it."

"Right now, what we want is information," I said, taking immediate advantage of Milana's willingness to pay back Othello's kindness. "Is there anythin' else ye can tell us about Terry?" I asked. Sure, I was pleased as punch that Milana would be able to follow through on her dream, but that didn't solve the immediate problem. Based on Milana's timetable, Terry had only been missing a few days. It was possible Terry had wanted to share the good news with her sister—but planned to wait until she had something concrete under her belt, like an editorial spread in a magazine or a perfume campaign. Something that proved she'd really made it.

Milana picked up a pen and clicked it a half-dozen times. "There is. There's a nightclub I suspect will lead you to the Sanguine Council, one way or the other."

"Why didn't ye tell us that before?"

"Because before I thought you were two well-meaning women looking for a missing girl. Telling you to walk into a lion's den would have been irresponsible of me, and potentially deadly to you. But if you have a friend who could kill Hercules, you may have what it takes to get the girls back, or at least find out what happened to them."

The way Milana said the last made my skin crawl. Sure, I'd considered the possibility that we wouldn't find Terry alive—even the possibility that we'd never find her...but the idea that vampires had her made me sick to my stomach.

Vampires were the *worst*.

And we were about to meet some. On purpose.

Ugh.

"Fuckin' fangers," I snarled.

CHAPTER 24

*W*e got ready at the hotel, Othello and I exchanging turns fiddling around in front of the mirror, donning eyelashes, eyeshadow, mascara, and so on. Not that Othello needed any to make her beautiful; her face had a natural allure to it that only got better when she hit you with that come-hither smile of hers. I, on the other hand, needed a fair amount. My skin had always been clear, with a light smattering of freckles littered across my cheeks and nose, but my bone structure came with harsh lines that had to be toned down—bold cheekbones, a rigid jawline, and a slightly dimpled chin...not to mention a host of bruises and scrapes that I had to carefully conceal. Between my features, my scars, and my height, I had to work extra hard to come across as feminine without putting my assets on display—something I usually avoided unless I hoped to use them to my advantage.

Tonight, for example, we were hunting vampires who preyed on young, attractive women. Which meant our best bet to beat them at their own game was to slut it up a little and play coy. Othello was already in her dress, a sultry black number with slits down the sides that offered brief flashes of leg, hip, and ribcage. It was as risqué as you could get while still revealing nothing. Dresses weren't my thing, however, so I'd gone for a sleeveless, indigo jumpsuit that hung from a collar of fabric around my throat and hugged my body in all the right places.

Once ready, we called a cab; Serge was still monitoring Chapman's hotel, texting Othello frowny face emojis every half hour to keep us updated. Assuming everything went down according to schedule, the Grigori would be coming for the seed in the next two days, which didn't give us much time. But after the fiasco with Darrel and Gomorrah, I wasn't sure if that timetable was still intact. Which is why, if I hadn't heard anything from Serge by morning, I planned to go knock down Chapman's door. If the Grigori or the Unclean tried to stop me, so be it, but I'd promised Hemingway I would get the seed, no matter what.

And I always kept my promises.

*T*he nightclub, *Twice Shy*, was one of those glitzy, upscale places with a line perpetually wrapped around the corner. Fortunately, Othello had called ahead, using her GrimmTech connections to get us a table and bottle service in the VIP section. When I asked why she hadn't called in all sorts of backup from either GrimmTech or her friends in St. Louis—an obvious solution to our predicament—she'd explained that her role at GrimmTech didn't allow her that kind of freedom.

"Research and development, moving assets, putting in work orders..." she said, pausing for emphasis, "all perfectly legitimate. But if they knew their boss was running around getting herself into dangerous situations, the board would have a heart attack. Going out for a night on the town, however, is expected, even encouraged."

"Ye shouldn't risk 'em gettin' pissed at ye, then," I insisted, still worried for her. "This could be dangerous. Why don't ye go back to work, and I'll call ye if I need anythin'?"

"Don't worry about me," Othello said, smirking. "If anything, I'm safer than you are."

I decided not to argue that point. Somehow whenever I argued with Othello I ended up repeating her words back to her a few minutes later. Only later would I wonder what she'd said that had changed my mind. If I didn't know better, I would have assumed she were some flavor of Freak—a mentalist, or something equally irritating. In hindsight, it made sense that she and Death were dating. Who else would have the balls to stand up to her?

It's not like Hemingway could die.

"And your friends in St. Louis?" I asked.

"Busy," Othello said. "Nate's running things out there, but many of us have split off and are operating independently. I considered calling in reinforcements from Kansas City, but Callie has her own shit going on." Othello continued speaking, mostly to herself at this point, "Besides, neither of them could exactly be considered independent these days, whether they wanted to help or not."

"Who's Callie?" I asked.

"A wizard who used to work with the Vatican. You'd like her…" Othello studied me for a second. "If you two didn't kill each other, first."

I cocked an eyebrow.

"She's…competitive."

I grinned. "Enough said."

Together, Othello and I made our way to the back of the nightclub where, overlooking the main dance stage, a series of shady-looking booths were arranged so those who wished could watch the crowds dance below—the perfect VIP section for elitist assholes, date rapists, or vampires.

Pick your poison.

We sidled up next to one another in one of the booths and watched as a beguiling young woman with pink hair and an outfit that made ours look tame danced her way over to us, a massive bottle above her head, sparks flying from its top.

They died as she poured the champagne into fluted glasses that had been lined along the table's edge. The girl seemed a bit baffled by us—two attractive women sitting alone at a booth, unfettered by male attention. It was common in New York City to see wealthy, beautiful women out and about, but less common to see them entertaining themselves. Othello flashed her a smile and waved her down to a crouch, shouting above the blare of the music—a haunting, bumping breed of techno that struck me as remarkably European. "I have a question for you!"

The girl nodded demurely and smiled.

"I was hoping to speak to the owner. Is that possible?" Othello slid a wad of bills across the table, clasped together by a thick gold band.

"Of course! He usually comes in a little later in the evening. Do you want me to send him your way when he does?"

"Please."

"Alright, let me know if I can bring you anything else," she said, palming the cash with the expertise of a card hustler, "I'll be nearby if you need anything."

After she left, Othello and I scoped out the nightclub in its entirety. The vibe struck me more like one of those underground dance clubs you find in Los Angeles, with people dancing in a huddled mass, eyes pinched shut, bobbing to the rhythmic pulse of the music. Red lights overhead tinged everything, flickering over the crowd in waves.

"What did Milana say to look for again?" I asked, ducking close so Othello could hear me without straining.

"She said the owner has ties to the Master of the city, and that most of the girls who were taken had recently come here. It was the only link she could find."

I studied the crowd. "They picked the right place. With this light, everyone's eyes glow red, and pale seems to be the fashion. D'ye t'ink they took the girls from here, or followed 'em back?"

"Here, probably. If they used their gaze, and the girls were already a little drunk, they could probably be talked into just about anything."

The gaze Othello referred to was a vampire's hypnotic stare, a sort of mind control that put people under a temporary spell. Resistance varied, but alcohol would certainly make someone more susceptible—lowered inhibitions had their drawbacks, after all. I took another drink of champagne, savoring it. Luckily, I was immune to that little trick.

I'd hate to waste good champagne.

"Keep your guard up," I warned her.

Othello nodded, then stiffened. "What is *he* doing here?"

I followed her gaze, catching sight of a slender man in a stylish suit jacket and jeans, the bright red hue of his dress shirt intensified beneath the strobing lights, his shoulder-length hair brushing the edges of his jacket. He seemed to sense someone staring and glanced up, locking eyes with first me, and then Othello. They widened.

"Who is it?" I asked.

Othello's expression had landed somewhere between concern and relief, as if she couldn't quite decide how to feel. She waved the newcomer up, inviting him to join us, but he jerked his head and pretended to be fascinated by a gaggle of girls posted up down the line of the bar.

"That's what I was afraid of," Othello muttered.

"What?" I leaned in, trying not to let my frustration show. "Who is he?"

"He's a friend. I think. It's hard to tell with him, lately."

I reached up and took Othello's chin in my hands, plumping her cheeks as I forced her to look at me. Her eyes went wide with surprise. "Who is he?" I growled. "Don't make me keep askin' ye."

Othello swatted my hand away playfully and smirked. "His name's Alucard. He's a vampire who works for the Council. And if he's here, things are about to get really ugly."

"Why's that?"

"Because lately he's become a bit of a wild card. He and Nate went their separate ways a little while ago. He's still one of us…but he and I shouldn't be seen together."

"Why not?"

"It's a pride thing. I work for Nate, and he's trying to establish himself with the Council. Still, I'm surprised he's avoiding me here. He must be up to something."

I tossed down the remainder of my champagne. "Alright, I'll go find out."

Othello's hand on my arm stopped me from rising and walking away. "Quinn! That's not a good idea."

"Ye want to know why he's here, don't ye? And ye say he's a member of the Council, which means he may know what's goin' on and where the girls were taken. I don't have connections to St. Louis, so it makes sense that I should go."

Othello looked conflicted but released my arm. "Alright, but hurry back. And for God's sakes don't flirt with him. Even if he sparkles."

I scrunched my nose. "Please. Everyone knows that's not how it works. Besides, I hate vampires."

Othello's laughter chased me down the stairs.

At least one of us was having fun.

CHAPTER 25

I settled in on Alucard's left, sliding onto one of the barstools, and propped my elbows on the bar. The bar area was surprisingly deserted; the bartender spotted me and quickly ambled over, eager to make some money. "What can I get you?"

"I'll take a Cosmo."

Alucard shifted his wandering attention to me. "How very *Sex and the City* of you," he drawled in an accent fresh out the bayous of New Orleans.

Fuck sparkles. Othello should have warned me about *that*.

"How very metrosexual of ye to notice," I shot back in my own brogue.

Alucard snickered. "So, what's a gorgeous thing like you doing in a dive like this?"

"Waitin' for someone handsome to come talk to me," I replied.

Alucard dipped his shoulder, hunkering down so he could speak without shouting, the flirtatious expression on his face completely at odds with what he said next, "Did Othello send you?"

I matched his expression, playing with the ends of my hair, which I'd teased and curled to give a little volume. "She wants to know what you're doin' here," I replied.

"Feeling's mutual. This club ain't the safest place y'all could have ended up for a night on the town."

"Aye. Good t'ing we were lookin' for trouble."

Alucard's eyes narrowed, but he kept up appearances, scanning the bar as if eyeing his competition, or staking out other girls to talk to. "Did she tell you who I am?"

"Aye. And what ye are."

He grunted. "Which means you're a Freak. And that she trusts you. Othello doesn't go around spilling secrets, last I checked, and she'd never offer me up to a Regular. Especially one so..." He paused, and the leering smile became momentarily real. "Tall."

I rolled my eyes. "Fangers aren't me type, sorry. I'm partial to long walks on the beach, and you're so pale you'd blind people...and that's without the whole goin' up in flames t'ing."

Alucard raised both eyebrows. "Maybe Othello doesn't trust you."

"What's that supposed to mean?" I asked, scowling.

"Nothing. You can ask her later. Anyway, as much as I'm enjoying this stimulating conversation, why don't you let me in on what you two are doing here?"

"Ye first," I said.

Alucard shrugged. "I'm here on business."

"Council business?"

"Maybe," he replied, coolly. "What's it to you?"

"We're lookin' for a friend. A girl who was taken by local vamps. Her and a few other missin' girls were last seen here, and we heard the owner has an in with the Master of this city."

Alucard's eyes flashed. "You two are gonna get yourselves killed," he growled. "Get Othello and get out of here."

I took the drink the bartender offered me and smiled, glad to diffuse the sudden tension for a moment. "Put it on his tab," I said. Alucard didn't look pleased, but he didn't argue, either. "Listen, ye have no idea who I am, so I'm only goin' to tell ye this once: don't ever tell me what to do unless you want to end up mounted on a wall somewhere."

"The owner doesn't know the Master of this city," Alucard said, as if speaking to a small child.

"Huh?"

"The owner *is* the Master of this city."

Well, that put a damper on things. I sipped the liquid brimming along

113

the lip of my dangerously full martini glass to hide my surprise. Othello and I had been under the misapprehension that a few rogue vampires had been abducting girls from this bar. But if the Master owned the bar, that meant he'd probably approved the whole thing.

We weren't up against a few New York City vampires.

We were up against them all.

"Now do you understand?" Alucard asked.

I sighed, then nodded.

"Look, I'll check on this friend of yours, and the other missing girls. But for now, you'd best get out of here, alright?"

"Leave?" I swirled my martini glass. "No t'anks."

"What?"

"I promised Terry's sister I'd find her. I don't care who it is, or how many fangers I have to blow away," I said, grinding my teeth together as I spoke, "I'm not lettin' 'em have her."

Ordinarily, I might have taken Alucard's advice. Killing a whole host of vampires was a tall order, with or without my abilities. Vampires were fast, mean, and they had a nasty tendency to survive anything short of staking, dismemberment, or fire. But, both as a woman and as someone who knew what it was like to be under a manipulative vampire's thumb, leaving the girls to their fates was simply not an option.

I'd rather die first.

Alucard stared at me for what felt like a minute before chuckling to himself. "I don't know where they hide you girls, but if I meet one more woman who sends shivers up my spine, I think I'll retire."

"Does that mean you're gonna tell me why you're here?" I asked, my anger still leaking through my voice.

"Nope. C'mon, let's go have a chat with Othello. Maybe I can talk some sense into her, instead."

I hurried to catch up as he took off towards the VIP section. "I thought ye were avoidin' her?"

"Not at all. I just didn't want to draw attention to myself. Sitting up high, chatting with you two? Pretty conspicuous."

I bit back a comment about his shirt, which seemed pretty damn eye-catching to me. Hell, for all I knew, he was color blind. I wondered if vampires were drawn to shades of red, like bulls. I was about to ask him when I noticed Othello had company—a disturbingly tall man in a dark suit, his flaxen hair long and tied back in a neat ponytail with a silk ribbon.

He turned to face us as we approached, and I saw Alucard stiffen in recognition. I did the same, but for an altogether different reason. It seemed the owner had arrived earlier than expected. Which meant I was looking at The Master of New York City—a vampire I'd met before.

His name was Magnus.

CHAPTER 26

I'd first met Magnus outside the House of Blues in Boston almost a month ago. He'd surprised the shit out of me in an alleyway after I'd used a Super Soaker full of holy water to douse a naughty bunch of vampires who'd needed to be punished. In the end, they'd been staked to walls like butterflies on display.

That last bit wasn't me, I swear.

Magnus had taken an immediate interest in me—you know, my likes and my dislikes, my hobbies, my blood type—and had gone so far as to chase me down the alley. A few days later, the pushy bastard had done me a solid by taking out the wizard who'd kidnapped my aunt, the same wizard who'd decorated the walls with vampire corpses. I hadn't heard from Magnus since, although I'd heard rumors about what he'd done to the wizard.

Let's just say karma is a bitch.

In hindsight, I wasn't that surprised to find out he was the vamp in charge; I'd known Magnus was a Master vampire who owned a mansion in New York State, and there probably weren't too many Master vampires out there. I simply hadn't connected the dots until now.

Sometimes I'm a little slow, but I always get there in the end.

"Miss MacKenna," Magnus said, rising to his full height, towering above me by about six inches—and I was the tallest of us there. "I never would have expected to see you here. And in such," Magnus paused to eye Alucard up and down before dismissing him in an instant, "interesting company."

If Alucard was rankled by the insult, he didn't show it. If anything, he seemed to shrink in on himself, sidestepping into the shadows to let us continue our conversation uninterrupted. I considered dragging him back, but it didn't seem worth the effort. If he wanted to chicken out in front of the big, bad Master vampire, he could.

Wuss.

"I didn't realize ye were the one pullin' the strings around here," I replied. "It's an *interestin'* place." I emphasized the word exactly as Magnus had when smack-talking Alucard.

Othello's head weaved slowly back and forth between the two of us, trying to figure out how we knew one another. Her eyes were glazed over, which made no sense; the bottle of champagne had barely been touched since our first pour, and she would have known better than to look in Magnus' eyes, whether she knew he was a vampire or not. "Are ye alright?" I asked her.

"Quinn?" Othello asked, staring two feet to my right.

"Miss Othello here was just telling me all about your missing friend. Terry, was it? It seems she's under the impression that one of my people is responsible."

"What did ye do to her?" I growled. I knew Othello would never willingly share that sort of information.

"Nothing permanent, I assure you. Ordinarily, I'd have my own means of interrogating her, but it seems she has experience with my kind. Fortunately, you humans have a few tricks of your own. The wonders of pharmaceuticals. She was too busy avoiding my gaze to watch her own drink."

I gasped. "Ye roofied her?" I took a step forward, my fists clenched.

"That's far enough."

A pair of men stepped out from the shadows to my right—sort of the go-to vampire entrance, in my experience. Neither of the two men frightened me, vampires or not; I could probably take either in a one-on-one fight. Unfortunately, it wouldn't be one-on-one, and it wouldn't be a fight. Between the two of them, they could probably stop me from making it to Othello without causing a big scene, and I couldn't risk her getting caught in the crossfire. I held up my hands. "Fine, what do ye want, then?"

"It's not so much about what I want. I believe you'll recall the wizard I took out on your behalf? Mr. Gladstone?"

I scowled at his description of events. "Ye mean the wizard who killed the band of vampires and hung them up like trophies? The one *I* handed to ye on a silver platter?"

Magnus shrugged. "Semantics."

"What about Gladstone?" I asked, tersely.

"Well, I tortured him, obviously. No one gets away with what he did to our kind without being punished. But the more he raved, the more I realized that—behind that puggish face of his—there was a rather brilliant mind. A fixated mind, to be sure. But nevertheless." Magnus took Othello's hand and helped her to her feet. She wobbled precariously, struggling to stay upright. "He's been very useful, you see. Did you have any idea how badly he hates Nate Temple? Ironically, Othello had all sorts of praise for the man. I think maybe they should compare notes. It's time I reward Gladstone for his good behavior. Even wizards like to open presents."

"Ye get your fuckin' hands off her before I snap your throat, you filthy blood monger," I cursed, practically spitting from anger. The idea that Gladstone was still among the living after what he'd done to me and mine made me furious. The idea that Magnus thought to use Othello as a bargaining chip to please the bastard enraged me even further.

Basically, I was in full-on Boston mode.

Magnus shook his head and waved to his guards. "I hate vulgar women. So unattractive."

The two guards moved in on either side to take my arms. I realized I would have to fight—that, if I didn't, Othello would end up getting hurt, anyway. Or worse. I had two guns on me, one holstered alongside each calf, obscured by the voluminous pantlegs of the jumpsuit I wore. I wondered if I'd have time to draw them, fire, and run to Othello's side. I judged the distance and cursed. There was no way.

That's when Alucard made his move.

CHAPTER 27

*T*he two guards fell as one, twitching on the ground, with Alucard standing over them. He held something dark and squirming and wet in both hands. I squinted, then gasped as I realized what he held.

Hearts. He was holding their fucking hearts.

"Magnus, Master of New York City," Alucard said, tossing the hearts to the floor and rubbing his palms clean on the smooth leather upholstery of the nearest booth. "You have violated Council law."

"The Council has no laws, you fool," Magnus replied, disdainfully. "At least none that apply to a Master in control of his territory."

"See, that's where you're wrong." Alucard began the laborious process of licking his fingers clean, eyeing Magnus as he did it. You'd think there'd be some weird sexual thing going on, but objectively it was downright creepy. "The Council has one law that everyone, even Masters, adhere to. Don't. Rock. The. Boat." He emphasized each word with a step forward, until he was directly in front of me.

Magnus considered this and shrugged. "Fair. But I don't—"

"Let me stop you right there. You, Maggie...can I call you Maggie? Word's out," he continued, before Magnus could respond, "and word is you've gotten a little reckless. Played things a little loose. You've drawn attention to yourself, and—by extension—to the Council. Maggie," Alucard said, in a piteous tone of voice, shaking his head in disappointment, "you rocked the boat."

Magnus sneered. "Tell the Council I'll pay their little tithe. I know that's what this is really about. The Council could care less about whether or not I play with my food."

Alucard shrugged. "I don't know anything about that. Above my pay grade. But don't worry, I don't play with *my* food." Alucard indicated the two guards, who'd gone still at some point during the conversation.

"Please. As if they'd send a rogue vampire after a Master. That's a nice parlor trick you pulled off with my men, with their backs turned, but I won't give you the same opportunity."

"Maggie, when I'm done with you, you'll give me anything I want. Like that woman you've got there. Tell you what, hand her over and I'll let you live another night. I had my eye on her from across the bar." Alucard licked his lips.

I scowled at Alucard's back. What was he playing at? Was he really trying to pretend he didn't know Othello and that he wanted her for a late-night snack? I realized for this to work, I'd have to play along.

"Neither of ye miserable bastards are goin' to lay a finger on her," I growled.

Alucard glanced over his shoulder at me. "Hush, the adults are talking."

I pursed my lips.

He was definitely going to pay for that later.

Magnus scoffed, ignoring me altogether. "You think you're even going to walk out of here alive after all this? I own this bar. I own every living soul inside it. If you try and leave, my men will tear you into pieces and kill everyone here just to cover it up. You think the Council is unhappy with me now? I'll carve through this city until the sewers run red with their blood."

"Is that so? Well then, let's—"

"Alucard?" Othello whispered, seeking out the voice of her friend. "Alucard is that you?"

Magnus flinched and the grip on her arm tightened. He searched Othello's face, then Alucard's. "You're him, aren't you? Temple's Daywalker."

Alucard reached back and mussed up his hair. "Well dammit, Othello," he sighed, sounding mildly annoyed. Then he shot forward, so quickly all I saw was his afterimage, his coat flying back behind him like a cape. Magnus moved with the same frightening speed; he tossed Othello over one shoulder and leapt down among the crowd, which panicked and spread in a loose circle. Before I could blink, six or seven vampires emerged from among them, guarding Magnus' retreat. Alucard took a slow look around the room at all the people who'd end up getting caught in the crossfire if he tried to give chase. His shoulders tensed; he was going to do it, consequences be damned.

So, I fired a round into the air.

I wasn't about to let him have all the fun.

CHAPTER 28

*T*he crowd ducked for cover as one, then bolted for the exit, nearly trampling each other as they fought to get out of harm's way. The vampires Magnus had left behind to cover his retreat remained, facing Alucard, except now there were no innocent bystanders in immediate danger. The music died with a squeal as the DJ fled.

Alucard shot me a questioning look. "Did you do that on purpose?"

"Ye were goin' to tear through them to go after her," I said. "This seemed like a better solution."

"We have to get her back."

I grunted. "Obviously."

One of the vampires launched himself at Alucard, fangs gleaming, hoping to take advantage of the momentary distraction. I put a bullet in the fanger's shoulder and sent him howling across the dance floor.

"Excuse you," I said, mimicking Alucard's accent. "The adults were talking." I glared at Alucard. "And don't ye ever say some sorry shit like that to me again, ye hear?"

The vampire I'd shot wailed and began tearing at the flesh of his shoulder, which was smoking. He was most likely hunting for the bullet, which had lodged itself in the pulp of his arm and was inexorably searing through his tissue. Magnus' crew of vampires watched their companion writhe, their faces slack with shock and fear.

Alucard didn't even bother to look at the fallen vamp, let alone respond to my threat. "He'll be too far away by now to run him down."

"I know where he's headed," I replied, with more confidence than I felt. It was likely that Magnus would hole up in his mansion upstate...but that wasn't a guarantee. Still, it was a better alternative than inciting a bloodbath.

I hoped.

The vampires were growing restless, spreading out to encircle Alucard and make themselves harder targets. The one I'd shot had finally fetched the bullet fragment and torn it free, flinging the shattered metal shard across the room with a hiss. That was the problem with carrying small caliber pistols—they were easy to conceal, but lacked that extra oomph.

Alucard spun on his heel. "Cover me," he said.

Three of the vampires, including the one I'd maimed, turned their attention to me. "I t'ink I'll be a little busy," I replied. I raised both guns and aimed, prepared to finish what I'd started; I could agonize over our options later.

Right now, I had cockroaches to kill.

I loved guns.

Not in the hardcore gun aficionado way—you know, like those collectors who got their rocks off by firing an obscenely large, loud automatic rifle into the sky, Rambo style. My love was purer than that, not to mention more practical. I loved guns the way some people love the outdoors. The sharp, brittle sound they made going off, the acrid stench of the smoke wafting from the barrel, the kick that threatened to rock me back —all of these contributed to an incomparable experience.

Maybe that's why, when I use them, I always have a manic grin on my face.

Which really freaks people out.

The first vampire to come at me saw that grin and—in the instant before I put a bullet through his nasal cavity and brain—turned a whole shade paler than I thought was inhumanly possible. He dropped to his knees, cradling his ruined face, then slumped over.

The other two were more cautious. They approached from two directions, ducking low as they ran up the stairs so I couldn't pick them off. I didn't bother wasting the bullets. Clipping them wouldn't do me any good. I needed to hit them in their most vital areas if I wanted to keep them down permanently.

One of the vampires, a woman, came from my right, streaking low with her hand outstretched as if to yank my leg out from under me. The tactic made sense—if she were up against another vampire or a shifter, the battle would be a test of speed, endurance, and strength. Taking out my legs was the safest bet. But she wasn't up against either of those. She was up against me.

At the last possible moment, with her fingers mere inches from my leg, her speed gave out and her gravity-defying lunge became a graceless slide. I drew back and stomped on her hand, smashing it into the floor with a satisfying crunch. She yowled, eyes pinched shut in pain.

The man, on the other hand, had gone high. He ran nimbly across the railing, his balance perfect and poised, arms wide as if he were about to give me a hug. He leapt at me, prepared to tackle me to the ground and use his prodigious strength to squeeze me until I popped. I ducked and he flew overhead, his graceful dive ending in a belly flop that shattered the table and our bottle of champagne.

"If there's one t'ing that pisses me off," I said, "it's alcohol abuse." I fired at the man's back, putting three bullets center mass. He screamed until his lungs filled with blood he'd stolen from someone else. I stomped on the woman's hand again. She wailed. I knew from experience that, this close to me, she'd be as helpless as anyone else with a shattered hand. As pitiful and in as much pain.

I drove my heel down on her fingers, this time.

A quick look around showed that of the three who had come after me, two were down, probably dead. That left four others for Alucard. I didn't envy him those odds. But when I sought out the fighting below, I found him staring at me, standing among a pile of bodies, their blood lapping against his shoes.

"Took your time," he observed, wryly.

"Oh, go fuck yourself."

He grinned, flashing fang. "You need help interrogating that one?" Alucard asked, nodding towards the woman huddled on the ground at my feet.

"Nope." I dragged the woman to her knees and flung her against the railing. Her right arm flew between the bars. I rested the block of my heel against her shoulder where it met her torso and applied a little pressure to that joint, pinning her. She groaned, eyes fluttering as she fought to stay conscious. "Stay with me, dearie," I said. "I have questions and you're the only one left who can answer them."

If Alucard was bothered by my approach, he didn't seem inclined to say anything. If anything, he appeared interested in my technique. He went to the bar and fiddled around, hunting for something while I plied the female vampire with questions. She was in the process of telling me everything she knew about Magnus, his mansion, his security, and even about the missing girls, when the sound of sirens heading our way interrupted us.

"Shit," I said. I looked around. There were dead bodies everywhere. Even if they were vampires, no Regular would be able to tell the difference until they ended up on the autopsy table—and even then, it was unlikely they'd be disregarded completely.

Alucard returned and approached. "Did you find out where they took Othello?"

"Aye."

"Good." He reached through the bars and snapped the woman's neck.

I felt my stomach roil, but said nothing. They were his people. If he wanted to play judge, jury, and executioner, who was I to interfere? Alucard met my eyes. I could tell he was prepared for a tongue lashing, but—when that didn't happen—he grinned in relief and waved for me to follow.

"What about the bodies?"

Alucard nodded, absentmindedly. He crossed over to the bar where three bottles sat open, a rag doused in gasoline dipped in each. He produced an old-school lighter from his jacket pocket—one of those antiques you find that rarely work—and lit the ends of each. "Want to do the honors?" he drawled. "They'll go up like matchboxes. Cops won't even find their teeth."

I shook my head. Guns I could handle. But homemade incendiaries? Hard pass. Alucard shrugged and chucked a bottle into the VIP area, igniting the booth Othello and I had sat in. The next hit the DJ's equipment, sending sparks flying as electric wires went up in flames. We made our way to the back exit. The sirens were getting uncomfortably loud. Alucard sent the last sailing into the bar itself, letting it crash against the bottles of alcohol standing on the shelves. The fire caught and spread and, in a matter of seconds, all I could see was smoke.

"They'll wait to get the firefighters in here," Alucard said. "Should give the place time to catch."

"Well let's get out of here, then," I said. "No sense gettin' caught. Besides, ye have blood on your shoes."

Alucard glanced down as he and I left, ducking into the rear alleyway, dodging the rats that scurried away from a nearby dumpster. "There're worse things to step in, I reckon. Especially in this town."

The rats disappeared down the nearest sewer drain.

He had a point.

"You weren't using wooden bullets when you took those people down," Alucard remarked, though it sounded almost like a question.

"Nope," I replied. If I was being honest with myself, I didn't even really think of vampires as people. I didn't begrudge them their struggle to survive, but their methods didn't appeal to me—they were leeches feeding off the fringes of society. Under the circumstances, though, I decided it was best to keep that to myself.

"So how?" Alucard asked.

I realized he was trying to figure out how I'd managed to hurt the vampires with the bullets I'd used; normal bullets wouldn't have slowed them down in the slightest, let alone driven them mad with pain. I grinned and held up my guns. "Did ye know Othello got ordained?"

Alucard frowned. "Yeah, so she could officiate at Ashely and Gunnar's wedding, but..." His eyes went wide. "Seriously?"

"Our God is an awesome God..." I sang in a lilting tune, grinning. Originally, I'd planned to bribe a priest for a blessing or two, but Othello had vetoed the idea, claiming she probably had spiritual authority equal to any priest. She'd said a series of prayers over my duffel bag full of guns and ammunition, including the two little beauties I'd used to kill Magnus' crew.

"What about what I saw you do back there?" Alucard asked. "When you fought them. Not even fledgling vampires flail about like that."

I grunted. "Never seen a cat land on its ass, even though everyone says they should be able to land on their feet?"

Alucard shuddered. "I've seen a cat do awful, unforgiveable things."

I cocked my head at the vehemence in his voice, staring at him until he grew uncomfortable.

Alucard sighed. "It's been a rough couple of years."

I waited for him to elaborate, but then—when he didn't—I set off down the alleyway. He hurried up beside me, thrusting his hands into his pockets. "So, what are you, anyway?"

My right cross sent him careening into the dumpster.

Because I always kept my promises.

Especially to myself.

CHAPTER 29

I made Alucard sit in the hotel living room while I changed. There was no word from Serge, but I couldn't risk him knowing that Othello was in danger. I couldn't predict what he'd do when he found out and—without Othello to remove his leash—he'd be little more than a liability, anyway. Besides, I needed him to keep an eye on Chapman until I could get his boss back. If I had to tell Hemingway that I'd let his girlfriend get kidnapped by a homicidal, blood-drinking maniac *and* that I'd let the seed to the Tree of Knowledge slip into celestial hands, I was pretty sure he'd see my death, after all.

Or, you know, cause it.

"So, what were ye doin' in town, really?" I called as I shuffled out of my jumpsuit, peeling the top half away from my body. I did a quick inventory of my injuries from earlier and was relieved to see none had gotten any worse—speaking from experience, there was nothing worse than bleeding out because you were too busy to notice.

"Chasing down a hunch," Alucard replied.

"A hunch?"

"Things with the Council are...fluid, right now. There's been a lot of turnover. The higher ups are hoping to stem the tide. They want to know who can be trusted to keep things the way they are. Or *were*," he added, smirking at me.

"And Magnus couldn't be trusted?"

"Magnus wasn't even on their radar."

"So, why'd they send you?"

"Who said the Council sent me?" Alucard sounded amused.

I ducked out with an incredulous expression, strapping a hip holster on over my brown suede pants. Alucard's eyes flicked from my hips to my face. A slow, languorous smile spread across his face. I glared. "I'll deck ye again," I said.

Alucard laughed, but raised his hands in surrender.

"So, if the Council didn't send ye," I said, "then why did ye come?"

"The Council is looking for candidates for a new position. A Master of the Midwest—someone they can trust to hold down the fort. Which means they're shopping around for Masters with good track records ruling large territories. Vampires who aren't connected to everything that's been going down there, lately."

I nodded, but frowned. "How does Magnus fit in?"

"Magnus is one of those candidates."

"So ye came here to what, vet him? Make sure he'd do a good job?"

Alucard cocked his head. "I came here to kill him. Quietly."

"Why?" I asked, surprised.

"Because I want the job," Alucard said, as if that explained everything.

And, in a way, it did.

"Well, this won't be quiet," I said, fetching a pair of combat boots from the living room floor. Othello's and my clothes were strewn all over the hotel room, but I didn't give a shit; I'd come back to the hotel for two reasons. Changing was only the first.

"No, it won't be," Alucard agreed. "But Magnus tried to kill me."

"Arguin' self-defense may not work, either," I noted, slipping the boots on.

"The Council doesn't need to sanction what I do," Alucard explained. "They simply need to understand it. Magnus tried to have me killed. Which means my retaliation," Alucard drew that word out, relishing it, "should make perfect sense. I wouldn't be a good candidate if I sat back and let him attack me without paying the price."

"So, we're goin' to storm the Master's mansion?" I asked.

"Sure are. Why, you got a problem with that plan?"

"No, I was makin' sure ye and I were on the same page, that's all." I returned to the bedroom and fetched the real reason I'd come back to the hotel; I slung the duffel bag strap over one shoulder and wobbled into the living room. "Ready whenever you are."

Alucard eyed my accessory, clearly amused, "Armed for bear, huh?"

I grunted, thinking of Christoff in his massive Russian Grizzly bear form. "No way. Bears are way tougher to kill."

Alucard rose and hooked his thumbs along the pockets of his jeans. "I'm starting to think I'm not the only one who's had a rough couple of years. I can't believe you're the reason Othello's been off grid, of late. Nate is going to lose his poor little mind."

"Well," I replied, "I'm sure he'll manage. Sharin' is carin', after all."

Alucard barked a laugh. "I see you haven't met him."

I frowned. "Once. He hijacked my Uber." While Alucard was busy laughing so hard he was practically in tears, I went to retrieve my phone from the bedroom. "We're goin' to need a car. It's a two hour drive to Magnus' place." A thought occurred to me. "We'll be pushin' daylight by then. Are ye sure you'll be alright to help?"

Alucard nodded. "Don't you worry about me, *cher*. I'll be fine."

"Do those little pet names get ye laid?" I asked, eyes narrowed.

Alucard shrugged, tonguing the tip of his incisor playfully. "Ain't no need for a car, by the way. I've got a guy coming. Should be here any minute."

"Someone you trust?" I said, rolling my eyes.

Alucard chuckled. "Sure. I mean, if you can't trust a priest, who can you trust?"

Well, *that* sounded promising.

CHAPTER 30

$\mathcal{T}$he driver pulled up in a rickety, rectangular Oldsmobile—one of those sad, dependable cars that people drove when gas cost less than a pack of bubblegum. It wasn't flashy, but then I got the impression that flashy wasn't the point; you could park this thing anywhere and no one would think to mess with it—cop or criminal. It was too pitiful to tow or to vandalize.

"Where'd you get this piece of junk?" Alucard asked.

"Paid for it," the driver said in a gruff, no-nonsense voice through a crack in the passenger window. "Who's she?"

"Of course you did. Pop the trunk," Alucard said, exasperated. "She's one of Othello's people."

"And we're bringing her along?"

I bristled, prepared to say something snarky, but was distracted by Alucard, who snatched the duffel bag from me and tossed it in the trunk. He slammed it shut, then eyed me up and down. "Your call, Legs. You want the front, or the back?"

"I'll take the back," I said, deciding it was best to avoid a confrontation with the guy behind the wheel before we even got on the road.

Alucard nodded, but stopped to open the door for me before climbing in himself. I scowled at him the whole time, but let it happen; some women might get rankled when a man opens a door for them, but I was lazy enough to appreciate the gesture.

"I saw her take out three of us in a little under a minute," Alucard said as he hopped in, his words almost inaudible over the roar of the Oldsmobile's antique engine.

A pair of red eyes flicked up to gauge me from the rearview mirror. The driver shifted gears and pulled away from the curb, turning slightly to make sure he was clear to merge. In profile, he had one of those heavyset, powerful faces that belonged on busts of steel magnates or oil tycoons. His thick neck, salt and pepper buzz cut, and sturdy shoulders gave off a similar impression. After a few minutes of driving, he turned his attention to me again.

"The name's Roland," he said.

"Quinn," I replied, tersely.

"Glad to see you two getting along," Alucard teased. "So where are your wolves, Roland?" Alucard shifted around to look at me, grinning like a demented child. "Roland here has two shapeshifting girlfriends. I've been trying to get him to tell me his secret for days now."

"I asked them to stay in St. Louis for a little while," Roland said. "Gunnar and Ashley have built something worthwhile there. A good pack. I want them to experience that. Build trust."

"Is that the real reason? You sure it wasn't because you couldn't keep up with their...needs?" Alucard let the last word drop, intentionally baiting the older man.

"I want them to know what it means to be part of a pack," Roland said, although I was sure I could see a very faint blush spreading across his cheeks. He must have fed recently. "I don't want them to feel like they're missing out by spending all their time with a vampire."

Alucard grunted. "Nonsense, if you ask me." He pointed to Roland, but looked at me. "Ever heard of a Shepherd?"

"Aye," I replied. "They say one used to work in Boston, where I live, years back."

Roland's shoulders stiffened imperceptibly.

"Well, I don't know about all that. But this fine gentleman used to be one."

My eyes shot to the older man. Shepherds were reportedly a group of wandering warrior priests—individuals responsible for protecting the

Church and its flock from the things that went bump in the night. They worked exclusively for the Vatican. No one I'd talked to knew how many there were or how to spot one. Over the decades, they'd become supernatural bogeymen—rarely seen, often feared. Meeting a Shepherd, even an ex-Shepherd, was not something I'd ever expected to happen.

"See," Alucard continued, "the way I figure it, religious types always end up doing this to themselves. They can't help it. It's a martyrdom thing. He's feeling guilty, that's all."

"Guilty for what?" I asked, trying to deflect the growing tension I saw building up in Roland's posture.

"For having lots of sex. What else would a Catholic feel guilty for?"

I glowered at Alucard, whose smile only widened.

"Oh, don't tell me...you're Catholic, too?"

"Alucard," I said sweetly, testing out his name for the first time, "do ye need me to remind ye what happens when ye start askin' dumb questions?"

Alucard brushed his fingers along his jawline, which had begun swelling up almost immediately after I'd put him on his ass. He sighed, but settled back in his seat with a chagrined expression. "Catholics. They're so..." his eyes twinkled mischievously as he glanced back at me, "touchy," he said, overemphasizing the word.

Roland shot his companion a dirty look before returning his attention to the road. "I got gas before picking you two up. Might as well rest if you can."

Roland's advice reminded me that I'd been up for nearly twenty hours now. If I didn't get some shut eye, I'd be running on nothing but adrenaline, so I spread out along the seats and closed my eyes, ignoring the occasional bumps in the road. I fell asleep to the grumble of the Oldsmobile's motor and the sound of Alucard humming something twangy.

CHAPTER 31

I dreamt.

The rhythmic pulse of red and blue washed over a quiet residential street, but the sirens were silent. Neighbors peered from the slits between their blinds, but refused to step outside. Two people—a man and a woman in thick, woolen jackets—passed a lighter back and forth, the smoke from their cigarettes drifting lazily in the twilight air. The man, far taller, with hulking proportions, nudged his companion and pointed with the lit cherry at a nearby street sign. Druid Street.

The area was residential, two-car garages occupied by conservative models a few years past their prime. The woman took a long pull of her cigarette and blew it out in a sharp exhale. They didn't speak.

They didn't have to.

I dreamt.

A short, muscular man with greying hair played with his children, wrestling his eldest daughter to the ground, pinning her there with one hand while he used the other to poke and prod, causing her to laugh and squeal. The younger sibling leapt on his back, giggling, yanking on his shirt and hair. The father shrugged his son off once, then again. The game went on, observed by a woman lounging on a nearby sofa, a cup of steaming tea cradled in her hands.

A knock interrupted the scene of familial bliss.

The father sniffed the air and rose, putting his children behind him.

He growled, the pitch low and inhuman.

I dreamt.

Overlooking a cliff's edge, high above the pounding surf, a woman in a sundress leaned into the wind, arms outstretched, her tow-colored hair fluttering behind her. Far below, another woman approached, her raven-colored hair as dark as the other's was fair, dressed as if she'd recently left a funeral. When they met, they did not embrace. In fact, they stood several feet apart, as if afraid to touch.

They had not seen each other in a long time.

They had hoped never to see each other again.

I dreamt.

In a dark place, so dark it had weight—like staring into the infinite depths of outer space, the darkness oppressive and vast and fascinating—something stirred. In the pitch blackness, shape wasn't discernible, but there was something there. A primordial presence, denser than that lightless world it inhabited, grinding forward with the patience of a black hole swallowing starlight.

It had places to be.

CHAPTER 32

*R*oland's rumbling baritone woke me as I felt a wave of nausea creep up my gut, my half-remembered dreams sending goosebumps prickling up my arms. I focused on Roland's voice, hoping it would pass, pretending to be asleep, my eyes only slightly open.

"So, what's the plan?" Roland asked.

Alucard shrugged, the outline of his body barely visible in the darkened cab. We were driving through an unpopulated part of upstate New York, the streetlights few and far between, our headlights barely making a dent in the gloom. I'd have turned on the high beams if it were me, but I bet Roland's vampire anatomy came with a factory setting that included night vision.

"Magnus has wards all around the grounds," Alucard answered a moment later. "There's a squad running security. Humans who can walk around during the day, posted on the outer perimeter. I'll leave them to you."

"That why you didn't want to use a Gateway? The wards?"

"Pretty much," Alucard said, "Depending how far out he placed them, we could end up having to go several miles. Driving seemed like the better option."

Roland mumbled something I couldn't make out.

"I'm not asking for their help," Alucard said, vehemently. "I need to handle this on my own. Besides, if Nate got involved it would be seen by most as a declaration of war." Alucard sighed. "Still, I owe you for coming on short notice. And Haven for loaning you out. Otherwise it would have been up to me and the girl."

"You sure she's up for it?"

"She's tough. I didn't get a solid read on what all she can do, but she's a good shot and can throw a punch. Doesn't hesitate. I can take down Magnus and the rest, but not while trying to save Othello at the same time. This way, we divide and conquer. Besides, she's so into me that if I told her to go home, she'd probably follow me anyway. Like a puppy."

"Like a what?!" I asked, pouncing up, prepared to slam Alucard's head into the windshield.

Roland's bellowing laughter made me even more irate. "Ignore him," the ex-Shepherd said. "We heard your breathing change when you woke up. He knew you were listening."

Alucard winked at me. "Just a joke, *cher*."

"Ye know, I've killed vampires for less," I hissed, only partly joking.

Roland chuckled. "To be honest, so have I. A lot less."

"About that," I said, "what's a former Shepherd doin' runnin' around with someone like him?"

"Someone like him?" Roland asked, amused, his crimson eyes glinting. "If you haven't noticed, I'm a vampire, too."

"I'm not blind," I said. I replayed Alucard snapping the neck of the vampire I'd been interrogating—noting again the satisfaction he'd gleaned from it. "I meant someone without a conscience."

Alucard jerked his head around, then turned to face the window. I wasn't sure why, but I felt like I'd hurt the big bad fanger's feelings.

"Alucard is not all monster," Roland said. "I've worked with monsters, men with souls darker than the demons they were supposed to save people from." Something about the way he said it made me wonder how fresh that wound was.

"I wasn't criticizin' him," I clarified. "Havin' a conscience is overrated. I'm just curious."

The tension in Alucard's shoulders eased, but he remained facing the window. "I used to be Master of New Orleans, you know," he said. "I traded that in for something I didn't know I wanted. A family. Friends I could trust. But you never really come back from the war, you understand? Not all the way. Still, you're wrong. I have a conscience. I care about my friends and my family. But everyone else? Collateral damage. Can't be helped."

"Like the crowd at the club?" I asked.

"Crowd?" Roland interjected. "What crowd?"

"They were between me and what I wanted," Alucard said, ignoring his companion.

"Aye. But goin' through 'em would've made t'ings far worse."

Alucard nodded. "And, if nothing's happened to Othello, I'll say thank you when this is all over. Gladly. But if she's not okay, it'll be on us for not taking that risk."

I sighed. He was right, of course; if Othello ended up hurt because I'd opted to save a crowd full of strangers, I'd never forgive myself. On the other hand, Othello had picked me for my discretion, for my ability to weigh risks and rewards. Deep down, I know she'd have wanted me to step in, regardless of what happened to her.

"That's the price you pay for keeping your soul," Roland said.

I arched an eyebrow. "Ye believe ye still have a soul?" I didn't ask this judgmentally, more out of curiosity. Most vampires I had met didn't seem overly concerned about having a soul, even going so far as to flaunt the fact that they didn't have one.

Roland shrugged. "I still have my magic. Maybe He hasn't forsaken me just yet. Or maybe it's up to me to prove I can carry this burden with grace. Either way, I'm glad you stopped my friend here from doing something I know he'd regret."

Alucard smirked. "See, that's why I keep you people around. Otherwise I'd be tearing out throats left and right."

"Well, once we get there, ye have me permission to execute every single one of 'em," I said, coolly. "Of course, if ye want to leave a few of them crawlin' on their knees, beggin' for the Almighty's forgiveness…" I leaned forward until I could see Roland's profile, "we can put this absolution theory to the test?"

Roland grunted. "Maybe next time."

CHAPTER 33

*T*he mansion gates were wide open.

"What do you think that means?" Alucard asked Roland.

"It's a trap," I said.

"Definitely a trap," Roland agreed. "Didn't run into any wards. And now no guards."

The mansion itself was visible in the distance, rising above a copse of trees on either side of the road. The sun had yet to rise, but the lights from the windows made the mansion stand out like a beacon. Alucard didn't seem to care, but Roland kept an eye on the horizon, likely gauging how long they'd have until the sun rose. My guess was another couple of hours.

"I don't like it," Alucard said, one hand propped against the dash as he studied our immediate surroundings. "I was really hoping to do this Nate's way."

"Nate's way?" I asked.

"Yeah. Blow shit up and apologize later. I'm not sure why, but it always seems to work out for him."

"Speak softly and carry a big stick," Roland said, as if that made total sense. Catching our befuddled expressions, he continued, "That's how you keep people you care about safe. Temple hasn't mastered the first part, but he's got plenty of firepower to use as a deterrent. You need a bigger stick."

Alucard glared at the ex-Shepherd. "I think my stick is plenty big enough, thank you very much."

Roland shrugged.

"Let's go," Alucard grumbled.

"Wait," I said. "Pop the trunk." He did, and I went around back and snatched up my duffel bag. If we were about to walk into a trap, I wanted to be armed. I ducked back into the car and glanced at my traveling companions. "Oy," I said, a thought occurring to me, "d'ye t'ink he might've rigged explosives? Ye know, along the road."

The two of them looked back at me, eyes wide.

"What?" I asked. "It's what I'd do."

"Maybe we should walk from here," Roland suggested.

"I think I'd rather fly," Alucard said.

"Hah hah," I said, rolling my eyes.

As if vampires could actually fly.

*W*e made it to the door without incident, although it had been entertaining watching the two vampires test out the ground with their boots, shuffling dirt about every so often when it bubbled up conspicuously. Honestly, the fact that they hadn't considered it meant Magnus probably hadn't either, but it never hurt to be cautious.

"So, do we knock, or…?" I asked.

Roland slammed his balled fist against the door several times.

"Did you seriously just knock on his door?" Alucard asked.

"Just because we're here to kill him doesn't mean we can't be polite," Roland said. "Besides, some of us have to be invited in."

I couldn't tell if he was trying to be funny, or serious.

The door creaked open a moment later and a stunning young woman, her eyes glassy and unfocused, greeted us, "Welcome to Kensington Manor. Please, come in."

The three of us shared a look. You know when something is about to go terribly, terribly wrong—that *oh shit* feeling you get right before it happens? That was written on all of our faces. We'd come prepared to go to war, and now it felt like we'd been invited to dinner.

I didn't like it. At all.

We followed our guide inside, walking past a sitting room and ascending to the main foyer. From what I could tell from the outside, the mansion—three stories tall and as wide as a grocery store—had at least a couple dozen rooms. A few hundred priceless paintings and statues. Probably an indoor swimming pool. The display of wealth was obscene, but not particularly surprising—with a few hundred years of saving, my 401K would probably cover something like this.

Well, maybe a few rooms like this.

Two staircases wound their way around either side of the main room, joining together high above our heads. Magnus stood at the railing in a dark blue frock coat that would have looked at home in the Edwardian era. Behind him stood a small harem of women, each displaying anesthetized expressions similar to our guide, who joined them. Magnus rapped his cane on the wrought iron rail with a resounding clang. "Welcome to my home, I—"

"Where's Othello?" I asked, ignoring the pleasantries. One, because I didn't have time for them. And two, because I hated it when vampires did the whole *I was born in blah, blah, blah and back in my day we took six days to say hello* bit. You'd be surprised how old that got—no pun intended.

Magnus glanced at me with disdain before turning his attention to my companions. "Ah, Alucard, once Master of New Orleans. And the former Shepherd. Haven's acquisition. I've heard some interesting things about you. About both of you. I—"

The sound of gunfire interrupted his pithy monologue as my first round burrowed itself in the meat of his arm. The second took him in the stomach. "I'm sorry," I said, "but I asked ye a question."

Magnus straightened and stared down at the blood leaking through his clothes, clearly furious. Unlike his fledglings, he didn't seem particularly bothered by the bullets. Magnus pointed his cane at me. "How dare you come into my Manor and—"

This time I shot him in the leg.

I glanced over at my companions, who were staring at me in complete shock. "What? He's not listenin' to me."

A horrific giggle I recognized erupted from the stairwell on our right. "Ooh, I like her!"

We turned as one, eyeing the scrawny man sprawled out along the stairs, propped up like a pinup model, kicking his legs. His scars appeared even more ragged and disturbing than they had the last time I'd seen him—I thought I could make out words gouged into his skin.

Alucard hissed and took a step forward. "What are *you* doing here?" he asked in stunned disbelief.

"Who, me?" the man asked, his smile so wide it threatened to tear his face in two. "I'm playing the stock market. Human stock. Vampire market. Investments, my friend. It's all about investments."

"We aren't friends, you creep," Alucard snarled.

"So much animosity," the scarred man admonished, flipping onto his back and sitting up. "With a friend like me, you could have all the twisted things your Daywalker heart desires. Respect. Power. Freedom." His eyes glittered. "No more leashes. In fact, you could have pets of your own. Would you like that? Your Beast Master all tied up...waiting to do what you tell her, begging. Wouldn't that be a treat?"

I had no idea what he was talking about, but I could see the scarred man's words were having an effect. Alucard's body language was rigid, as if he were fighting against his own instincts. I decided it was as good a time as any to interject. "Oy, why d'ye and that mountain attack me the other night, ye miserable shit?" I asked.

"Oh, it's you! I'd forgotten. Things slip my mind so easily these days. But you disappeared! Where'd you go, I wonder?" He thrust a couple fingers into his mouth and yanked on his own teeth, pulling his jaw down. He withdrew them with a giggle. "Oh well! You're here now. Let's make the best of it, shall we?"

"Who is he?" Roland asked, nudging Alucard, who nearly jumped at the contact, looking guilty.

"He's an enemy," Alucard replied. "Someone we dealt with a long time ago. He's the original deal-maker. Rumpelstiltskin."

Of course, he was.

Because that's the kind of trip this was turning out to be.

CHAPTER 34

*M*agnus, fully recovered, but sporting some seriously gruesome stains, interrupted our discussion by yanking one of the girls from the crowd. "Tell me, Miss MacKenna...is this your friend? The one Othello spoke of?"

I glowered at him, refusing to speak.

"No?" Magnus threw her aside by one arm. I heard the girl's bone snap from below, and watched in horror as she sunk to the ground, cradling her shattered forearm without so much as a sob. "How about this one?" Magnus snatched another girl.

I ground my teeth together, aching to put another bullet between his eyes. Two things stopped me: the distance and the consequences. At this range, I might end up hitting the girl he held by accident; I was a good shot, but not that good. The other problem was—either because Othello's blessings had worn off or because Magnus was a Master vampire—my bullets didn't have what it took to end the motherfucker.

"Not this one either. Shame." He flung his newest victim back into her companions, many of whom collapsed in a heap without a sound, despite the pain of having a whole person chucked at them.

"Stop this!" I screamed, my trigger fingers tingling from need.

"Tell me how you managed to get past the rules of Guest Right, and I'll stop."

Guest Right. A set of laws imposed on Freaks entering one another's territory—a sort of behavioral guide meant to keep Freaks from killing each other in their own homes. By all accounts, anyone who broke them would forfeit their power and, in some cases, their lives. Roland and Alucard's reaction suddenly made more sense; they hadn't expected me to take pot shots at Magnus any more than he had.

"Some rules don't apply to me," I responded, cryptically. The truth was I had no idea why I'd been able to shoot the bastard without repercussions of some sort—it had simply never occurred to me that anything would happen.

Magnus sneered and dragged a girl from the pile behind him. Her eyes were wide, but not frightened. She'd been dressed in a thin shift that revealed way more than I was comfortable with—her naked legs smooth and tan and corded with lean muscle. She was barefoot, but heavily made up, like a doll.

Terry.

"Oh, I see we've found our missing young woman," Magnus said, gauging my reaction. "But after all the blood loss, I find myself insatiably thirsty." Magnus leaned down, planting his lips against Terry's throat. I took a threatening step forward, but realized I could do nothing about it. Alucard and Roland seemed equally pissed, but attacking Magnus would render them powerless. All we could do was watch.

A man I hadn't noticed before ascended the staircase on our left. "Now, now, Magnus, settle down," he said. "The cameras haven't even started rolling yet. Go get yourself cleaned up, that blood is off-putting."

"Dorian," Magnus replied, rising to his full height to tower over the newcomer. "Don't presume to tell me what to do in my own home. Just because the Marquis requested you, doesn't mean you have any true authority here."

Dorian mock-saluted, the action as graceful and practiced as a bow. "All I'm saying is that, if you bleed that lovely young woman out now, we'll lose a juicy opportunity later on. Besides, we need everyone's cooperation to get things off the ground."

Roland grunted, speaking through gritted teeth. "This isn't good."

"What's the matter? Other than the obvious," Alucard said, his gaze inexorably drawn towards Rumpelstiltskin, who waggled his fingers in an obnoxious wave.

"That's Dorian Gray," Roland replied. "Callie told me about him. Likes to put on shows and events."

Dorian Gray. Another character fresh from the pages of a storybook. How many of these guys were there wandering the world? Had these legends been written into existence, or had they been there all along, and written about only afterward? I studied the man behind Oscar Wilde's legend and noted the same things he had—his incomparable beauty, the slight, ever-present sneer that reeked of self-satisfaction. Dorian Gray was a man it would be easy to love and easier still to hate.

"What kind of shows?" I asked, absentmindedly.

That pale, almost-blush returned to Roland's cheeks. "Orgies, for one."

I eyed the small horde of scantily clad women behind Magnus, who was having a heated argument with Dorian, still holding Terry close. Under the circumstances, it would be more like group rape—except how would we factor in? I suddenly became very aware of the layers I had on and what I would do to make sure they stayed that way.

I took another look around the room while Magnus was distracted, hoping against hope to find Othello nearby. Nothing, unless you counted Rumpelstiltskin, the dealmaker. He'd climbed up on the railing, now, mounting it like a horse. Like a bored toddler.

A thought occurred to me. I groaned and rubbed my temples. "Of course, it was ye," I said, mostly to myself.

"What was that, Quinn?" Roland asked.

"The wee scarred fucker," I said, pointing. "Alucard said he's the deal-maker, right?"

"So?" Roland asked.

"So, he's the one. T'wasn't the vampires at all. Or at least not all them." I called out to the little man, "Oy! Stilts!"

Rumpelstiltskin batted his eyes at me cartoonishly. "Yes?"

"Were ye the one who got Terry her interview with Austina?"

"That depends. Which one's Terry?" he asked, head cocked to one side like a dog's.

I pointed to the young woman in Magnus' arms.

"Oh! I sure did. Fame and fortune. Right up my alley."

"But she didn't even become famous," I argued. "Shouldn't that be a breach of contract?"

Rumpelstiltskin slid down the railing with a joyful squeal, landing on his feet. "Oh no. She had to *feel* famous. To *feel* fortunate. Never works on the stuck-up broads—they won't be happy until they've won an Oscar. That's why I steer clear of LA. But New York City? If they can cover rent, they think they've made it." He tottered on over, pumping his arms as he went. "I'll let you in on a little secret though, if you'd like? Free of charge."

I sneered down at the odious little man. For centuries he'd cashed in on his talent for offering people what they wanted in exchange for something they didn't think they'd ever need. And yet somehow, Terry and the other girls had ended up here, against their will, as living mannequins—a blood supply wrapped in smooth, shapely bodies. "Tell me what they agreed to."

Rumpelstiltskin snapped his fingers and pointed his fingers at me like a gun. "Bingo! Fine print! You know what I hate about making deals?"

I waited for him to go on, unwilling to give him the satisfaction of playing along with his crazy chatter.

He pouted, his eyes unnaturally wide. He kept them that way until my own began to water, then giggled. "I hate...hate," he said, emphasizing the word with a snarl, "making deals for other people. They don't appreciate the craft."

"What are you rambling about?" Alucard asked, taking a step forward as if he might snap the little man's throat.

"He thinks he can use me," Rumpelstiltskin said, ignoring Alucard altogether. "That his sleight-of-hand will keep everyone's eyes away from what lies behind the curtain." The little man clapped gleefully, hopping up and down. "But I know what Hell is." He stopped jumping and yanked at the skin of his face, pulling at his cheeks until the scars were thick and wide across his face, the words written in bold font. "I know what Hell looks like!" he screamed.

Dorian and Magnus turned at the scream, startled.

"It's all in the fine print," the little man whispered, drooling absently. He looked up, met my eyes, and winked. "They traded their futures for the only thing none of them cared about...their pasts."

With that, Rumpelstiltskin disappeared, his giggle lingering long after he left.

"Magnus!" Alucard called, his voice startlingly loud in the silence the dealmaker had left in his wake. "I think this has gone on long enough. Let's be done with the pleasantries. I'm ready to take you on."

Magnus cocked an eyebrow. "You're not a Master anymore. Why should I accept?"

"No, no, this is good!" Dorian said, excitement animating his hauntingly beautiful face. "It'll make for a great fight card. We have the Daywalker vying for the title belt, the ex-Shepherd turned vampire, and the..." Dorian peered out in my direction as if noticing me for the first time. "Excuse me, what are you?"

"She really doesn't like that question," Alucard advised, holding his arm out in front of me to dissuade me from firing at the legendary aestheticist.

"I wouldn't have shot him," I lied, glaring at my vampire companion while I subtly slid my finger off the trigger.

"Well, whatever she is, I'm afraid her odds aren't great," Dorian said. "But maybe we'll get an upset! The audience loves underdogs."

"Audience?" I asked.

"Of course. It's all been prearranged," Dorian asserted.

"What has?"

"Your fights to the death, of course! The newest edition of Freaky Fight Night."

CHAPTER 35

*R*oland crossed his arms over his chest. "What makes you think we'll play along?"

Magnus started playing with Terry's hair, coiling its ends around his finger. "I thought you came here trying to rescue people?"

Roland sneered. "And we're supposed to believe you'll let us walk away after all this?"

"No trust, I see. Old habits die hard don't they, Shepherd?" Magnus said, smirking. "I swear that *if* you win, you'll be free to go."

"And the girls? Othello?" I asked.

Magnus snapped his fingers. "Right, I'd almost forgotten. Follow me." The Master vampire turned, dragging Terry by one arm, and waded through the small harem, many of whom hadn't bothered to rise after being knocked to the floor.

Dorian waved us on up and trailed after Magnus. "Excuse me, ladies. Coming through," he said, gently urging them aside like you might a herd of sheep.

"Guess we're playing along, for now," Roland grumbled, heading towards the stairs. I took the stairs with Alucard, who seemed lost in thought after finding out his challenge would be accepted. I nudged him.

"What?" he asked.

"Can we trust him to keep his word?"

Alucard considered that, then nodded.

"So, what's got ye so gloomy?" I asked.

"None of this is making any sense. What's Dorian Gray doing here? Why the show?" Alucard shook his head. "By taking me on, he's gone all in on the first hand. He thinks he knows what cards I've got, but it's a risk. You don't get as old as he does by taking risks. So, what's in it for him? What's he got up his sleeve?"

Together we dipped through the crowd of girls, much as Dorian had. I made a silent promise to help them, although I had no idea how I was going to do it. They'd bartered with Rumpelstiltskin for a better future, and had lost their pasts in the process—their memories. Without that, what was left of them to save?

"You're still takin' him on, aren't ye?" I asked.

Alucard grunted. "Of course, I am. I can't back down now. How about you, planning on taking Dorian up on his offer?"

I grinned and raised the duffle bag up for good measure, hefting its prodigious weight long enough to ease the tension off my shoulder. "I'm always ready for a fight."

Alucard eyed the bag. "You want me to carry that, *cher*?"

"No, I wouldn't want ye to break a nail before your big fight," I said, winking.

Alucard rolled his eyes.

"Hurry up, you two," Roland said from perhaps a dozen feet ahead of us. "I'm pretty sure we're headed to a dungeon."

"What makes ye say that?" I called, disturbed by the idea that Magnus was leading us to a cold, dark cellar full of cages.

"I can smell it."

I didn't want to think about what a dungeon smelled like. Especially if it had something to do with Othello, which had prompted this tour in the first place. "Ye sure we aren't headed to the wine cellar?" I asked. "Surely there's a wine cellar?"

"I doubt it. Dungeons are much more popular. A nice real estate feature for Master vampires looking to relocate. It's a *feng shui* thing, not to mention a convenient disposal site."

Wait, was Roland making a joke? I arced an eyebrow at Alucard, who shrugged. "I was a Master in New Orleans. We had the bayou. Alligators did the job for us, no muss, no fuss."

"Fuckin' vampires," I said, with a sigh, earning a chuckle from my two companions. Their laughter faded quickly, though, our momentary reprieve from the seriousness of the situation over. The longer we walked, the higher the tension rose as we considered what Dorian Gray and Magnus had in store for us. I was so preoccupied, in fact, that I hardly noticed that we'd crossed to the rear of the mansion and had begun descending. I could smell it now—the damp, earthy aroma of wet stone.

"Ah, Mr. Gladstone," I heard Magnus call out from around a corner up ahead, "I see you're enjoying your new accommodations."

I took off past Alucard, who tried reaching for me but wasn't fast enough. Roland seemed too surprised to stop me, and within moments I'd turned the corner, my gun held high, prepared to put a bullet in the bastard who'd kidnapped my aunt. I found Dorian leaning against the wall, studying his fingernails, while Magnus—arms folded behind his back—stared up at the wizard. I followed his gaze.

I lowered my gun to my side.

Alucard and Roland were behind me in an instant, using their preternatural speed to cover the distance. Roland took a look at what lay beyond and hissed through his teeth. Alucard said nothing.

"I'm sure that, if he could," Magnus said, turning to face us, "Mr. Gladstone would extend his greetings. But, such as he is…" Magnus drifted off, meaningfully.

Such as he is. I flicked my eyes over Magnus' shoulder to where Gladstone hung, naked, suspended from a series of thin steel cables that pierced him through various parts of his body and attached on either side to the mortar. It was like he'd been crucified by a series of power lines, his limbs hanging limp where they weren't strung up—a leg swung listlessly back and forth.

His eyelids flickered.

"Did you know that you can invade the human body at several points without doing any actual damage to their organs?" Magnus said. "I got the idea from the Emergency Room at Lincoln Memorial. I was looking for a new blood supplier and met a young man who'd been shot six times without any permanent damage to his vital parts. Can you imagine?" Magnus glanced over his shoulder at the suspended man. "Still, I must say, he's holding up surprisingly well."

Roland was the first to speak. "Get that man down from there, you—"

"No," I interrupted. "He's good where he is."

Roland whirled to face me, but whatever he saw on my face made him pause. He shared a look with Alucard, who seemed relatively unperturbed in comparison. "You sure?" Alucard asked me.

I nodded. Thing is, part of me was truly disgusted by what had been done to the wizard. The human, feeling part of me. The part of me which got excited at Christmas and loved kittens and would give me the courage to save a child from a burning building. The good part of me. But the rest of me saw the man who'd mercilessly slit his own partner's throat, the man who'd nearly gotten someone I cared about killed, the man who'd been content to send a demon after priests if it meant the death of his archrival, the man who'd used my aunt as leverage in his bid to open a gateway to Hell. That part of me couldn't be happier to watch the motherfucker suffer.

"So. Othello?" I asked, yet again.

Magnus grinned. "Oh, my. I confess I hadn't expected that."

"Me either," Dorian Gray said, appraising me. "So callous. I love it. Like a whisper of perfume."

I raised my gun. "If ye make me ask even one more time…" I threatened.

Magnus chuckled. "Quite right." He snapped his fingers and Terry produced a magnetic key that looked eerily similar to the one I had for Chapman's hotel room. She turned to a door I hadn't noticed, tucked away in a small alcove, and swiped the card. The door sprung open and Terry backed away, still in a daze. "You'll find that Miss Othello is completely unharmed," Magnus said magnanimously. "Sadly, Mr. Gladstone has been her only company over the last few hours."

"Othello!" I called as I strode towards the door, my gun wavering between the two men as I went, in case either planned to make a move. Dorian raised his hands and backed into the wall, smiling intently for some reason, as if at an unspoken joke. Magnus joined Terry several feet from the door, looping one arm over her shoulders.

"Quinn! Is that you?" Othello cried out.

"It's me!" I stepped into the doorway. Othello rose and approached, tears in her eyes. She flicked them away with a dismissive gesture and wobbled unsteadily into my arms. I settled her against my shoulder and turned her around. Alucard was there before I could blink, offering to take her.

"I feel like shit," Othello said.

I let Alucard pick her up; he held her effortlessly, like a groom crossing the threshold, but seemed reluctant to get near me for some reason. "Aye, that's because Magnus roofied you," I said, choosing to ignore the vampire's hesitancy, "I'm so sorry it took us so long to make it to ye. It was all me fault," I admitted.

"Not just hers," Alucard said. "I'm glad to see you're alright."

"You're both here now, that's what matters. But Quinn?" Othello said, staring down the length of her body, her glare settling on the Master vampire at the end of the hall.

"What?"

"Why is that *piz'da* still breathing?" Othello asked in a clinical tone, like an executive in a board room.

It was a good question.

CHAPTER 36

I was first up.

"This is insane," Othello said, shackled with silver chains to a chair on my right within the walls of the impromptu arena Dorian had constructed in Magnus' backyard—judging from the size and the thick tarp interior, I was guessing Dorian had borrowed a circus tent for the occasion. Lights and cameras hung everywhere, strung from poles or mounted along walls. Dorian lounged on a plush, dining room chair, flicking grass off his loafers while a small tech crew ran around doing techy things. Based on how they moved and interacted with one another, I guessed they were human—part of Dorian's entourage, then. A wide set of computer monitors with various controls had been set up already, and occasionally Dorian fiddled with it, panning the cameras and calling out instructions to his people.

"Aye, but there's not a whole lot we can do about it," I admitted. "We could take 'em all on, but ye and the girls would be at risk. They'd use ye as shields. Besides, the lads can't attack first or they'll be stripped of their power."

I didn't bother sharing my inner misgivings. At this point, I'd given up trying to figure out motive. If they wanted to put on a show, I'd give them a show. We all would. Naturally, none of us had wanted to go along with Dorian's ridiculous plan, but after we realized that Magnus had called back a couple hundred of his vampires, and after he'd assured us the safe return of the girls as well as Othello for our trouble, it seemed like the best we could hope for.

I still couldn't understand what they hoped to achieve—what was the point? Why go through all this trouble? Something Rumpelstiltskin had said nagged at me, but I couldn't put my finger on it. Something about what was behind the curtain...I shook it off. That's what I got for listening to the ravings of a demented fairy tale legend.

Did I seriously just think that?

"What?" Othello asked, as if baffled by my response. But she wasn't looking at me. She was looking at the wires and monitors, practically drooling. "Oh, sorry. I was looking at the tech. Those are some really nice cameras."

I stared at her until she had the good grace to look at least a little ashamed.

"Thank you for coming to save me," Othello said.

"I would never leave ye behind. Besides, I owed ye one for steppin' in and rescuin' me from the Justices. Pretty sure their doctor would've opened me up to see how I worked if ye hadn't," I said, only half-joking. "Although I'm surprised your boyfriend didn't whisk ye away like he did Serge and I."

Othello's eyes widened.

"Oh shit!" I said. "Serge! Has he texted ye?"

"Check my phone. It's in my pocket," Othello said, wiggling her ass around so I could fetch her phone.

Before I could check it, the resounding thud of a hand patting a microphone echoed throughout the confines of the tent. "Freaks!" Dorian yelled, his voice amplified by the monitors around him, each of which displayed a different angle of his perfectly symmetrical, drool-worthy face. "Welcome to Fight Night!"

Without an actual crowd present, the introduction fell a little flat, but Dorian seemed pleased by whatever he saw on the monitors. He was probably live streaming the whole bout, which meant there may have been thousands, even millions, of viewers tuning in to watch, judging by the level and quality of the tech filming it all. Were these Freak Fight Nights common? Why hadn't I ever heard of them?

I shared a pained look with Alucard, who sat beside Roland in the stands that had been erected shortly after we'd been escorted into the tent itself.

So much for keeping a low profile.

"Please," Dorian called out, "welcome our first contender! The loveliest sadist you will ever meet, Quinn MacKenna!"

So that's what Dorian had been so intrigued about before; he thought I was some sort of psychopath for leaving Gladstone to rot in Magnus' dungeons. I scowled, irritated by his choice of words. Sadly, that's when they decided to turn the cameras on me. My scowl deepened.

I waved using the barrel of my M4.

"Go fuck yourselves," I said, enthusiastically.

"Ooh! So fierce!" Dorian bellowed, laughing. "Let's see if she can keep that up."

I promised myself that—no matter how this ended—I was going to make Dorian Gray pay before this was all over. I was plotting various forms of torture when I realized that he might have a point. Maybe I was a sadist, after all. I studied the remainder of my guns, which lay spread out at my feet; when I'd asked if there were any rules against modern firearms, Dorian had laughed in my face.

I'd taken that as a *no*.

"And now the challenger!" Dorian called.

I peered at the opposite side of the tent, wondering who or what I'd be fighting. My hands were shaking from adrenaline and nerves. It was weird; when the actual fighting started, I knew I'd be calm. Rational. Decisive. But at that exact moment, all I could think about was how much I'd rather be at the bar chasing a shot with a cocktail.

A gateway appeared—a jagged slash with flames licking at the edges, smoke spewing from the rent itself. A figure moved into view, almost too large to fit through the massive tear. Behind me, Othello drew in a sharp breath as the creature clambered through the hole.

"Welcome the creature who needs no introduction!" Dorian bellowed. "The mighty Gomorrah!"

"Fuck me," I breathed.

CHAPTER 37

I'd laid out my available firepower and organized them according to potential stopping power—the line began with the two sawed-offs and ended with my pistols. I hunkered down as Gomorrah cleared the gateway, slung the MP5's strap over one shoulder, and fetched the sawed-offs. The rent between the dimensions snapped closed.

I couldn't believe it had come to this; I never thought I'd regret turning down Serge's offer to get a bazooka. Of course, how was I supposed to know I'd need an anti-tank rocket launcher on a routine business trip?

I know, I know. Always be prepared.

Fucking Boy Scouts.

I rose, checking the magazines of the various weapons which gave me my best shot at making a dent in Gomorrah's mountainous exterior—I flipped open the double-barreled sawed-offs, popped two rounds in each, and swung them closed. I'd slung the M4 assault rifle across my body where it hung free at the small of my back and draped the MP5's strap over the opposite side to let it rest against my hip. I threw my hair up in a messy ponytail and ditched my trench coat. I needed my arms free, and—no matter how chilly it was outside, or how stylish the jacket was—my trench wasn't going to protect me from jack shit except maybe a cold.

For those of you who know and routinely use guns, you can imagine how ridiculous this all seemed. For those of you who don't, keep in mind that guns are bulky, heavy things with handles and barrels and other odds and ends which will inevitably poke or prod. Having so many on my person meant I had to waddle to move comfortably. It wasn't attractive, it sure as shit wasn't graceful, and I was on live television.

Because that's my life.

"Technically," I said as Gomorrah approached, "this would be a grudge match, I t'ink."

Dorian's jaw hung slack in surprise after hearing that. "Ladies and gentlemen, I stand corrected! It seems this is no ordinary bout! These two have faced off before!"

"You do not have the wolf man here to save you this time," Gomorrah said, his voice as craggy and discordant as I remembered.

"Maybe not," I said, "but then this time ye won't be blindsidin' me on a public street in the middle of the night."

A chorus of inhuman howls and booing echoed from an array of speakers above. Apparently, they'd gotten the audio up and running in time for the virtual crowd to react to my response. Gomorrah's eyeless face turned towards the sound of the noise, then sunk back down. I couldn't tell if my retort had gotten a reaction—you try arguing with a rock and seeing if it gives a shit.

Go on, I'll wait.

"What are ye even doin' here?" I asked. I'd considered questioning Gomorrah about the seed directly, but it didn't seem wise with all the Freaks out there gathered around their monitors; we had enough parties interested in Chapman's seed without advertising its existence to the whole world. Still, between Rumpelstiltskin and Gomorrah, it looked like the Marquis—whoever or whatever the hell he was—had history with Magnus, a relationship of some sort. I simply couldn't figure out what sort of relationship it was.

Did psychopathic Freaks have a Country Club Membership or something? An inaugural ball where they drank the blood of the innocent out of punch bowls and danced the night away to the devil's music?

"That is not your concern," Gomorrah replied. "Enough talking."

"Oh, right, sorry. I'd forgotten how chatty ye get," I quipped, rolling my eyes.

Gomorrah, true to his word, charged. He was surprisingly fast, covering the ground between us in a matter of seconds. I didn't bother dodging; I'd probably get so tangled in all my guns that I'd end up an even easier target than before. I'd already considered all my options and realized this wasn't a fight I could win by being faster, or stronger, or even smarter.

I waited as patiently as I could for the giant, boulder-like fist to come swinging at me from overhead—it seemed Gomorrah planned to crunch me down like a can of soda. It felt eerily similar to watching a nurse prepare a needle meant for my arm. I cringed as I watched his fist descend, one eye pinched shut, my fingers crossed, prepared to roll away if this didn't work.

You see, with his length of stride and his reach, I knew I wouldn't be able to match Gomorrah in terms of speed. And one look was all it took to know who would win in an arm wrestling competition. Which left being clever. Sadly, that only worked if you had time to plan in advance, to strategize and exploit your opponent's weakness. I didn't have the luxury of time, and as far as I could tell the only weakness Gomorrah had was his shitty personality. But, depending on how his first blow fell, I'd know if I had what I needed to win.

Luck.

And an anti-magic field that, for whatever reason, repelled Gomorrah's attacks.

Gomorrah's hand buried itself in the ground beside me, so deep the dirt hugged his rocky forearm.

I sighed in relief as the virtual crowd gasped in confusion.

Then I started shooting.

CHAPTER 38

*G*omorrah's surprise at having completely missed me gave me ample time to unload the first of my double-barreled shotguns at his exposed kneecap—basically a slab of stone held in place by sand and fire and glass. The noise from the speakers was deafening, but I blocked it out, strafing to my left as Gomorrah fought to pry his hand free from the ground. I tossed my first shotgun aside and leveled the second point-blank against his knee. I fired. Chunks of rock spewed outward; a few stone chips ricocheted, clanging against the barrel of the smoking shotgun. I flung it alongside its twin and swung my assault rifle around.

Gomorrah bellowed and tore his hand free. He whipped around, trying to backhand me into next year, but—as his hand soared well above me—he overextended and fell. I hadn't even bothered to dodge, which made it look all the more comical. In fact, I'd barely moved since the fight started. I set the butt of the M4 in the crook of my shoulder, aimed a little below Gomorrah's knee to account for the slight lift that would occur once I began firing, and widened my stance.

I let loose everything I had, squeezing the trigger in short bursts, emptying my clip until nothing remained of Gomorrah's knee but a small, bowling-ball sized crater. Granted, it was a hell of a lot less convenient than dropping Austina's bodyguard had been, but the principle was the same; without a leg to stand on, Gomorrah's threat level went from DEFCON 1 to half-mangled zombie. When the Unclean—as Hemingway had dubbed him —bastard tried to rise, he discovered that very thing for himself; he tottered and collapsed back to the ground as his leg collapsed, shattering in two.

The crowd had gone completely silent.

"Ladies and gentlemen, Freaks of all ages...what a stunning turn of events..." Dorian was calling out in disbelief.

I barely heard him.

Instead, I set my assault rifle aside and drew the MP5. While it had very little stopping power to offer compared to the guns I'd already used, it would work for what I needed. The behemoth had flopped over onto his back and was attempting to sit up, but, without his right leg to counterbalance, he seemed to be struggling. In fact, he looked so piteous I briefly considered offering to help.

Instead, I sprayed him in the face with a swarm of helpful bullets.

Now it was my turn to get booed by the crowd. Apparently, they were all for someone being crushed to a bloody pulp by a rock monster but couldn't support the idea of kicking someone when they were down...or shooting them, in this case.

Hypocrites.

I found the nearest camera, flipped them off, and continued firing until the vaguely human shape of Gomorrah's face was completely eradicated. I lowered the submachine gun and rubbed at my arms; shooting that many rounds nonstop would leave my biceps twitching for hours.

Some people, even some of the Freaks watching, might consider this overkill. Gomorrah couldn't even touch me, after all, so why go through the trouble of blowing his face to smithereens? Here's the thing: Gomorrah was a bully. And, unless you'd survived bullies, you wouldn't understand.

Those who jeered had never been forced to weather the blows and taunts of schoolyard alphas or fend off the hungry stares of their pack followers—the skittish wolves who gnawed on the leftover meat, teasing you with the names given by your tormentors, snickering whenever someone treated you like dirt. They'd never had to learn what it took to break that cycle.

I had.

I wasn't maiming Gomorrah for kicks and grins. I was doing it so any Freak out there who saw me out on the street knew to cross to the other side. Basically, I'd picked the biggest bully on the playground and kicked his ass so badly he wouldn't ever walk again, and then I'd wrecked his face.

Because when you fought me, prison rules applied.

This was a message to my viewership.

"I do not feel pain," Gomorrah said, his words slightly garbled now that he no longer had lips. "I cannot die. I will kill you." To emphasize his point, the Unclean mercenary flipped over onto his stomach and began to crawl towards me, grinding himself across the ground, gouging furrows into the grass.

I snorted, retrieved my shotguns, and strode over to my duffel bag to begin the laborious process of reloading; if the moron wanted to lose the rest of his limbs, so be it. Fortunately, Dorian saved me the effort, realizing what it was I intended. "I believe," he yelled, quieting the murmuring crowd, "this fight is concluded! The winner is Miss MacKenna!"

Not so lovely anymore, apparently.

I'd take it.

Still, since I had the attention of the crowd, I shoved two shells into one of the shotguns, smiled, curtsied, and shot Gomorrah in the face once more for good measure.

CHAPTER 39

*R*oland passed me on the stairs to take his place in the ring. "Quite a show you put on there."

"I was lucky," I said, shrugging.

Roland nodded. "Yes, you were. Lucky, and ruthless. Who trained you to shoot?"

I grimaced. "I had a mentor once upon a time. You'd have hated him. But he taught me a few useful t'ings." I didn't feel like going into any more depth than that, and I was glad when Roland didn't press. Talking about my old boss brought up bad memories.

Roland hesitated at the foot of the stairs. "Quinn," he said, then met my eyes for a long moment. I wasn't sure what he wanted, then realized he was testing his vampire gaze on me. I frowned. He blinked and a slow smile spread across his face. It looked good on him, albeit a little out of place. "I figured it was something like that," he said.

"Don't die, ye idgit," I said, frowning inwardly at his comment.

He chuckled and waved.

I punched in Othello's password as I walked along the stands to where Alucard was sitting. I'd snuck the phone out of her back pocket after my duel with Gomorrah while a squad of Dorian's people tried to figure out how to cart the pile of rocks off the field. Several of the tech crew and a few of Magnus' vampires shrunk back from me—or fled altogether—as I went, which I found so amusing I started to hop up and down the rows to see them scurry.

I almost felt like a celebrity.

Or, you know, like a ruthless dictator.

By the time I made it to Alucard, I'd already read through Serge's frequent texts, almost all of which consisted of frowny face emojis. The last two, however, weren't as adorable. The first was innocuous, but straightforward: The man is leaving the hotel. The second, which had arrived only a few minutes ago, was less so: Follow to Brooklyn Bridge. Smells bad. Very very bad.

I remembered Serge's keen sense of smell playing a role in the acquisition of my guns and cringed. If the Serbian had picked up a scent worth noting, it meant Chapman was getting himself involved in something truly dangerous. Had he decided to go ahead with the handoff? If so, the Brooklyn Bridge made sense; even in the hours before sunrise, it was trafficked enough to be considered public. Gaggles of tourists often clustered along the walkway that ran across the bridge, taking selfies.

I stared down at Gomorrah. Why would the Unclean behemoth be here, if Chapman were about to give away the seed? Shouldn't the hired muscle be where the action was? Was I wrong about the whole thing? Chapman could be out for an early morning jog across the bridge for all I knew. Deep down, though, I knew better; Serge's nose and my gut couldn't both be wrong. For some reason, I heard Rumpelstiltskin's voice in my head, his eerie, warbling giggle...sleight-of-hand. Behind the curtain.

I cursed.

"I t'ink I know why they're doin' all this," I said, settling in beside Alucard. "Why they're so concerned about airin' these fights, and the deal Magnus struck with Rumpelstiltskin. All of it."

The vampire scooted a few feet down the bench. "Do tell," he said.

I marveled at the space he'd put between us. "Did ye pull a lunchroom cafeteria move on me, just now?" I asked.

Alucard's brow furrowed. "A what?"

"Ye scooted away from me like I have cooties," I accused.

163

"Cooties?" Alucard drawled.

I stared at the vampire. Was Alucard so old that he'd never encountered the concept of cooties? Talk about a generational gap. Next, I'd have to explain the merits of boy bands, pagers, encyclopedias, and *Blockbuster*.

"What's the matter with ye?" I asked.

"Nothing is wrong with me. But after your little show down there," Alucard said, "and the trick you pulled in the dungeon, I'm wondering if it's safe to sit too close to you."

"Ye *do* t'ink I have cooties!" I yelled, eliciting faint giggles from those nearby. I turned a glare on the eavesdroppers and laughed when they shrunk back in fear. I grinned and held out my arms to the vampire. "Come give us a hug, ye filthy bloodsucker."

Alucard gave me his best flat-eyed stare.

"Fine," I said, with a wink. "I didn't want to hug ye, anyway."

"Is it a secret?" he asked. "What you can do, I mean."

"Why don't ye ask Roland? He t'inks he's got it all figured out."

Alucard studied the field below where Roland waited calmly for his opponent to show, one hand on the hilt of his sword. "Roland figured you had some sort of magical protection. Something to keep you safe. But I don't buy it. When I tried to grab you in the dungeon, nothing stopped me or shoved me aside, I just missed. You didn't move faster, either. You made *me* slow down." Alucard shrugged. "I'm not sure what kind of engine you've got, but until I know I'm not fuel, I think it's better to keep my distance."

"You're one to talk," I accused. "To ye lot, we're all fuel."

Alucard smirked. "I never said I wasn't a hypocrite."

I rolled my eyes and patted the seat next to me. "You're safe, ye big baby." Alucard hesitated but slid over. I was tempted to slug him, but decided against it; we all have cause to fear the unknown.

"So, you said you sorted it out?" Alucard asked a moment later. The tech crew had finally managed to move Gomorrah with the help of Magnus' vampires—they'd gone with the light-as-a-feather-stiff-as-a-board method. A few stragglers fetched the chunks of stone worth carrying and waddled across the field with them. I wasn't sure what they'd do with Gomorrah himself—the big bastard hadn't spoken or moved since I'd pelted him in the face that final time—but I was hoping it involved him becoming someone's lawn ornament.

"Do ye know anythin' about a seed?" I asked.

Alucard looked at me like I'd lost my mind.

I sighed. "Alright, let's just say there's this magical artifact tradin' hands as we speak, and one of the parties involved employs your man with the scars, as well as that stone bastard they're cartin' off the field."

Alucard's interest perked up, and then his eyes narrowed.

"Exactly," I said. "Now tell me, if ye wanted to divert attention from somethin' like a handoff that could mean the end of the world, what would ye do?"

"You think they staged this whole thing to keep everyone's eyes elsewhere? That they recruited Dorian Gray to set up these fights?"

"Well, not these fights. A fight. We just happened to show up," I said. "Ye heard how excited he was when he heard you call out Magnus? You're even more of a draw. It's all sleight-of-hand. Like plannin' a robbery the night of the Superbowl," I said, trying to think of an analogy that the vampire would understand.

Alucard gave me a funny look.

I threw up my hands in disbelief. "Are ye tellin' me ye don't know what the Superbowl is? What have ye been doin' for the last 50 years?"

Alucard rolled his eyes. "*Cher*, I'm from New Orleans. Trust me, I know all about the Superbowl. I'm only wondering what you plan to do about this handoff, assuming you've got it right."

"If I'm wrong, it won't matter. But if I'm right, I have to stop it," I replied. "Which means I need to get back sooner rather than later."

"I think what we've got going on here might be more of a priority, all things considered. We've got to get Othello and the girls out of here. Not to mention ourselves."

I locked eyes with Alucard. "Big picture? Gettin' back and makin' sure nobody gets their hands on the artifact may be more important. Like end of the world important."

"Says who?" Alucard asked, skeptical.

I paused to consider that question. "If I said a Horseman of the Apocalypse, would ye believe me?"

Alucard's already pale face went one shade lighter. "Which one?"

"Death."

"Well, fuck."

"What?" I asked.

"Nothing. I was sort of banking on Hemingway showing up to rescue

Othello and saving us all the trouble of fighting these assholes. But my luck has never been that good."

I snorted. "So…"

Alucard pulled out his phone. "Hold on, I'll see what I can do."

I stared at him.

Who was he going to call, *The Avengers?*

CHAPTER 40

*D*orian finally seemed to have the field where he wanted it and gave the signal to turn the cameras back on. While trying to keep my mind off what was going on with Chapman and the seed, I considered the various ways Dorian must have entertained his audience during the intermission. Did he have advertisers? What kind of marketing campaigns were geared towards Freaks? Were there commercials for werewolf grooming products? Vampire orthodontists? Sleep masks for Cyclopes?

Now *those* I would watch.

"And we're back!" Dorian called. "Sorry to keep you waiting, but I promise this next fight will be worth the delay! Especially considering our second bout of the evening features someone many of you have waited years to see bleed! Please join me in welcoming the infamous ex-Shepherd, Roland Haviar!"

The cheers and jeers reached a fever pitch. As a former Shepherd, it made sense that the Freak community had an issue with Roland—the Vatican's soldiers had become supernatural bogeymen for a reason, after all. Now that he was a vampire, however, I was sure there'd be those who considered him a trophy—a superstar playing for their home team. Hence the mixed response. I found myself gripping the edges of my seat, consumed by the pageantry of it all. Now that it wasn't me down there, I had to admit, the whole Fight Night concept was thrilling, in a way.

So long as Roland didn't end up dead.

"And the challenger!" This time the gateway didn't appear so much as explode outward. A whirling cloud of grainy salt spun out from the flaming rent and piled in a massive mound on the middle of the field, followed by a fountain of blood. "The leader of the Unclean and sister to the fallen Gomorrah," Dorian called over the din created by the creature's entrance, "Sodom the Defiler!"

The pile of salt and the puddle of blood merged, coalescing into a tall, thin creature with vaguely feminine features—if the woman in question were eight-feet-tall, had freakishly long limbs, no eyes, and a name that made everyone who wasn't into anal cringe.

For the record, I cringed.

"Where the hell do they find these guys?" Alucard muttered beside me.

"I t'ink ye just answered your own question," I replied, earning me a snicker.

Roland, for his part, looked unconcerned. He drew his sword and angled it in a fighting stance that I recognized from my brief stint studying *kendo*; I'd given up on the ancient Japanese art of sword fighting when they informed me it would take months to learn how to properly draw the damn thing. Ain't nobody got time for that.

Except, apparently, Roland.

The ex-Shepherd studied his opponent, who left trails of salt crystalizing behind her as she stalked along the edges of the field, the blades of grass so smothered in white that they looked like slivers of bone poking up from beneath the earth. I wondered if she'd have any clever one liners of the "now you die" variety, but she seemed even less interested in talking than her brother had been; she sprung, launching herself at the ex-Shepherd with shocking speed—by far too fast for most vampires, especially a fledgling, to dodge.

Fortunately, Roland was no slouch.

The ex-Shepherd dropped to one knee, dodging below the briny abomination's claws, then sprung up, slicing Sodom from groin to gullet. Roland stepped through the gaping hole he'd made, the salt spray dusting his clothes, and cleaned his sword off on his slacks as Sodom pitched forward onto the ground. I was impressed, and I wasn't the only one; the speed and execution of Roland's counterattack had left the crowd speechless. I wasn't sure who the favorite had been leading up to the fight, but I was willing to bet a few gamblers were sweating bullets right about now.

At least until Sodom's two halves remerged, the blood pooling together, salt spilling, until she was whole once more. The Defiler rose, seemingly unfazed. Apparently—unlike her durable but inflexible brother—losing limbs wouldn't slow her down much.

Good thing I hadn't drawn that matchup, huh?

Roland took a few steps back and studied his opponent. I could practically see the wheels spinning in his head. If he couldn't cut her into ribbons, he'd have to come up with a different strategy—something less straightforward. The ex-Shepherd returned his sword to its scabbard in a practiced motion, but that's precisely what Sodom had been waiting for. She thrust her arm forward, somehow even faster than before, the limb elongating into a lance of crystalized salt and blood. Roland danced backwards, barely managing to dodge the tip of the lance, almost tripping over his own feet.

"It's too soon," Alucard murmured, "he's still getting used to using his abilities. He can't rely on outpunching that thing."

As if he'd heard Alucard's distant mutterings, Roland abruptly switched tactics, diving to his right and flinging out his hand. Magic spewed from his fingertips, a ball of broiling flame splashing against Sodom's back. The flame was darker than any I'd ever seen, tinged an unnatural shade of red. If the crowd had been quiet before, they were dead silent now—too shocked to see a vampire wielding a wizard's magic to react. I noticed the vampires in attendance sharing bewildered looks with one another.

"Ladies, gentlemen, and Freaks! It looks like this match has gotten interesting!" Dorian yelled. I agreed. If Roland could use magic like that, he stood a chance of bringing Sodom down permanently. A wizard's magic was often limited only to his imagination and power reserves. Roland didn't strike me as the overly imaginative type, but he did strike me as a survivor.

He'd make do with what he had.

The crowd hooted as flames licked Sodom's back, eager to see more, but the noise diminished as the flaming ball sunk into the monstrosity, infusing it with light. Sodom turned on the ex-Shepherd and cackled. Seriously, cackled.

"Fuck," Alucard cursed.

"What is it?" I asked, baffled.

"It's Roland's magic. Everything he casts is tinged with blood. His gateways and his spells. That thing he's fighting can absorb anything he throws at it."

"You're fast," Sodom said, her voice like the hiss of sand on stone, angling herself to face Roland head on. "But not very clever."

Roland searched the ground for a moment until he found a small rock. He raised it, turning it this way and that. "Is this part of your brother, you think?"

Sodom screeched in outrage and barreled towards the ex-Shepherd. Roland fell into a fighting stance. I could see him considering his options, trying to come up with a new plan of attack—but Sodom didn't give him that kind of time. She swiped out with a leg but then, when Roland leapt to avoid it, continued with a backhand that sent him flying. Roland bounced once, then twice, but came up on all fours and launched himself at his opponent Wolverine-style, his claws extended as if he planned to tear her apart with his bare hands, his fangs bared, eyes flashing red.

Sodom's lance-like arm took him in the side and pinned him to the ground faster than I could blink. She marched forward, forcing the tip deeper, tearing through Roland's stomach. The ex-Shepherd screamed in pain and outrage. He tore at the offending lance like a wild animal, thrashing and flailing.

"What's happening?" I asked, turning to Alucard.

"He's lost control of himself," Alucard said, eyes narrowed.

"What can we do?" I asked. I refused to sit in the bleachers while Roland was toyed with and killed. The ex-Shepherd was a good guy, after all.

For a vampire.

Alucard's phone rang before he could answer.

And that's when the wolves showed up.

CHAPTER 41

*T*wo massive wolves built unlike any I'd ever seen—with eyes as red as any vampire's—burst through the tent, tearing holes through the tarp as if it were wrapping paper. The longer of the two launched itself at Sodom's head, while the shorter went for her legs.

Over the screams and shouts, I realized Alucard's phone was playing Duran Duran's "Hungry Like the Wolf." The vampire slid his thumb across the screen and held it to his ear, shouting over the commotion. "Took your sweet time, I see!" he said, grinning like a maniac.

He listened for a few seconds and laughed. "Yes, I see that. I'm guessing pent up sexual frustration?" Another laugh. "So, you'll be right behind, I hope? Excellent. See you soon."

I punched Alucard in the arm.

"Ow! What was that for?" he asked.

"Who was that on the phone?" I demanded.

"Oh, don't worry about it."

I punched him again.

"Hey! You said you were in a rush, so I phoned a friend."

I glared at the vampire. He didn't know what cooties were, but he could reference *Who Wants to Be a Millionaire*? "Who did ye call?" I asked, again. It wasn't so much that I minded him calling in reinforcements—that part I was all for. But I wasn't a fan of being left in the dark.

"You'll see, *cher*. C'mon, let's go get Othello and the girls out before things get too crazy."

"Crazier than this?" I asked, waving my hand at the field, where the two wolves were squaring off against Sodom, who'd fallen back to recover from a series of bite wounds. Roland's wound was healing, but the wild look in his eyes still hadn't faded. Meanwhile, Dorian seemed content to let the show go on. In fact, he was directing his people to bring more cameras into the fray so they could capture each of the fighters in action from various angles.

Alucard chuckled as he raced down the bleachers with me hot on his heels, but didn't bother responding. A few of Magnus' vampires tried to stop us, but Alucard made short work of them, carving his way towards the field, leaving corpses in his wake. Seeing him in action, I was reminded yet again that—as a former Master—Alucard was a class above the fangers I was used to squaring off against. Part of me was glad to have him on my side, while the other part of me plotted ways to kill him if it ever came to that.

I'm not perfect, people. But I am practical.

We found Othello on her side on the ground, having been tipped over at some point during the hubbub. Alucard reached for the chains, undoubtedly planning to tear them off, but reared back at the last instant with a hiss. "Silver. That was clever of them," he said.

"Ye didn't have a plan for that?" I asked, hands on my hips.

Alucard rubbed at the back of his neck. "I'm guessing there's a key?"

Othello glanced up at me and rolled her eyes. "Can you help a girl up in the meantime?"

I hoisted Othello back to her original position in time to see one of the wolves who'd attacked Sodom go soaring into the stands, not far from where we'd been sitting. Apparently, Sodom had gotten over the surprise of facing three opponents. Fortunately, it also seemed like Roland had gotten control of himself. I watched as the older man sliced through Sodom's legs with his blade, and the remaining wolf pounced on the Defiler's chest, landing a dozen feet away, putting as much distance between the two halves of Sodom's body as possible. I thought it was a good strategy—the further she had to travel to heal, the longer it would take her to recover—at least until Sodom dissolved completely and rejoined several feet away, undamaged.

"They should've sent *her* after John Connor," I said, half-joking, half-terrified.

"What?" Othello asked.

"I never know what she's talking about," Alucard said.

"Seriously? *Terminator?*" My gaze oscillated between the two of them.

"Is that a movie?" Alucard asked.

"Of course, it is," Othello said, sighing. "I should have known."

"Uncultured swine, the both of ye," I said, before returning my attention to the fight.

The wolf who'd been thrown joined her counterpart and together they faced off against the salt monster, their teeth bared in a snarl. I realized what it was that seemed so odd to me about these wolves: they were somehow longer, and therefore taller, than any of the others I'd seen. Stretched. It was like spotting a long-distance runner amid sprinters, as if you could sense they had been designed to do something else.

Like chase you throughout the night and devour you by morning.

Ironically, Roland, easily the smallest of the three, seemed to be in charge. I realized something in his demeanor had changed while I'd been busy studying the wolves; he'd knelt and pressed his palm against the ground, his eyes pinched shut. Sodom took a threatening step forward, but then stopped, cocking her head to the side like a dog. A moment later I heard something, too—distant creaks and groans. Alucard whirled towards the sounds but couldn't seem to place them.

Suddenly, the hiss and spit of the lawn's sprinkler system filled my ears. Water spewed from the tiny steel sprinklers, arcing everywhere. The wolves, quickly getting soaked, shook off the liquid until their fur stood on end, like massive Pomeranians. Meanwhile Sodom, the invulnerable salt monster, shrieked as she dissolved into a murky pink puddle.

I eyed Roland, who rose with a satisfied smirk. He caught me looking his way and shrugged. "What a world, what a world, huh?"

"See! See!" I said, pointing at the ex-Shepherd. "I'm not the only one!"

Dorian's camera equipment, so close to the fighting that they'd been caught in the water works, began to malfunction, and I could hear him screaming at his techs to retrieve them before everything went haywire. A horde of Magnus' vampires, meanwhile, had formed a loose circle around the field, preparing to come at us in waves if we tried to flee. The Master of New York City himself, however, had yet to make an appearance.

One of Roland's wolves raised her snout and howled in victory, joined swiftly by her companion. Except, after a moment, I realized they weren't the only wolves baying. There were others—answering howls—resounding from outside the tent.

In the hundreds.

CHAPTER 42

*T*he wolves flooded in through the hole created by Roland's
saviors, tearing it wider as they moved to encircle the tent, like a
cavalry in formation. I saw a few of Magnus' vampires try to stem the tide,
only to get run over or torn to shreds. In a matter of moments, the vampires
were surrounded by the largest pack I'd ever seen.

Two wolves marched through the opening on their hind legs, their
bodies somewhere between wolf and man but deadlier than either,
confirming a rumor I'd heard but had never entirely believed. One was
white, the other dark. Male and female, respectively, judging by their sizes. I
realized I was looking at the pack alphas—their leaders.

The white wolfman approached, ignoring the vampires scrambling in
his wake. Or maybe he simply couldn't see them; the monstrous mongrel
only had one eye, after all. His companion trailed behind, eyeing the bloodsuckers and licking her chops as if anticipating a meal, a necklace of bones
draped around her neck.

Alucard met them halfway, waving as he jogged over. "Glad you could
make it," he said. "Gunnar. Ashley." Alucard bowed slightly to both, who
returned the gesture.

"We would have been here sooner," Gunnar, the thick-chested white
wolf, replied, "but Nate kept pestering us with questions."

"He wanted to come, but we told him he wasn't needed," Ashley said, baring her fangs in a canine grin. "Well except for the gateway, of course."

Alucard chuckled. "Oh, that's beautiful. He's probably so pissed right now. Plotting his revenge."

Gunnar nodded his shaggy head and studied the arena clinically. "So, this is your idea of a vacation, is it?"

The former Master of New Orleans shrugged. "I like to live on the edge, what can I say?"

"Excuse me," I said, "I hate to interrupt, but can we hurry this up?" I folded my arms over my chest. "Some of us have places to be."

Ashley snarled at me. "What's your hurry?"

Alucard held up a placating hand. "Don't mind her, that's just how she is."

I started scouring the field for where they'd taken my bag full of guns. You know, just in case I felt like shoving a muzzle up someone's ass here in a few minutes.

"What's wrong, Quinn?" Othello asked, picking up on my urgency.

"I t'ink Chapman's goin' through with the handoff. If we don't hurry and get back, we may not be able to stop him."

"Gunnar! Ashley!" Othello called, getting their attention. "She's right. We have to hurry."

The wolves saw the silver chains wrapped around Othello and growled, clearly displeased. They glanced at each other. Ashley spoke first. "Understood."

"The pack will help you," Gunnar affirmed, though I noticed he was looking at Othello, not me.

Guess I'd upset the pooches.

Oh well. So long as they didn't piss all over my carpet, I'd get over it.

Roland walked over to us, trailed by two very naked, very wet women. He waved at me as he approached. "Quinn, I'd like to introduce you to Paradise and Lost." The women waved enthusiastically at me. A little too enthusiastically, if I was being honest; breasts that perky didn't really need the help. "Did I hear you needed to get somewhere?"

I opened my mouth to reply, but was interrupted by a series of terrified screams from the opposite side of the arena, where Magnus had appeared with his harem of kidnapped girls, each held by one of his vampires. The Master of New York City held Terry casually by the throat. She seemed remarkably more aware than she had in the mansion, her eyes wide and startled with fright.

"It smells like wet dog in here," Magnus said, sniffing the air in distaste. "Is it too cliché to tell you mangy mutts to get off my lawn?"

The wolves growled as one, sounding vaguely like the rumble of thunder in the confined space. In answer, Magnus tightened his grip on Terry's throat. She whimpered. Gunnar and Ashley faced the Master together, their movements uncannily synchronized.

"Is she one of the ones we need to rescue?" Gunnar asked.

"Yes," Alucard replied. "They've been taking the girls from the city for some reason. Rumpelstiltskin's involved."

Gunnar's hackles rose, making the massive son of a bitch look even bigger. In fact, Ashley was almost dainty in comparison. But those eyes... those were a crazy bitch's eyes.

"Enough chatter," Magnus said. "As entertaining as this all is, you have no jurisdiction here, Wolf King. Fortunately for you and your pack, I'll overlook your interference in Council-sanctioned business. Your Daywalker challenged me to a duel, after all."

"Is that true?" Gunnar asked.

"It is," Alucard answered. "Only way I could think of to get terms established."

"Then we can't interfere," Gunnar said, sounding resigned.

"Ye what?" I demanded, irate. What the hell was the point of having all these wolves around if they couldn't help us take out Magnus and his band of merry vamps?

"It's how they do things," Othello explained.

"And if Alucard loses? What then?" I asked.

"Then we leave," Ashley said through gritted fangs. "Or we go to war with the Council. Neither are great options."

"What about Roland?" I demanded. "He had wolves step in."

"It's not the same," Gunnar responded. "His fight was part of Dorian's little game. Not a sanctioned duel."

Othello saw me shaking in anger and frustration. "Quinn, they want to step in as bad as you do. Trust me."

I glanced at my companions, noting the tension in their necks and shoulders, and realized Othello was right. I took a deep, calming breath, trying to see things from the wolves' perspective. Their pack was massive, but even they stood no chance against the Council's retribution if they took on a Master in his territory to save a bunch of Regulars. It was total and utter bullshit, but it was also completely true. Power structures needed checks and balances, which is why duels like these had been established in the first place—otherwise the bloodshed would never end.

Which meant our survival hinged on Alucard winning.

Goodie.

Gunnar settled his massive paw on Alucard's back and pushed him forward. "Go get 'em, Glitterotti."

Alucard rolled his eyes as he headed towards the center of the field. "Hah hah." He stripped off his leather jacket and began rolling up the cuffs of his shirt, the red color stark against his pale skin and dark hair. "Same rules apply, right, Maggie?" Alucard called out. "I win, Othello and the girls are ours? We walk away?"

I could tell he was saying this more for Magnus' men than Magnus himself; if Alucard won, Magnus would be dead. Still, it was necessary. If Magnus lost and the vampires took it on themselves to avenge him, the girls would be the first to die. This way, no one would be tempted to do something stupid.

Magnus' eye twitched. "Of course. However, I'd like you to know that as soon as I'm done tearing out your throat, I'm going to execute the girls one at a time while Miss MacKenna and the ex-Shepherd watch. Then I'll find out if either of them can last longer than Gladstone. He's at fifteen days, and counting."

"Always the threats with you people," Alucard said, rolling his shoulders. "Let's see what you've got, Mags."

CHAPTER 43

*T*he two vampires fought with such ferocity and speed that all I really caught were the blows themselves. Magnus, with his height and experience, clearly had the advantage in terms of close-quarters fighting. But what Alucard lacked in range, he made up for in tenacity; I watched him take a right hook to the face, only to gouge into Magnus' forearm with his teeth a moment later, tearing at the bastard's arm like a pit bull with a chew toy. By the time the Master shook him off, Alucard had a gob of flesh to spit out.

To be honest, I may have gagged a little.

Of course, Magnus didn't seem to care nearly as much as I would have about missing three percent of his body; he sprung forward and landed a kick that sent Alucard listing sideways, then used his momentum to slam Alucard's face into the dirt. Magnus held him there, his arms quivering with tension.

"Is that all you have, Daywalker?" Magnus ground out through clenched fangs.

Alucard snarled and spun, snatching Magnus' wrists as he went, and ended up on top of the Master vampire. He fired punches, clipping Magnus' face and tearing divots into the earth when he missed. Magnus laughed maniacally, blood marring his pale face.

"Better!" he yelled.

The Master vampire thrust his arms to either side and shot up, hovering nearly ten feet off the ground. Alucard lost his balance, slid off, and rolled back onto his feet. Magnus rotated slowly until he faced his adversary.

I glanced at my companions only to find that none of them seemed remotely surprised. The bastard was defying gravity—not to mention everything I'd ever learned in school about physics—and no one but me was the least bit shocked. I cursed, realizing I'd never really seen two vampires go at it—at least not at this level. What determined who had the upper hand? Was it age? The strength of the one who turned them? The quality and consistency of their diets?

I was seconds away from asking Roland when Magnus roared and flung himself at Alucard, clawed hands outstretched—but the Master vampire never reached him. Alucard, floating several feet in the air, had pierced through Magnus' gut so forcefully that his arm had come out the other side, his fingers wet with blood and bile. He spun in slow circles, like a jewelry box ballerina.

A pale, bloody ballerina.

Who could fly.

"You aren't the only one who figured out that trick, Maggie," Alucard said, teeth bared.

Magnus grunted and coughed up blood, splattering it across Alucard's shirt. "I wondered how strong you would be. The legendary Daywalker. And yet, still so much weaker than I had anticipated."

Alucard frowned and yanked, drawing his hand out and leaving a gaping wound behind. The Master gasped and plummeted to the dirt. The fight, it seemed, was over. The crowd of vampires on the other side of the tent began murmuring amongst themselves.

Alucard landed next to Magnus' limp body. "Your Master is through! Release—"

Magnus' laughter interrupted Alucard's command. Alucard spun, but not in time to avoid Magnus' hand as it wrapped around his throat. Except it wasn't Magnus at the other end.

Not really.

What had Alucard by the throat resembled Magnus the way an eagle resembles a sparrow. Sure, they were both birds. They both had wings and flew. But one was easily the better hunter, the faster flyer, with the longer, sharper beak.

Where Magnus once stood there was now an ungainly, bald figure with bat-like ears and thick, wide shoulders. His face was pockmarked and sunken, with row upon row of rat-like teeth, eyes beady. Black veins pulsed visibly beneath his skin—veins I'd seen before.

When he spoke, it was with Magnus' voice, "You know, when Gladstone told me he was an alchemist, I confess I was more amused than anything." The hand around Alucard's throat began to squeeze and I saw what little color Alucard had begin to fade. "But then he tells me the legend of the Nosferatu. I'd heard this ridiculous myth before, obviously, but—come to find out—it was true all along. Vampires given alchemical potions created by wizards to augment their strength and appearance. To make them more frightening. Can you imagine? Those must have been dark times."

"What time is it?" Gunnar asked in a hushed voice.

"Seriously?!" I hissed.

"It's still too early for the sun to be up," Othello said, ignoring me.

I frowned. Were they planning to fry all the vampires in attendance? I glanced at Roland, then Alucard, who was moments away from blacking out. It would solve the immediate problem, but unless we could get those two to safety, it wouldn't make much difference. Roland, on the other hand, seemed to take to the idea.

"I think I can do something about that," he growled. "Hold on." The ex-Shepherd held out a hand and, high above us, a gateway began to form, its edges hemmed in blood. Then, before I knew it, a beam of pure, brutally bright sunlight shot out at an angle, hitting Alucard full in the face.

"Ye missed, ye idgit!" I shouted angrily.

Then something very fucking strange happened.

It seemed Roland hadn't missed at all.

Because Alucard was a Daywalker.

And I was about to learn what that meant.

CHAPTER 44

*M*agnus fell back with a hiss, clutching his hand, which had gotten seared by the sunlight from Roland's gateway. Even though it only came from one point, I still had to shield my eyes to see. "Where the fuck did ye find a sunlamp like that?" I asked.

"Egypt. The Gobi Desert."

Gunnar chuckled. "That's brilliant. This ought to be fun."

"Fun?" I asked, whirling.

The Wolf King pointed. I followed his clawed finger, settled my hand above my eyes, and squinted in time to see Alucard rise. Remember when I compared Magnus' transformation from a sparrow to an eagle? Well, Alucard's was more like seeing a sparrow turn into a fucking phoenix. Or an angel.

Only, like, a proper angel, the kind I'd always wanted to see—a being made of fire and light, wings unfurled, eyes streaming flame, alien and breath-takingly beautiful.

I turned to Othello. She giggled at whatever my facial expression conveyed and nodded. "I told you not to be dazzled by him, didn't I?"

"Aye. But I didn't realize ye were bein' literal," I confessed.

"My children!" Magnus called, interrupting our conversation, his eyes wide with fright at the sight of Alucard in his new form. "The interlopers have broken the rules of the duel! Kill the women! Kill the wolves!"

Before the vampires could react to their boss' command, Ashley barked and a contingent of wolves I hadn't even noticed leapt up to attack those vampires holding the girls. I realized they'd been slinking closer and closer during the fight, preparing to strike the whole time.

Pandemonium broke loose as wolves and vampires squared off against one another. Paradise and Lost shifted and bounded after a few vampires making for the hole in the tent, hoping to escape. I found Ashley directing her wolves with a series of verbal commands. Yips and barks, mostly.

"I thought ye said ye wouldn't go to war?" I asked Gunnar, who seemed to be preparing to join the fray.

"And let those girls die? We'd never do that. Besides, we were never going to let Magnus live. He could go to the Council and report whatever he wanted. Without Alucard or Roland to support our side of things, we'd end up on their hit list. This way, we control the narrative. Gotta love a bureaucracy," Gunnar glanced down at me. "Nice meeting you." Then he took off, leaping at a small cluster of vampires who were trying to get to the confused and screaming girls. I saw Terry among them.

Roland tapped my shoulder. "Hey, do you still need to be somewhere?"

I looked around at the chaos around me and felt completely torn. On the one hand, Othello and the girls were still in danger, even if it seemed like our side had the advantage. On the other, if I didn't try to stop Chapman I'd have let Hemingway down and, in the process, failed to stop Armageddon.

No pressure.

"Do it," Othello said, rising from her chair, the silver chains falling away like tinsel. "I'll make sure we get the girls back home."

Roland and I gaped at her.

"What? Oh, right." Othello held out her hand to reveal a tiny, thin tube— no bigger than a juice box straw—of pulsing blue lights. "Nanobots," she admitted. "Forgot I'd left some in my back pocket from when Hemingway and I…actually, nevermind. Not important," she said, clearing her throat and blushing.

I turned to Roland, shaking my head. "Alright. Can ye make a gateway to the Brooklyn Bridge?"

Roland nodded. "Do you need backup?"

"Oh! Right!" I ran towards Dorian's monitors, not surprised to see that the immortal had fled and taken his most expensive camera equipment with him; I was willing to bet he'd have a lot of pissed off customers demanding their money back after that service disruption. I got what I needed and hurried back to Roland's side. "Alright," I said, patting my duffle bag. "Ready whenever ye are."

Roland grumbled something but weaved his hands in the air until a gateway appeared in midair, a few feet in front of me.

"Um, could ye lower it, maybe?" I asked, grinning. "I'd rather not have to jump."

The grumbling continued, but eventually it was low enough that all I had to do was step through. I turned to Othello. "Be careful."

"You too," she said, gripping my arm for a moment before releasing me and walking over to Ashley, who seemed to be in control of the situation.

"Whenever you're ready, Miss," Roland said teasingly, his rough baritone not too dissimilar from Bogart's.

I grinned. "Here's lookin' at ye, kid." Then I ducked through the portal—glad to get away from the mayhem of terrified screams, pained grunts, and piercing yelps.

Only to step into a warzone.

CHAPTER 45

*T*he sky above the Brooklyn Bridge was on fire.

I stepped out onto the walkway that ran the length of the bridge—which ordinarily allowed pedestrians to peer down at passing traffic as they crossed from Manhattan to Brooklyn. Except there weren't any pedestrians. Unless you counted the man with a sword.

"Get thee behind me, Satan!" The man screeched, swinging at me.

I ducked and spun away on instinct, shocked to find the man dressed in dark military fatigues, covered haphazardly in pieces of armor—like one of those amateur Renaissance Faire attendees who want to participate, but are too broke to fully commit. Except his armor looked eerily functional, as did the sharp ass sword he was wielding.

He took another swing at me and I danced backward, stumbling awkwardly with my duffel bag weighing me down. "What the hell is the matter with ye?!" I screamed at him.

Before he could answer, a winged shape careened down, and a set of clawed feet snatched the man around his breastplate and took him screaming off into the night sky, which—as I mentioned before—looked as if it was on fire.

Everywhere I looked, there was fighting. Men and women wearing various pieces of armor and wielding various weapons, each of them uncannily fast, took on creatures straight out of a Guillermo del Toro film—

monsters with scales, too many or too few eyes, tails, wings, anything imaginable. A nearby fight had devolved into a stalemate as the woman held her enemy back with an upraised crucifix, her lips reciting what I could only assume was a prayer.

Nephilim.

The name came back to me from my conversation with Karim. These were the Nephilim. Which meant they were fighting demons. Actual demons. I glanced up at the sky. It wasn't burning—it was full of figures made of light.

The Grigori.

What the hell was going on?

I tossed my bag on the ground, opened it, and fetched the assault rifle and sawed-offs. I didn't have much time, or even a plan, really, except to find Chapman and get the fuck out of there. But I wasn't about to walk across the bridge unarmed. Though it physically pained me, I left the rest behind and tore off towards the other end of the bridge, where it looked like the fighting was fiercest. My bet was that Chapman, if he was here, would be smack dab in the middle of that mess.

I rushed past the woman reciting scripture. Her eyes widened, and she momentarily forgot what she was saying. With her defenses down, the demon attacked, launching itself at her, swinging its barbed tail at her face. I left them to it, feeling only slightly guilty for ruining her concentration.

Whoops.

I dipped, dodged, and even dove in my effort to get across the bridge. Demon and Nephilim alike, fortunately, were too busy taking each other on to molest me as I went, although I did have to hunker down every now and again and wait for one or the other to fall off the edge of the bridge or take their battle to the sky.

To be honest, part of me felt compelled to help the Nephilim—especially when I saw an opportunity to put a demon's eye out or yank someone to safety—but Karim's assessment of their militancy, not to mention the asshole who'd swung at me without warning, made me reconsider; getting mowed down by friendly fire would be an embarrassing way to die after all the shit I'd gone through in the last few hours.

Near the first of the bridge's two platforms, I saw several demons gathered together, launching themselves at two Nephilim huddled behind their shields. I tucked myself up against the iron grating, holding myself up by the steel cables, and waited. The trick to making it to the other side, I knew, was to be as sneaky as possible. I was super outclassed here, and I knew it. One false move and I could end up falling off the bridge and dying in the East River—not the most glamorous way to go.

A jingle from my pocket tore through the din of the fight ahead and—as one—the demons and Nephilim swiveled to find the source of the noise. Me. I blinked, cursed, and fumbled in my pocket for my phone.

"Of all the stupid fuckin'…" I muttered.

"Who is that?" One of the Nephilim asked.

"Is she one of ours?" A demon hissed, nudging the scaled creature beside him with a barbed elbow.

I swiped to answer the phone. "Little busy here," I said.

"Miss MacKenna!"

"Serge! Where are you?"

"Serge follow. Near Brooklyn side of bridge. They are—" a chorus of noises on the other side of the line made it difficult to hear what Serge said next. "Must hurry," he finished.

I groaned, hanging up the phone. The platform I was near was the one on the Manhattan side—which meant I had the length of the bridge to go before I made it to where Chapman and Serge were. I eyed the demons and Nephilim ahead, who seemed to care less about who I was than how I'd made it this far.

"You shall not pass," one of the Nephilim said, hoisting his shield and sword.

I rolled my eyes and swung my assault rifle around, aiming for his breastplate. "Okay, Gandalf, whatever ye say."

The Nephilim charged, bringing his shield up to deflect my rifle fire. I wasn't trying to kill one of God's soldiers or anything, but I damn sure wasn't about to get impaled by one, either. I drew my pistol and aimed for his legs; a flesh wound would likely be enough to slow him down. I fired three rounds and watched in disbelief as he used his sword to deflect all three.

Because apparently God's soldiers were also ninjas.

The Nephilim roared, only a few feet from me, and I dropped to one knee, sighting down the scope of my assault rifle; I needed to put him on the defensive until I could come up with a plan. At that precise moment, however, a scream drew us both back towards the platform.

The demons, it seemed, hadn't been idle. The other Nephilim was desperately fighting for her life, fending off furious blows from three fronts. I grimaced. If this went on much longer, she wouldn't stand a chance.

"Peace be with ye?" I yelled at the Nephilim nearest me, recalling the lessons of my Catholic childhood as I extended my hand. Honestly, I had no idea if he'd take the truce offer or try to stab me, but I was willing to risk it if it meant avoiding a fight I couldn't win.

I was good, but my God-given talents didn't include superhuman reflexes.

The Nephilim spun around and eyed my hand with disdain, then confusion. He reached out and clasped it. His hand was surprisingly cold and dry. "And also with you," he replied. "Don't make me regret this." With that, he took off to help his partner.

I joined the fray, skirting the edges of their battle in my attempt to reach the other side of the platform. I was almost past when one of the demons noticed me. I ducked under its grasping arms and swung the stock of my rifle into its jaw. It fell back, dazed, and then stared down at his belly and the steel blade sticking out of it. The female Nephilim grinned in triumph, ripping her sword free before neatly slicing off the demon's head.

She took a quick look around, and I realized she was bleeding heavily from a wound in her side. She saw me looking and waved me off. "Go now, while you can. This is no place for mortals." As if to emphasize her point, a howling demon charged her like a bellowing rhinoceros, its face a mass of bulbous protrusions and spiny appendages. I took her advice, turned, and fled, praying I'd make it to the other side in one piece.

CHAPTER 46

I did make it in one piece, but only just. I slogged forward, dragging an injured leg behind me, clutching my two sawed-offs in either hand, my assault rifle shattered and discarded a few hundred feet back. That's what happens when you can't dodge a falling light pole fast enough, in case you're curious. I'd managed to pry myself from underneath it, but my rifle hadn't survived, and now my poor leg felt like I'd gotten it caught in a car door; I had a feeling the bruise would be the size of a melon, if I survived the night.

The lights in the sky were much brighter now, so bright it was almost as if the sun had risen. The Grigori hovered above, watching the fighting, but never interfering. I didn't know why, but guessed it had something to do with the whole balance thing Hemingway had talked about; if they got involved, then the other side would have no choice but to do the same. Maybe that's why the Nephilim and the demons were the ones going at it— kids will be kids, but once the adults start throwing punches, shit gets real, fast.

I called Serge back, but he didn't answer. Hopefully he was keeping himself safe somewhere out of sight. Without Othello's go ahead, he'd be a sitting duck. Fortunately, it seemed the fighting here had all but ended. A few Nephilim were down, flopped over the railing or pitched on the ground. There weren't any demons, but plenty of blood and ichor to suggest there had been—from what I could tell, when a demon was slain they simply evaporated. Pretty efficient recycle system, all things considered.

No muss, no fuss.

I shuffled past the corpses towards the platform. Once closer, I could make out a few figures standing at the railing facing the GW bridge. The first I recognized immediately—Darrel the Angel had on the same khaki trench coat he'd donned in the subway station. The second, huddled between the Darrel and another man, was Chapman. He cradled a planter in his hands and seemed to be listening to the words of the only other person there I didn't immediately recognize.

As I approached, the third figure turned to me.

I felt my stomach lurch.

Detective Ricci cocked his head and waved.

CHAPTER 47

*R*icci slid his hands into his pockets and faced me. "Well, this is an unexpected surprise!"

I stood there, mouth agape.

"Do you know her?" Darrel asked, eyeing me warily as if assessing a potential threat.

"She was on the lookout for one of the missing girls I'm 'responsible' for finding," Ricci said, using air quotes. "A prickly bitch, if memory serves. But easily put off—the script is pretty much always the same. I blame being overworked, offer sympathy, maybe a little hope. Eventually they assume the worst and stop calling." The detective shrugged.

Darrel's disgust was evident, but he said nothing.

Chapman still faced the water, seemingly oblivious to our conversation.

"I don't understand. Why are ye here?" I asked, still struggling to understand.

"I'm putting in my bid, obviously," Ricci said. "I had hoped to do so with a little less fanfare," Ricci waved a beefy hand at the fighting taking place further down the bridge, "but Mr. Chapman didn't leave me much choice."

"He'd already made his decision," Darrel said. "You have no business here, Marquis."

Marquis.

I sidled up against the nearby railing and took a deep breath, finally noting the chill in the night air and how much I ached—until now I'd been oblivious, running on pure adrenaline. I could feel a migraine coming on, a dull barb of pain lodged just above my right eye, and that migraine had a name.

The Marquis.

Unless there were multiple aristocrats running around New York City's Freakish underworld, that meant Ricci was somehow behind Rumpelstiltskin's abductions of the girls, Gomorrah's assault on my rental car, and Dorian's Freaky Fight Night.

But none of that made any sense.

"I thought ye were a good guy," I said, still reeling from the revelation that Ricci was anything other than a mildly incompetent detective. "Ye visit that kid in prison..." I muttered. "That's what the old cop said. That ye were a good person..."

Ricci looked confused at first, then brightened. "Oh! Right. I didn't realize the old geezer was paying that much attention. I'll have to do something about that." Ricci began popping his knuckles, one at a time. "That was one of my better ideas. Mentor a mortal, get him to kill his best friend, and pump him for information once he's in prison. That little Dominican punk introduces me to all the best people."

I shook my head in disgust and disbelief. "But why?"

Ricci arced an eyebrow. "Why?"

"She means 'why go through the effort'?" Darrel clarified, his expression softening as he looked at me. "She doesn't know what you are."

Ricci glanced at the Grigori in surprise, then back at me, laughter glittering in his eyes. "Oh, that's rich. You waltzed in here and you don't even know who you're talking to?"

Chapman turned, finally, and met my eyes. "He's one of the Fallen," he said, sounding tired. "One of the angels who rebelled against God and lost."

Ricci looked like he'd swallowed a sour candy but nodded. "True, although not entirely accurate. I'm more of a stand in, a representative, if you will. If I were here in my true form, things would get...Biblical." Ricci chuckled at his own joke. "Unlike the Watchers, when we step out among mortals, the alarm bells tend to go off. So, I took this one over. A little pudgy, if you ask me," Ricci said, cradling the fat of his belly, "but the fringe benefits are excellent."

I shook my head, unable to wrap my head around what I was being told.

Detective Ricci was one of the Fallen? As in, Lucifer's angels? I suddenly felt incredibly out of my depth.

And a little like going to confession.

"Wait," I said, holding a hand up to clarify, "So ye possessed a detective? But why him?" I asked. "What's the end game?"

Ricci paused as if considering whether to answer me. I realized Darrel also seemed interested in the Fallen's answer—as if he, too, wanted to know Ricci's motives.

Ricci shrugged. "I'm sure you've noticed a few changes in the world, lately. More selfishness. More hatred. More terror. The times they are a changin'," he said, mimicking Bob Dylan's twangy voice. "The end times are coming, and I'm not the only one who's noticed. There's a lot of activity downstairs, and a lot of eyes on the Midwest. Pretty soon there'll be a reckoning, and I intend to have a nice chunk of the Eastern seaboard carved out for myself before that happens."

I frowned. "How does bein' a detective help with that?"

"I rub elbows with unsavory people. I look the other way when there's something in it for me. I make deals. Network." Ricci grinned. "You'd be surprised the level of influence you have when people trust you."

Unsavory people...looking the other way. I squeezed the railing so hard I could feel the metal burrowing into my skin. "You've been working with Magnus. Helping him kidnap the girls. Rumpelstiltskin works for you."

"Oh, you've met Magnus?" Ricci said, sounding pleasantly surprised. "Oh yes, the girls! Magnus had a rather elaborate plan to turn them into a high-end escort service. It's frowned upon in New York City, but women in those positions are privy to so many secrets." Ricci shrugged. "At some point, you simply indulge your people. He wanted girls he could control, so I made sure he got girls."

My migraine grew incrementally worse the more Ricci spoke. I could see it now—his web of informants and ex-cons and Freaks—all of them making it possible to corrupt, to control. It was insidious, but also ingenious; it wasn't a convoluted plot to overthrow the world...it was politics 101.

My lips curled upwards in a slow smile as I realized I knew something Ricci didn't, something that would throw a wrench in his plan. "Magnus is dead by now, ye know," I said, spitefully. "Dead, or wishin' he was."

Ricci's eyes flashed. "I doubt that very much. Besides, how would you know that?"

"I believe Dorian called it 'Freaky Fight Night,'" I said. "Ring any bells?"

Darrel looked confused. "What's she talking about?"

"This bastard," I said, pointing accusingly at Ricci, "tried to pull attention away from what ye were doin' here by pittin' his minions against a bunch of Freaks for entertainment."

Ricci threw his hands up. "Guilty as charged."

The Grigori's brow furrowed. "So that's why we haven't seen any reinforcements," he muttered.

Ricci grunted. "I'm surprised Magnus was even involved in the fighting. He's not the type to get his hands dirty. Besides, the two I sent should have been more than enough."

"D'ye mean Sodom and Gomorrah?" I asked, grinning. I stepped away from the railing and took a step forward. "Because Sodom is irrigating someone's lawn right now, and Gomorrah is decorating it."

Ricci sneered. "And why should I believe you?"

"I don't care if ye do," I said, stalking forward until I was within spitting distance. "All I care about is what John plans to do with that seed. Ye can go fuck yourself."

"I don't—" Darrel began.

"And ye can do the same. Leavin' me and mine to clean up your mess and take on the Unclean by ourselves. Tryin' to take the seed when ye know it'll kickstart a war." I stared at Chapman, who hung his head, staring at his feet. "What did ye offer him?"

Darrel looked indignant. "We—"

"Death," Chapman said, interrupting the Grigori. He lifted his head and met my eyes, and I saw that desperation I'd seen before, only this time it was somehow worse. "I just want to *die*," he hissed in an anguished voice.

Oh. Yikes.

CHAPTER 48

I glared at the legendary nurseryman. "What the fuck d'ye mean ye want to die?" I asked.

"Not simply die," Darrel responded, drawing my unwelcome attention. "He wishes to be given his rightful place in Heaven. Something we, too, wish for him after everything he's done." I rolled my eyes. I could sense a sales pitch when I heard it; the Grigori was trying to remind Chapman what he was getting out of the deal while appearing altruistic in the process. The angel sounded like every guy who'd ever offered to buy me a drink at the bar under the guise of improving my night—strings were always attached.

"I spent my whole life trying to be a good man," Chapman said, ignoring the Grigori. "I never married. I helped people. I worshiped and I sacrificed. At first, I thought this was my reward," he said, indicating himself, his youthful face and body. "To live forever. To help people forever. But then there were the wars. Between men. Between ideologies. All that death. Such senseless death. And the politics," Chapman spat, "the games the gods play with mortal men and women…I can't take it. I don't want to be a part of this world anymore."

"But what if you could live without that pain?" Ricci interrupted, sensing his opening. "What if we gave you the power to end everyone's suffering? To bring down the gods?"

"You know that's an empty promise," Darrel said.

Ricci's eyes lit up with malice. "The Horsemen will ride soon enough. You know that as well as I do. Who's to say whether Johnny here won't play a role in that? Especially once he chooses the side that's bound to win—no matter what your silly book says."

Chapman's gaze never strayed from my face. I could sense he was pleading with me, asking me to understand, to empathize. To support his need to see it all end, one way or the other.

"Stop bein' a coward," I said, cutting off the other two. They both jerked around to look at me, wondering who I was siding with. I took another step forward until Chapman and I stood within arm's reach of one another. "Bein' a good man isn't about askin' for a reward. If you're good, you're good. If ye aren't, ye aren't." I grimaced, but plowed ahead, refusing to sugarcoat things for the man no matter what he'd been through—I wasn't that sort of person. "If ye want it to end, I understand. But man up and do it yourself. Don't drag the world down with ye."

"That's not—" Darrel began.

"I've tried," Chapman said with a bitter smile. "I've been all over this country, you know. I've worked in clinics, treated soldiers, signed up for relief efforts. I've put myself in harm's way so many times. Eventually, once I realized I wasn't destined to die that way, I tried to end it myself." Chapman reached into his back pocket and pulled out a whittling knife. He slung the blade free with a practiced flick and ran its edge across his forearm before any of us could stop him.

Chapman switched the planter to his knife hand, tucking it safely under one arm, and held out his wounded arm for me to see. A dark, amber liquid dribbled out from the wound, congealing along its edges.

Sap. He bled sap.

"I'm not even human, anymore, you see," Chapman said. "John Chapman died centuries ago. I'm just the spirit he left behind."

Darrel rested a hand on Chapman's shoulder. "Give us the seed and we'll follow through on our end. I promise."

Chapman nodded, then hung his head once more.

"Sadly," Ricci said, hooking his thumbs in his belt loops and rocking back and forth, "I can't let you do that."

"You can't take it by force," Darrel replied, facing the Fallen. "Without Appleseed's blessing, the seed will never take root. There's nothing else for you to do here. You lost."

"See, that's where you're wrong," Ricci said. He glanced up at the sky, which had lightened somewhat, and studied the Watchers—cloistered so high above our heads they could have been mistaken for stars. "If he won't give it to me, and I can't take it, I'll have to make sure you lot can't have it, either."

And the fucking stars began to wink out.

CHAPTER 49

*D*arrel stared up in disbelief. "What have you done?"

"Call it a preemptive strike," Ricci replied.

"What's happening?" Chapman asked. "What's he doing?"

"Do you know how one gets a title in Hell?" Ricci asked, clearly enjoying himself. "One pays one's dues, obviously, but in Hell a title isn't some arbitrary thing. It's more like a position. A rank. It means you're in charge. In practical terms, that rank determines how many legions of demons are under your control." Ricci smiled. "Can you guess how many legions are given to a Marquis?"

I gaped as the sky brightened enough to see by, sunrise only a few minutes away. I had no idea how many demons were in a legion—I'd always hated conversion tables in math and science. But, from what I could tell, I was guessing the answer to Ricci's question was somewhere between a shitload and a fuckton.

Give or take a buttload.

Winged demons the size of fighter planes, so many they threatened to blot out the horizon, were battling the Grigori above our heads. Between their size and sheer numbers, they were overwhelming the Watchers, forcing them to descend as they fought to survive. Which, unfortunately, meant the aerial battle was swiftly getting closer.

"We should probably leave 'em to it, don't ye t'ink?" I asked Chapman, half-jokingly.

Chapman looked devastated. It took me a second to realize that a man like him—someone who had devoted himself to helping people—would only blame himself for all this. In his mind, his selfishness and his desire to end his own life had caused this mess—and he couldn't handle it.

"Oy!" I shouted. He jerked his head up. "Pity yourself later. Ye didn't know this was how t'ings would turn out, but now ye should realize the trouble that seed can cause." I pointed up. "That's what Hell on Earth looks like, and I for one am not ready to see everythin' and everyone I love get caught in the crossfire."

Chapman studied the sky and nodded. "You're right."

"Give the seed to me now," Darrel interjected, holding out his hand for the planter. "I'll see it and you are taken care of."

Chapman locked eyes with me. "No, she's right. Things have gone too far. I won't be responsible for the end of the world as we know it. For starting another war." He turned away from the Grigori. "Let's go."

A blinding light flashed before our eyes.

"Motherfucker!" I cursed.

If this shit kept up, I was going to have to insure my eyes.

"We had a deal, John Chapman," Darrel said, his voice vibrating with power, surrounded by a brilliant, golden aura. "And you will honor it."

"Uh oh," Ricci said, cackling. "Sounds like you two pissed off the night-light. I think I'll take this body somewhere else and let you sort this out amongst yourselves. No sense ruining a good meat suit." Ricci sauntered off, leaving his demons to take care of the Watchers. "Take care!"

Almost as if waiting for him to depart, demons and Watchers alike began falling from the heavens, crashing into the bridge, exchanging blows on the way down. If I'd thought the fights between the demons and the Nephilim had been vicious, I was quickly proven wrong. Those tussles were nothing compared to this: the demons Ricci had summoned this time were much larger and deadlier, while the Watchers themselves had flipped the switch from "Observe and Report" to "Smite First and Ask Questions Later"—the angels flung golden lightning from their fingertips, bolts that disintegrated all they touched.

Chapman and I ducked for cover behind a steel beam as a scaled demon with the wings of a bird and the face of an insect took a shot to the side that sent it screaming into the side of the bridge. The bridge shivered, and I saw a few steel cables snap. One whipped around with such force it sliced a Grigori messily in half. As the sun rose and the chaos up above escalated, I began to worry about what would happen once the bridge became more trafficked and whether the Regulars would see the storm up above for what it was—a battle between Heaven and Hell. How could anyone miss this?

"You can't hide from us," Darrel said, hovering a few feet away, glowing, his body almost unrecognizable, lightning dancing along his knuckles, sparking off the ends of his fingers. "We're out of time. Hand over the seed."

Chapman and I exchanged looks.

Then we ran.

CHAPTER 50

*H*ave you ever been chased by a bumble bee? You know when you duck for cover, protecting your exposed areas, and there's that awful buzzing whirling around your head like a siren of impending doom, and you wish you could swipe it out of the air, but you're equally worried that you'll miss and piss it off even more?

Yeah, fending off Darrel was exactly like that.

Except less buzzing, and more yelling.

"Get them!" Darrel commanded, flying after us. "They have the seed!"

One of the Grigori broke away from the battle in the sky to come after us, a contingent of demons hot on its heels. Lightning flashed, tearing into the bridge's wooden slats behind us; the exposed metal screws smoldered as we tore off towards Brooklyn. I hadn't given any thought to how we'd lose them once we left the bridge, but I knew we couldn't hang around; Darrel's angelic powers hadn't worked on me before, but I doubted Chapman had that kind of protection. Just because he couldn't die didn't mean he'd stay on his feet if one of those lightning blasts hit him.

One of the Grigori came soaring in from our left, pulling up casually alongside us, a hand extended. I raised my shotguns and unloaded all four barrels, praying to God that they'd take the angel out.

Oh, the irony.

Steel projectiles exploded outward, passed through the angel's body, and came out the other side as—I kid you fucking not—glitter. "Well that's fuckin' great," I said, panting as I fought through the pain of running on my injured leg. I tossed the guns aside. They were too heavy to carry and, unless angels were deathly allergic to shiny confetti, more or less useless.

The Grigori, perhaps more than a little annoyed that I'd shot at him, pointed at me. A single bolt of lightning arced towards me, only to slam against my anti-magic field, ricocheting wildly in different directions. I wasn't sure what to make of that; usually when magic of some sort hit my field, it fizzled out. But, much like Gomorrah's inability to hit me, it seemed the angel's lightning was more repelled than nullified.

"How are you doing that?" Chapman asked, huffing. He wasn't really dressed for this sort of thing; brown loafers weren't the best running shoes he might have chosen. Not that I could talk; I hadn't packed cross-trainers.

"I don't know," I confessed. I wish I did. If I knew how I was doing it, maybe I could control it. Use it to get us out of here, somehow. The idea was half-formed in my mind when one of the demons—this one squid-like with knives at the end of its tentacles—caught up to the Grigori. The two flew at each other. The demon took the worst of it and slammed into the wires that hung above us, thrashing about like a lobster caught in a net, the blades attached to its body clipping steel cables and beams alike in his frenzied attempt to break free, gouging them all. Somewhere behind us, another shockwave arrived, sending Chapman and I stumbling to the ground. Chapman dropped the planter, and it rolled towards the edge, but mercifully halted against a sheet of steel grating.

Darrel landed next to Chapman. The Grigori dropped to one knee, the light from his body suffusing Chapman's face as he looked up. "I never did understand you humans," Darrel said. "None of us ever have. That's why we must have the seed, don't you see? How can we be asked to watch beings we cannot understand?" The angel settled his hand on Chapman's shoulder. "Give it to us."

Defiance hardened Chapman's jawline as he ground his teeth together and shook his head. Darrel's serene expression transformed into something hateful. "Fine," he said. I covered my eyes as another flash of blinding light pulsed—but that didn't block out the sounds of Chapman's screams. When I looked back, I saw his skin smoking. Chapman groaned and tried to get up, but Darrel kicked him in the shoulder hard enough to send him flying onto his back. The angel stood over him, one hand held out. "You wanted to die. Consider your prayers answered."

"No!" I screamed, flinging my own hand out. I felt my field expand in answer to my rage and frustration, like a balloon blown outward. Darrel flew back, thrust away with enough force to send him soaring into a steel beam, denting it with his body.

Above us, the sounds of fighting diminished as Grigori and demon alike took note of what I'd done. I struggled to rise, fighting off the wave of exhaustion that threatened to pull me under. I needed to get to Chapman. Get Chapman, get the seed, and go. A brief glance upwards told me that my chances of doing so were less than stellar; Heaven and Hell were headed straight for me.

When did I get so popular?

I crawled over to Chapman as quickly as I could. If they were coming after us, maybe my field would stop them. I felt the tunnel vision settling in. The migraine I'd been fighting this whole time seemed seconds away, which meant a blackout was inevitable. I cursed, only a few feet from Chapman's smoldering body. What a way to go out, chased down by angels and demons alike, and I wouldn't even be conscious to see it.

I reached for Chapman's hand as the darkness descended.

I came to a moment later, screaming in pain.

Chapman, clutching my hand, stood over me. The pain was a dull roar thudding in my ears, emanating from the hand Chapman held, as if I'd stuck it in a tub filled with ice and water—my nerves on fire, begging me to let go. Above, demons and angels howled in rage as they were forced back. By trees. Trees the size of California redwoods, their roots surrounding us, branches soaring out with such speed and force that they impaled those who got too close. The trees continued to grow until their shade blocked out the morning light, covering the Brooklyn Bridge with a virgin forest. Boy, the morning commuters would be in for a surprise. The pain in my hand threatened to make me pass out again. I tried to withdraw it, but Chapman refused to let go. He looked down at me, his eyes burning green, so bright he didn't even look human.

Those eyes were the last thing I saw before I felt the world slip away again.

CHAPTER 51

I felt someone prod me and groaned.

"Hey! Let her rest," I heard someone say. A woman. A voice I knew but couldn't place. I struggled to remember who I was. Where I was. I opened my eyes, and then immediately shut them—too bright.

"She's awake now, might as well see how she's feeling," I heard another voice say in response. This voice, like the one before, had an accent—though neither were the same. I tried to sit up and panicked when my muscles wouldn't respond; I realized I'd been tied down and panicked even more. I fought against the restraints that bound my arms, legs, and torso.

"Whoa, whoa, easy there! We'll get them off you, *cher*, don't you worry. You were having little seizures there for a bit. Had to be extra careful." I felt the bands on my wrists disappear and raised my hands to my eyes to block out what little light made it past my eyelids. I wasn't sure why I was so sensitive to it all of a sudden, but knew better than to tough it out.

The other restraints were removed shortly thereafter.

"What happened? Where am I?" I asked, my throat dry and scratchy.

Silence, then the woman spoke, her Russian accent faintly detectable. "We were hoping you might tell us. Serge found you on the bridge and we were able to get you to the hospital...but you were non-responsive. Comatose." I could hear something in the woman's voice. Sadness. Grief. "We were all really worried. This morning it was like someone flipped a switch. Lots of brain activity. Then the seizures started. You've been quiet for a couple hours since, though."

"I didn't mean to wake you up, *cher*. Just wanted to make sure you were comfortable."

"Alucard's been with you the whole time."

Alucard. The flaming vampire angel. The name brought back a flood of memories. "Did he…" I drifted off, my throat too parched to continue. A cup of water was pressed into my hands. I took a grateful sip. "Did he watch me sleep like a total creeper?"

The woman chuckled. She seemed so familiar, but my memory was fuzzy, sluggish. Like I had woken up during the last action scene of a movie, but couldn't recall how we had gotten here.

"Very funny," Alucard drawled.

"I'm really glad you're alright," the woman said, with a sob.

"Othello was very worried about you," Alucard said.

Othello. My friend. Right. I reached out for her until she took my hand. I braved the light, found it somewhat bearable, and opened my eyes wide enough to look at her. I smiled. "I'm never takin' a job offer from ye, ever again."

Othello sobbed again as she nodded, laughing.

"So, can you tell us what happened?" Alucard asked once Othello got herself together.

"What do ye mean?" I asked.

"On the bridge."

Another rush of memories. Ricci's smug face. Darrel preparing to kill Chapman, hand outstretched. Chapman standing over me with inhuman eyes.

"There was a battle. Angels fighting demons. I'm not sure how, but I t'ink Chapman stopped them."

Alucard and Othello exchanged puzzled glances.

"What?" I asked.

In answer, Alucard fetched the remote from the table next to my hospital bed. He turned on the TV and plugged in a number. A weatherman waved his hands to mimic the movement of a storm front due later that evening. I cocked an eyebrow at the Daywalker, noting how the sunlight poured through the window and across his face.

"Wait. Alright, now look."

The weather report finished, the news had switched to a scene of the Brooklyn Bridge from a helicopter's point-of-view, panning from left to right. Crews of workers hung along suspension wires and scuttled around the base of the bridge. A few of the men held chainsaws. I thought I could see a bulldozer working its way back across the bridge. And, on the far end, there was a small forest of the thickest, tallest trees I'd ever seen.

The headline read: Eco-terrorists Lay Siege to New York City Bridge. Below, the text smaller and easier to miss: No Group Has Yet Claimed Responsibility.

I reexamined the bridge and the various stages of reconstruction. "Othello? How long have I been asleep?" I asked.

"Five days," she said, settling a hand on my arm.

I hung my head, realizing I'd spent more time in a hospital gown on this trip than in regular clothes. "Could ye two do me a favor?" I asked. I glanced up at them, noting their doting expressions. "Could ye find me a drink? And make it a stiff one."

Because nothing goes better with a coma and seizures than Scotch.

I was sure I'd read that somewhere.

CHAPTER 52

Q lucard filled me in on everything that happened after I went through Roland's gateway as we left the hospital. Apparently, Gunnar and Ashley's pack had forced the majority of Magnus' vampires to surrender before too much blood was shed. The sight of Magnus' creepy, rat-like head dangling from Alucard's flaming fist might have had some-thing to do with it, also.

I pressed for details, but—midway through Alucard's explanation, some-where between his graphic description of tearing one rival vampire in half with his bare hands and decapitating another—we realized we were in the middle of a hospital.

Full of people.

With ears.

A nurse reached for a phone, punched in two numbers and froze. Alucard had leaned over and met her eyes, holding her pinned there. "Forget we were ever here," he said, softly.

She nodded.

I glanced up at the woman, who still seemed a little dazed, and grinned. "We are not the droids ye are lookin' for."

Alucard pushed me forward and described the rest of what had happened in a whisper.

They'd managed to save the girls, but Roland and Alucard had to put them under their spell to calm them; most had been too hysterical to question. Othello had booked a private wing of a rehab facility while I was unconscious and put the girls under constant guard, claiming they'd been exposed to a mind-altering chemical that had amnestic side effects. She'd employed doctors, scientists, and even hypnotists—without the slightest change in their condition. She'd been about to give up and call their families when my seizures started.

"Maybe seeing their loved ones will help," she said as we descended in one of the elevators, sounding defeated.

"I have something I'd like to try, before you do that," I said. "I have a lead to run down first, but if you give me twenty-four hours, I'll see what I can do."

"Gladly," Othello said. "Anything you need."

Serge greeted us on the curbside and I felt like kicking déjà vu in the testicles. The only person missing was Hemingway. I held up my hand, urging Alucard to stop pushing my hospital-mandated wheelchair. "Wait, where was your boyfriend durin' all this?" I asked. I'd completely forgotten about the Horseman, but in hindsight the clash at the bridge should have been right up his alley.

Othello shook her head. "I haven't been able to get hold of him. The last time we talked, he was planning to visit Kansas City. Something was going on there that warranted his attention."

Alucard grunted and resumed pushing. "Roland ran off pretty quickly after the fight. Probably Callie related."

Othello shrugged, but didn't look inclined to disagree. If she was worried about her boyfriend, she didn't show it. But I guess that made sense; how much trouble could Death really get into?

"That Callie girl sounds like fun," I said. "We should grab drinks."

Othello snickered. "No drinks for at least a week, remember? Doctor's orders."

I glowered at her. "You're not invited."

Funsucker.

CHAPTER 53

I hurried across the heavily congested street, slipping between two taxis. With the bridge still under repair, Manhattan had become somewhat gridlocked as commuters sought other access points. Which meant getting uptown had been a major pain in the ass.

I was hoping it would be worth it.

John Chapman, also known as Johnny Appleseed, buzzed me in.

I ascended to the second floor and sought out his apartment number. A door opened down the hall and Chapman himself waved me in. He'd shaved, which made him look younger, and a bit less edgy. Or maybe that was simply me projecting; after our last encounter, all desire to run my hands up and down his body had fled, and now I had a hard time looking at him without shivers running up my spine. Even his voice gave me goosebumps—he'd called me the day after I returned to my hotel, given me his address, and asked me to drop by. Said we needed to talk.

"It's good to see you," he said, flashing me a smile.

"Aye," I said, sneaking past him while maintaining as much distance as possible. "So, what is it ye wanted to talk about?"

Chapman shut the door and frowned. "Is something wrong?"

I frowned. "The last time I saw ye, ye were makin' trees pop up out of nowhere." I didn't bother mentioning his eyes. "I blacked out, fell into a coma, and had to be saved by my driver. And I'm pretty sure all that is somehow your fault."

Now it was Chapman's turn to frown. "You mean you didn't do it on purpose?"

"Do what?" I asked, exasperated.

"Lend me your power."

I gaped at him.

"I'll take that as a *no*," Chapman said, slowly, looking troubled. "I'll admit I'm surprised. That night on the bridge..." he drifted off, the memory of what happened playing across his face in real time. "I've never felt like that before. It was the most intense sensation. I had seeds in my pockets. Decoys, in case things went wrong. I knew as soon as I touched them that I could awaken them. That I could make them grow."

"I don't understand," I said, shaking my head in confusion.

"I didn't, either. I've never had that sort of power. I can urge things to grow. To flourish." He waved a hand at his apartment and I realized we were surrounded by greenery, some of the plants exotic, indigenous to much different climates. "But nothing like what I did on the bridge. It was like you were flooding me with power. I didn't want to leave you behind, but once I stopped touching you and the power faded, I decided to take the seed and run. I was betting they wouldn't come after you. That...and I was a little afraid to touch you a second time."

I turned away, trying to sort through what Chapman was telling me. He wasn't lying; the awe of what he'd done was written all over his face. Somehow, when we'd touched, his power had reacted to my field. Or something. I had no way to know exactly what happened. Since leaving the hospital, I'd given myself a once over—my various wounds had healed, although I still had a slight bruise on my thigh and abrasions on my wrists from the restraints. As far as I knew, my field was unaltered, although I sensed it was slightly more pliable than it had been before. It seemed like every time I was forced to expand it, the field became easier to manipulate.

"I didn't give ye power on purpose," I confirmed. "I'm not even sure how I did it."

Chapman nodded. "Well, I'm glad you did, either way."

I turned back around. "So, you're not lookin' to get killed anytime soon?" I asked, snidely.

"No," Chapman said, shaking his head. "I'm not sure why, but after you lent me your power," he held a hand up before I could reiterate myself, "I know you didn't do it intentionally, but it was yours, whether you knew it or not. But regardless, what I felt…it reminded me what it is to be alive. I'd forgotten. You live long enough, especially when you don't live by the same rules everyone else does, and you lose track of things. Time, for one. But also, what motivates people. Desires. Goals."

"Ye have a plan, then? For what's next?"

Chapman grinned. "I do."

I waited for him to elaborate. When he didn't, I shrugged. "Fine, keep your secrets, tree man." I realized that I no longer knew his reason for seeing me; I'd assumed it had something to do with his display of power on the bridge or his decision to betray the Grigori, but neither seemed likely. "What did ye want to talk to me about, anyway?" I asked.

"Oh, right. I wanted to ask you a favor. Come with me for a second, would you?" Chapman headed down a hallway that branched off from his living room without waiting for my reply. I followed, too curious to be annoyed.

Chapman ducked through a door on the right, flicked on the lights, and disappeared. I trailed, turned the corner, and stood, slack jawed, in the middle of the hallway. Inside the room, on a series of daises, were various glass cases containing apples. Spotlights shown down on each, and I had the feeling Chapman had installed security to keep them safe—the way you might with jewelry or priceless works of art.

Chapman stood near the back of the room, waving me forward. "Come on. This isn't what I want you to see."

"What is this?" I asked, waving idly at the displays. "I mean, I know ye have a t'ing for apples, but…"

Chapman rolled his eyes and stepped forward. "I told you already, there are a lot of gardens out there." When he realized I wasn't satisfied with that answer, he began pointing to each apple in turn. "The Apple of Discord, which caused the Trojan War. One of Hesperides' golden apples, very recycle friendly. The apple that defeated Atalanta. The apple that founded Avalon. The apple Loki stole. The apple that almost killed Snow White." Chapman jerked his head back over his shoulder. "Now come on. I've got something better to show you."

Oh, yeah, sure.

Of course, he did.

I followed numbly, plodding behind as he guided me back to a closet at the rear of the room. For a brief moment, I wondered if his "something better" was going to turn out to be a private unveiling of his own personal candied apple on a stick. I sincerely hoped not; I'd hate to have to kill Johnny Appleseed so soon after he'd decided to enjoy life.

Fortunately, Chapman stepped into the closet, then back out again without so much as an inappropriate joke. He cradled a familiar planter in both hands. He beamed down at the pot, then held it out to me like a proud parent. I cocked an eyebrow but glanced down to see what all the fuss was about. Inside the planter, edging out beneath the dirt, was a single, solitary stem attached to a leaf made out of gold.

"I found it before I left the bridge. I'm not sure how, but I think some residual power remained, because when I touched the soil, the seed began to grow."

"Wasn't that what the other sides wanted?" I asked.

Chapman nodded. "It is, but I never had the juice to make it grow. I was simply its keeper. I bet it would have taken the Grigori, or even the Marquis, ages to get that to happen, if ever. The Tree of Knowledge was willed into being by God, after all. And yet here it is," Chapman said, running his finger gingerly over the leaf, which seemed to curl and extend as if inhaling a deep breath.

"So, what is it ye want from me, then?" I asked, utterly confused.

"I need you to take it away. To keep it safe." Chapman tried to hand the planter to me, although I could see it pained him to do so.

"Are ye fuckin' serious? No way!" I waved him off with both hands. "Why would ye want me to do that?"

"Because," Chapman said, patiently, as if speaking to a small child, "both sides want it, and they think I have it. If I disappear, they'll think the seed has disappeared, as well. And because you have power. Enough power to keep it safe. Even," he continued, catching my look, "if you don't know what kind of power that is, yet, or how to use it. I think it's in safe hands if I leave it with you. But you have to promise me to look after it. Not to give it to the buyer you were working for. It can't become a bargaining chip. It's too powerful for that." Chapman stroked the edge of the planter lovingly before placing it in my unwilling hand.

"Hello, mother," it said, the voice tiny and thin, like a young girl's.

I almost dropped the damn thing.

"Oh yeah," Chapman said, grinning. "It does that."

CHAPTER 54

I met Othello in the lobby of the rehabilitation center.

"Quinn! How are you feeling?" Othello asked, almost as soon as I'd walked through the door.

"Good. Still recovering, but good." Mostly I was trying to recover from the shock of playing house with a talking plant, but I couldn't go into that with Othello. Besides, she had enough on her plate worrying about Hemingway, who still hadn't called. I was hoping my little stunt here would cheer her up; I knew being responsible for the girls who'd been snatched up by Magnus' vampires was weighing on her.

"So, what is it you wanted to try?" Othello asked.

"Hold on," I said. I pulled out the burner phone I'd bought the day before —my old one had died a miserable death on the Brooklyn Bridge, pieces of it were probably still floating down the East River—and called the number on the card I'd retrieved from my pocket on the way in. A few seconds later, two individuals stepped out from the lobby bathroom. The first was familiar to both Othello and me.

"Milana!" Othello said, surprise forcing her voice an octave higher than normal.

"Hello. It is good to see you again," Milana said, bowing slightly at the waist. "Miss MacKenna filled me in on recent events. I'm very glad to hear you've found the girls."

Othello gave me a chiding look, but I pretended not to notice. I mean, I could have told her what I'd intended, but I owed her for dropping Serge on me—even if she'd inadvertently saved my life in the process. I turned to the matronly woman standing beside Milana and dipped my head. "I want ye to know that we're very grateful to ye for comin' to help," I said, with as much respect as I could muster.

"Yes, well, my daughter was very adamant. Supposedly, she felt this might pay back a debt of some sort. We Greeks always pay our debts," the woman—known in mythological circles as Mnemosyne, mother of the Nine Muses and goddess of memory—said.

Somehow, I managed not to make a crack about what else the Lannisters and the Greeks had in common—but it was a close thing. I rested my hand on Othello's shoulder. "Oh, I'm sure Othello here will be more than glad to keep up her end of the bargain."

Milana looked pleased. While Othello would have gladly passed along her knowledge of the Fight Club in St. Louis, part of me realized that—unless she gave Othello something in return—Milana would always feel indebted to her. The solution had come to me after something Rumpelstiltskin said about the fine print. I realized that the girls may have given away their pasts, but that one's past and one's memories were two separate things. After meeting with Austina, I'd researched the Muses on my own, which is how I'd known about Mnemosyne. After that, all it had taken was a brief conversation with Milana to iron out the details.

"Alright, then," Mnemosyne said, holding her arm out for Milana to take. "Lead on. Let's remind these mortals who they are."

And so, we did.

CHAPTER 55

I held Tanya's mom while she sobbed into the cotton of my blouse, which was, fortunately, dark enough to hide the stains. I patted her awkwardly. "There, there."

Othello had booked Terry and me a first-class ticket home shortly after Milana and her mother came to visit. The girls had all recovered, miraculously, their memories whole and healthy. Bizarrely, however, they seemed to have lost track of various things: old scars, pierced body parts, tattoos, and—in one case—a more appealing nose. We confessed we couldn't explain those any more than we could explain the weeks that had passed without their notice, but no one seemed overly inclined to bitch, especially once Milana explained that models who had clean, untouched bodies were that much more likely to find work.

Personally, I'd take the scars.

"Thank you so much for bringing her home," she said, still crying as she pulled away.

I smiled. "You're welcome."

"I'm not home for good, Mom," Terry said, earning a glare from her mother and a surprised glance from her sister. Tanya had been subdued since our appearance, but was clearly glad to see her sister safe and sound.

"What is that supposed to mean?" her mother asked.

Terry reached out and took her mom's hand, smiling. She reached out for Tanya's, who accepted it with only a moment's hesitation. "Listen, I know you like having me around. I would, too." Terry grinned. "But I have a plan. One I didn't have, but should have had, before. I'm with an agency, working for a great company in New York. I've got a few job interviews lined up next week. I'm going back. And I want you to support me." Terry squeezed her mother's hand. "If I blow it, I'll come home. But I have to know you're here for me or I'll be too miserable to give it a real shot."

"I still don't understand," Tanya said. "How can you not remember what happened?"

Terry frowned and I saw her struggling to recall the details of her weeks long abduction. I watched her face with a sense of unease. If she ever did recall what the vampires had done to her, I doubted she'd be the same positive, outgoing girl she was now. Not everyone walked away clean from things like that. "I wish I could tell you. But I wasn't hurt. Actually, I feel great. Remember when I blew out my knee playing volleyball?" Terry lifted her leg and wobbled her foot around. "It's like it never even happened."

Tanya didn't seem satisfied but let the subject drop.

I breathed a sigh of relief, extricated myself from what was guaranteed to be an awkward family moment, and headed for the door.

"Wait!" Tanya yelled. After having sparred with me a few times, Tanya knew better than to hug me like her mother had, but her grateful smile was reward enough. "Thanks for bringing my sister back."

I nodded. "If I had a sister like ye watchin' out for me, I'd be really grateful," I said. "I'm sure Terry appreciates it."

Tanya nodded. "What do you think happened to her?"

I hesitated. On the one hand, I knew Tanya would have a hard time letting the subject drop. She might spend forever wondering. But her sister making a deal with Rumpelstiltskin, being abducted by vampires, and saved by werewolves? It sounded ridiculous, even to someone as familiar with crazy as I was—and that was without mentioning the divine intervention of a goddess.

"I t'ink she's your sister and, no matter what happened, she may want to move on. Maybe it'd be best to let her," I said.

Tanya studied my face for a moment, then sighed. "You're probably right."

"Besides," I said, glancing over Tanya's shoulder to where Terry and her mother were hugging, "sometimes ye have to take the bad with the good."

217

Tanya followed my gaze, grinned, and shrugged.

I nudged her forward, waited until all three were wrapped together, snug in their gushy Hallmark moment, and left before someone tried to offer me tea while we talked about our feelings.

There was a reason I didn't have many girlfriends.

CHAPTER 56

I spent the next several days off the grid, excluding a brief exchange with Othello during which we discussed Terry's homecoming and Ricci's suicide. Apparently, the detective hadn't reported in to work the following day—they found his body a few days later hanging from the rafters of his apartment. My guess? The Fallen had cut his losses and the detective, faced with the truth of what he'd done, had taken the most painless way out.

Othello promised me she'd speak to her contact about me getting into Fae, and we ended our conversation by discussing Hemingway's absence. She assured me he was fine, and I assured her that I believed her. If either of us were lying, I couldn't tell. We hung up feeling mildly better about things, which is all that really mattered.

Thankfully, good weather followed me home, so I'd spent the last few days touring the city. I hadn't realized how much I'd missed it, or my apartment, or my bed. I'd briefly considered stopping by Christoff's bar but decided my social life could wait for me to fully recover—besides, I wasn't ready for all that green. In fact, the only person I hit up once I got back was Dez, who admonished me for being gone so long and insisted we get dinner later in the week.

I still wasn't sure what had happened with my anti-magic field or why it had reacted to Chapman the way it did. Eventually I'd have to confront Dobby and force the truth out of him, but for now I contented myself with testing my field, expanding it a little at a time, trying to recreate what I had done on the bridge to protect Chapman.

Speaking of which, the folk hero asked me out on a date before I left New York, claiming he'd booked a dinner reservation for two at a five-star restaurant in Manhattan. In the end, I turned him down; there was no point, considering I couldn't touch the man without going into shock—and I couldn't look and *not* touch, if you know what I mean.

Ironically, it seemed Johnny Appleseed was no longer my only suitor. Alucard sent me a letter in the mail—yes, a handwritten letter, with a wax seal and everything—from Italy, where he and Roland were spending some quality time with the Sanguine Council. The contents were friendly, nothing too forward, but in his postscript, he'd asked if he could call on me in Boston. I hadn't replied yet. One, because my handwriting is terrible, and two, because I wasn't sure how I felt about the vampire. I mean, for starters, he was a vampire. But as a Daywalker who didn't need to drink blood, not to mention a handsome Southern gentleman who wrote letters, maybe I could make an exception.

But then, of course, there was Jimmy. After mentioning my phone woes to Othello, I'd been provided with a handy dandy...*thing* that did everything I thought a phone should and a few things I'm pretty sure *Skynet* would have patented. The best part: I kept my old number, and everything synced without a single hiccup. Of course, it turned out that—while in a coma— Jimmy had finally called me back. In fact, I had seven missed calls. Sadly, the voicemails hadn't survived.

I hadn't reached out to him, either.

You probably think I was merely being petty, but the truth was I wasn't sure how I felt about reigniting things with someone who was capable of ghosting me for a month. That, and I needed a few days to relax without any added drama—drama which, at this point, definitely included Jimmy.

Naturally, that plan went to shit. Yesterday I got home to an official summons from the Chancery on my dining room table requesting my presence regarding an inquiry into an "event hosted by Dorian Gray." It seemed someone in their organization had watched the damn thing and recognized me. I was half tempted to tell them to go fuck themselves, but decided, for now, I'd let Othello look into it. If she couldn't get me out of it a second time, maybe I'd be better off meeting with the assholes face to face. At least then I'd have someone to blame.

Coincidentally, Hemingway seemed to have reappeared and taken a page from the Chancery's book; I found a present from Othello and him on my couch today—a bulging black duffel bag with a bright pink bow and a handwritten note that said: *In case we can't make it to the party in time. Love, Othello.* Beneath it, in a hastily written scrawl: *Love your place. The plant is a nice touch.* Joie de vivre! *Hemingway.*

I scowled at the irony of Death's comment, folded the note, tucked it into my back pocket, and fetched the watering can I'd bought the day before. On the windowsill, tucked into a small alcove, stood a planter. Within, a stem, and two golden leaves facing in either direction.

"How goes it, Eve?" I asked, tilting the can over the lip of the pot.

"Oh, you know. Living the dream," Eve, the Tree of Knowledge, replied. "Did you know Happy Hours are banned in Boston?"

I nodded. "I did know that, actually."

"Well did you know that the Red Sox have patented their own shade of green?"

"I—"

"Or that the worst molasses-related accident happened here, killing 21 people?"

I sighed.

I'd fought and killed several bloodsuckers, taken on a rock monster older than half the mountains on the East Coast, survived a battle between angelic and demonic forces, and helped rescue a bunch of innocent girls from becoming mindless slaves.

All to get an Alexa without a kill switch.

Of-fucking-course.

But on the bright side...

I was bound to win free shots at trivia night.

VIP's get early access to all sorts of Temple-Verse goodies, including signed copies, private giveaways, and advance notice of future projects. AND A FREE NOVELLA! Join here: www.shaynesilvers.com/l/219800

Turn the page to read a brief excerpt from **OLD FASHIONED**, the third installment of the Phantom Queen Diaries.

Or get the full book online! http://www.shaynesilvers.com/l/207013

SAMPLE: OLD FASHIONED (PHANTOM QUEEN #3)

*T*he vicious pounding of a heavy fist on my apartment door woke me from a bleary-eyed sleep. I groaned, rolled over, and thrust my head under the nearest pillow, begging God to make it stop. But—seeing as how God didn't owe me any favors—the racket continued until I was compelled to plug my ears and swear, for the thousandth time, that I would never, ever, drink again.

Or, you know...drink less, at least.

I clenched my teeth, wondering why on Earth the maids had chosen to ignore the *Do Not Disturb* sign, before I remembered that I was in my own bed and not my Las Vegas hotel room; I'd flown in last night on the red eye after a wild weekend. The wildest weekend, in fact, I'd ever had. And—to put that in perspective—I should mention that my weekends routinely involve life-threatening danger, fucking *magic*, and copious amounts of booze.

But, silver lining, I'd checked a few items off my bucket list I'd never even thought to write down—like mud wrestling dragons, breaking into a Casino vault, fending off a horde of shapeshifting strippers, and dick-punching a celebrity. Fortunately, a great deal of that was fuzzy and half-remembered; I'd rarely found myself doing anything without a drink in hand, courtesy of Sin City's legendary hospitality. Unfortunately, that meant I owed my body 48 cumulative hours' worth of hangover…and the bitch had come to collect.

Basically, I felt like death.

If death had been run over by a trucker, thrown in the back of a tractor trailer transporting diseased animals, and left to rot in a desert until lizards lounged on his sun-bleached bones.

And someone…Wouldn't. Stop. Knocking.

"Fine, alright! I'm fuckin' comin'!" I screamed, my Irish brogue making me sound a lot less grumpy than I rightfully felt—a regrettable side effect of having an accent people dub "sing-songy." To be honest, that's probably why I cussed so much; I got tired of people treating me like a snarling puppy whenever I threw a temper tantrum.

Fun fact: no one calls you cute if you say fuck all the time.

I growled, kicked off my covers, and threw on a long robe; spring had arrived in all its glory a week ago, so I'd begun crashing in a Men's XXL jersey. But at six-feet-tall, and most of that legs, I couldn't afford to answer the door in my nightly attire, no matter how stylish my retro Red Sox jersey was. Not unless I wanted to give someone a show they hadn't paid for.

I shuffled towards the door, but tripped over a small suitcase I'd stolen from my Russian friend, Othello, a world-class hacker and COO of Grimm Tech—a company in Germany that produced, amongst other things, an assortment of toys with magical properties. I cursed and lashed out, kicking it across the room, then froze.

Shit.

I ignored the knocking for a moment and doublechecked to make sure the suitcase was unharmed. Inside was a copper disc that fit in my palm. I only had a rough idea of what it did, because by the time I started quizzing her, all Othello would say was that she was the most brilliant woman alive; she'd had several dozen shots of vodka at that point. Apparently, it was what she called a "galvanizer," whatever that meant. I don't know why I'd taken it, except maybe to poke fun at the most brilliant woman alive for not keeping her shit locked up in a secure vault somewhere.

That's right, just keeping her ego in check, one theft at a time.

Once I knew the case was undamaged, I shoved my hands over my ears to block out the incessant hammering and tried to decide how I would kill whoever was at my door. I had plenty of guns thanks to a special delivery from Death, yes that Death, one of the four Horsemen of the Apocalypse. I could easily whip out a weapon and put a bullet through the door.

Or there was always the good old-fashioned Chuck Norris approach—a windpipe-crushing roundhouse to the throat.

By the time I made it to the door, I was already plotting what I'd do with the body, and what I'd tell the police if I ever got caught. I wasn't sure my "they wouldn't shut the fuck up and leave me alone" defense would be enough to swing the jury. Could having the worst hangover of your life count as an insanity plea? Sadly, once I glanced through the peephole, my meticulously planned murder fell apart.

Because nobody gets off scot-free after killing a *cop*.

I inched open the door, hiding my makeup-less face behind my bangs—a wave of vibrant red that would hopefully distract my visitor from the bags under my red-rimmed eyes. "Jimmy, now's not a great time," I said.

I decidedly avoided mentioning my shenanigan-fueled weekend; I wasn't sure how many laws we'd broken, but—considering the immortal status of some of our attendees—I was willing to bet we'd end up on the far side of 25 to life.

"Get dressed, Quinn. And hurry," Jimmy snapped, his deep baritone rumbling through the crack in my door.

"Excuse ye?" I asked, poking my head out into the hallway, too annoyed by his abrupt tone to care about how wrecked I looked. Detective Jimmy Collins, a former lover and decorated member of the Boston Police Department, loomed over me, his expression cold.

Of course, that probably shouldn't have surprised me; I hadn't seen or spoken to him since an incident a couple of months back in which he'd died in an alternate dimension, only to be brought back to life through the intercession of a god. Since then, he'd definitely given me the cold-shoulder, dodging my phone calls like it was his job. Until, that is, he'd tried reaching out to me last week. Sadly, I'd been a little busy recovering from a coma—the unfortunate result of fighting angels and demons in pursuit of a holy relic that I'd stashed away on a windowsill in my living room.

I know what you're thinking…Vegas probably hadn't been the best convalescence I could have chosen after being officially brain dead for almost a week.

Sue me.

"It's police business," he said, the skin around his eyes tight, his jaw clenched. I ogled the man; I couldn't help it. Jimmy had a face and body fresh from a catalogue—broad shoulders and narrow hips, a strong jawline, and skin so smooth it seemed to emit its own light. He'd grown out his facial hair since I'd seen him last—the beard meticulously faded, offsetting his wide cheekbones.

"Listen," I said, batting my eyes at the not-so-nice detective, "I'll admit t'ings got a wee bit out of hand. But it was all in good fun. We didn't even realize we were stealin' from the mob until after it happened. And, before ye ask, we gave it all back. Even the strippers promised not to press charges, so…" I drifted off as Jimmy's expression shifted from irritation to disapproval. "Um…what sort of police business, did ye say?" I asked, sensing he had no idea what I was talking about.

"I didn't," Jimmy clarified, though I could see the wheels turning in his head.

"Well, ignore all that, then. What can I do for ye?" I asked, sweetly.

"I don't have time for this, Quinn. Get yourself dressed. I'll wait in the hall."

I scowled. "Aren't ye forgettin' somethin'?" I asked. "Like 'hello, Quinn, nice to see ye, sorry for never callin' ye back'?"

"That's not why I'm here," Jimmy said, studying the hallway as though someone might step out at any moment. "Like I said, this is police business. You've been…requested. I tried getting in touch with you for over a week, but you never called me back, so now I'm here to collect you in person."

"Is that why you're actin' like an arse right now?" I asked. "Because I didn't call ye back right away? I was out of town and me phone broke. I planned to call ye back soon."

"Before or after you stole from the mob? And..." Jimmy leaned in, sniffed, and recoiled. "Drank your weight in *Clontarf?*"

I glared at him, then surreptitiously sniffed myself, wondering how Jimmy had picked up on the exact brand of whiskey I'd been drinking all weekend long. I certainly couldn't smell anything, although I wouldn't have expected to; I'd showered and brushed my teeth before going to bed just a few short hours ago. I scowled, trying my best not to think about the fact that he smelt pretty good by comparison, his cologne clean and sweet, like honeysuckle, although there was something else there—the faintest aroma of stale smoke. "I'm a grown woman, Jimmy Collins. If I want to get into trouble and drink with me friends, then that's what I'll do."

Jimmy rolled his eyes. "I don't care what you do or don't do, Quinn. If I had it my way, I wouldn't even be here. But right now, my orders are to take you to a crime scene. So, let's dispense with the pleasantries and move it along."

I ran my tongue across my teeth, trying to contain the mixed emotions I felt welling up inside: anger, frustration, disappointment. "Alright, then," I said, finally. "Ye stay the fuck outside. I'll be out in a minute." I slammed the door in his face, seething and—if I was being honest with myself—more than a little heartbroken. It wasn't like I had crazy high expectations or anything. I mean the man had gone out of his way to avoid me.

But I'd never dreamed our reunion would play out this poorly.

"Did you know that, in America, a divorce occurs every 36 seconds?" a voice, slight and feminine, rang out from my living room.

I sighed.

"No, Eve, I didn't know that," I replied. "But I'm not surprised."

Eve, my spoil of war and budding Tree of Knowledge, liked to impress me with her freakish knowledge of statistics—although I was beginning to suspect that her knowledge bombs came at a price; she often spouted out whatever information she thought was most applicable at the time, regardless of the social consequences.

"Did you know individuals between the ages of 18 and 29 generally have sex 112 times a year? That equals a little more than twice a week. What happens if you go longer than the average span, do you think? Are you feeling ill? Anxious, maybe?"

I turned on the shower and fetched a towel from my room, ignoring the pernicious houseplant.

"Did you know—"

"Did ye know that baby trees make the best firewood?" I fired back, before she could finish.

Eve was silent, and, for a moment, I thought my not-so-veiled threat might have finally shut her up. I stepped into the shower.

"I don't think your source is credible!" she called out.

I groaned.

Get the book online! http://www.shaynesilvers.com/l/207013

*Turn the page to read a sample of **OBSIDIAN SON** - Nate Temple Book 1 - or **BUY ONLINE (FREE with Kindle Unlimited subscription)**. Nate Temple is a billionaire wizard from St. Louis. He rides a bloodthirsty unicorn and drinks with the Four Horsemen. He even cow-tipped the Minotaur. Once...*

TRY: OBSIDIAN SON (NATE TEMPLE #1)

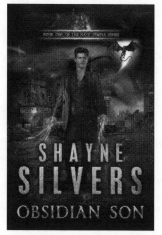

*T*here was no room for emotion in a hate crime. I had to be cold. Heartless. This was just another victim. Nothing more. No face, no name.

Frosted blades of grass crunched under my feet, sounding to my ears like the symbolic glass that one would shatter under a napkin at a Jewish wedding. The noise would have threatened to give away my stealthy advance as I stalked through the moonlit field, but I was no novice and had planned accordingly. Being a wizard, I was able to muffle all sensory evidence with a fine cloud of magic—no sounds, and no smells. Nifty. But if I made the spell much stronger, the anomaly would be too obvious to my prey.

I knew the consequences for my dark deed tonight. If caught, jail time or possibly even a gruesome, painful death. But if I succeeded, the look of fear and surprise in my victim's eyes before his world collapsed around him, it was well worth the risk. I simply couldn't help myself; I had to take him down.

I knew the cops had been keeping tabs on my car, but I was confident that they hadn't followed me. I hadn't seen a tail on my way here but seeing as how they frowned on this kind of thing, I had taken a circuitous route just in case. I was safe. I hoped.

Then my phone chirped at me as I received a text.

I practically jumped out of my skin, hissing instinctively. "Motherf—" I cut off abruptly, remembering the whole stealth aspect of my mission. I was off to a stellar start. I had forgotten to silence the damned phone. *Stupid, stupid, stupid!*

My heart felt like it was on the verge of exploding inside my chest with such thunderous violence that I briefly envisioned a mystifying Rorschach blood-blot that would have made coroners and psychologists drool.

My body remained tense as I swept my gaze over the field, fearing that I had been made. Precious seconds ticked by without any change in my surroundings, and my breathing finally began to slow as my pulse returned to normal. Hopefully, my magic had muted the phone and my resulting outburst. I glanced down at the phone to scan the text and then typed back a quick and angry response before I switched the cursed device to vibrate.

Now, where were we?

I continued on, the lining of my coat constricting my breathing. Or maybe it was because I was leaning forward in anticipation. *Breathe*, I chided myself. *He doesn't know you're here.* All this risk for a book. It had better be worth it.

I'm taller than most, and not abnormally handsome, but I knew how to play the genetic cards I had been dealt. I had shaggy, dirty blonde hair—leaning more towards brown with each passing year—and my frame was thick with well-earned muscle, yet I was still lean. I had once been told that my eyes were like twin emeralds pitted against the golden-brown tufts of my hair—a face like a jewelry box. Of course, that was two bottles of wine into a date, so I could have been a little foggy on her quote. Still, I liked to imagine that was how everyone saw me.

But tonight, all that was masked by magic.

I grinned broadly as the outline of the hairy hulk finally came into view. He was blessedly alone—no nearby sentries to give me away. That was always a risk when performing this ancient rite-of-passage. I tried to keep the grin on my face from dissolving into a maniacal cackle.

My skin danced with energy, both natural and unnatural, as I manipulated the threads of magic floating all around me. My victim stood just ahead, oblivious to the world of hurt that I was about to unleash. Even with his millennia of experience, he didn't stand a chance. I had done this so many times that the routine of it was my only enemy. I lost count of how many times I had been told not to do it again; those who knew declared it *cruel, evil, and sadistic*. But what fun wasn't? Regardless, that wasn't enough to stop me from doing it again. And again. And again.

It was an addiction.

The pungent smell of manure filled the air, latching onto my nostril hairs. I took another step, trying to calm my racing pulse. A glint of gold reflected in the silver moonlight, but my victim remained motionless, hopefully unaware or all was lost. I wouldn't make it out alive if he knew I was here. Timing was everything.

I carefully took the last two steps, a lifetime between each, watching the legendary monster's ears, anxious and terrified that I would catch even so much as a twitch in my direction. Seeing nothing, a fierce grin split my unshaven cheeks. My spell had worked! I raised my palms an inch away from their target, firmly planted my feet, and squared my shoulders. I took one silent, calming breath, and then heaved forward with every ounce of physical strength I could muster. As well as a teensy-weensy boost of magic. Enough to goose him good.

"*MOOO!!!*" The sound tore through the cool October night like an unstoppable freight train. *Thud-splat!* The beast collapsed sideways onto the frosted grass; straight into a steaming patty of cow shit, cow dung, or, if you really wanted to church it up, a Meadow Muffin. But to me, shit is, and always will be, shit.

Cow tipping. It doesn't get any better than that in Missouri.

Especially when you're tipping the *Minotaur*. Capital M. I'd tipped plenty of ordinary cows before, but never the legendary variety.

Razor-blade hooves tore at the frozen earth as the beast struggled to stand, his grunts of rage vibrating the air. I raised my arms triumphantly. "Boo-yah! Temple 1, Minotaur 0!" I crowed. Then I very bravely prepared to protect myself. Some people just couldn't take a joke. *Cruel, evil,* and *sadistic* cow tipping may be, but by hell, it was a *rush.* The legendary beast turned his gaze on me after gaining his feet, eyes ablaze as his body...*shifted* from his bull disguise into his notorious, well-known bipedal form. He unfolded to his full height on two tree trunk-thick legs, his hooves having magically transformed into heavily booted feet. The thick, gold ring dangling from his snotty snout quivered as the Minotaur panted, and his dense, corded muscles contracted over his now human-like chest. As I stared up into those brown eyes, I actually felt sorry...for, well, myself.

"I have killed greater men than you for lesser offense," he growled.

His voice sounded like an angry James Earl Jones—like Mufasa talking to Scar.

"You have shit on your shoulder, Asterion." I ignited a roiling ball of fire in my palm in order to see his eyes more clearly. By no means was it a defensive gesture on my part. It was just dark. Under the weight of his glare, I somehow managed to keep my face composed, even though my fraudu-lent, self-denial had curled up into the fetal position and started whimper-ing. I hoped using a form of his ancient name would give me brownie points. Or maybe just not-worthy-of-killing points.

The beast grunted, eyes tightening, and I sensed the barest hesitation. "Nate Temple...your name would look splendid on my already long list of slain idiots." Asterion took a threatening step forward, and I thrust out my palm in warning, my roiling flame blue now.

"You lost fair and square, Asterion. Yield or perish." The beast's shoul-ders sagged slightly. Then he finally nodded to himself in resignation, appraising me with the scrutiny of a worthy adversary. "Your time comes, Temple, but I will grant you this. You've got a pair of stones on you to rival Hercules."

I reflexively glanced in the direction of the myth's own crown jewels before jerking my gaze away. Some things you simply couldn't un-see. "Well, I won't be needing a wheelbarrow any time soon, but overcompen-sating today keeps future lower-back pain away."

The Minotaur blinked once, and then he bellowed out a deep, conta-gious, snorting laughter. Realizing I wasn't about to become a murder statistic, I couldn't help but join in. It felt good. It had been a while since I had allowed myself to experience genuine laughter.

In the harsh moonlight, his bulk was even more intimidating as he towered head and shoulders above me. This was the beast that had fed upon human sacrifices for countless years while imprisoned in Daedalus' Labyrinth in Greece. And all that protein had not gone to waste, forming a heavily woven musculature over the beast's body that made even Mr. Olympia look puny.

From the neck up, he was now entirely bull, but the rest of his body more closely resembled a thickly furred man. But, as shown moments ago, he could adapt his form to his environment, never appearing fully human, but able to make his entire form appear as a bull when necessary. For instance, how he had looked just before I tipped him. Maybe he had been scouting the field for heifers before I had so efficiently killed the mood.

His bull face was also covered in thick, coarse hair—he even sported a long, wavy beard of sorts, and his eyes were the deepest brown I had ever seen. Cow-shit brown. His snout jutted out, emphasizing the golden ring dangling from his glistening nostrils, and both glinted in the luminous glow of the moon. The metal was at least an inch thick and etched with runes of a language long forgotten. Wide, aged ivory horns sprouted from each temple, long enough to skewer a wizard with little effort. He was nude except for a massive beaded necklace and a pair of worn leather boots that were big enough to stomp a size twenty-five imprint in my face if he felt so inclined.

I hoped our blossoming friendship wouldn't end that way. I really did.

Because friends didn't let friends wear boots naked...

Get your copy of OBSIDIAN SON online today!
http://www.shaynesilvers.com/l/38474

Shayne has written a few other books without Cameron helping him. Some of them are marginally decent—easily a 4 out of 10.

Turn the page to read a sample of **UNCHAINED** *- Feathers and Fire Series Book 1,* *or* **BUY ONLINE (FREE with Kindle Unlimited subscription).** *Callie Penrose is a wizard in Kansas City, MO who hunts monsters for the Vatican. She meets Nate Temple, and things devolve from there...*

(Note: Callie appears in the TempleVerse after Nate's book 6, TINY GODS...Full chronology of all books in the TempleVerse shown on the 'Books by the authors' page)

TRY: UNCHAINED (FEATHERS AND FIRE #1)

*T*he rain pelted my hair, plastering loose strands of it to my forehead as I panted, eyes darting from tree to tree, terrified of each shifting branch, splash of water, and whistle of wind slipping through the nightscape around us. But… I was somewhat *excited*, too.

Somewhat.

"Easy, girl. All will be well," the big man creeping just ahead of me, murmured.

"You said we were going to get ice cream!" I hissed at him, failing to compose myself, but careful to keep my voice low and my eyes alert. "I'm not ready for this!" I had been trained to fight, with my hands, with weapons, and with my magic. But I had never taken an active role in a hunt before. I'd always been the getaway driver for my mentor.

The man grunted, grey eyes scanning the trees as he slipped through the tall grass. "And did we not get ice cream before coming here? Because I think I see some in your hair."

"You know what I mean, Roland. You tricked me." I checked the tips of my loose hair, saw nothing, and scowled at his back.

"The Lord does not give us a greater burden than we can shoulder."

I muttered dark things under my breath, wiping the water from my eyes. Again. My new shirt was going to be ruined. Silk never fared well in the rain. My choice of shoes wasn't much better. Boots, yes, but distressed, *fashionable* boots. Not work boots designed for the rain and mud. Definitely not monster hunting boots for our evening excursion through one of Kansas City's wooded parks. I realized I was forcibly distracting myself, keeping my mind busy with mundane thoughts to avoid my very real anxiety. Because whenever I grew nervous, an imagined nightmare always—

A church looming before me. Rain pouring down. Night sky and a glowing moon overhead. I was all alone. Crying on the cold, stone steps, an infant in a cardboard box—

I forced the nightmare away, breathing heavily. "You know I hate it when you talk like that," I whispered to him, trying to regain my composure. I wasn't angry with him, but was growing increasingly uncomfortable with our situation after my brief flashback of fear.

"Doesn't mean it shouldn't be said," he said kindly. "I think we're close. Be alert. Remember your training. Banish your fears. I am here. And the Lord is here. He always is."

So, he had noticed my sudden anxiety. "Maybe I should just go back to the car. I know I've trained, but I really don't think—"

A shape of fur, fangs, and claws launched from the shadows towards me, cutting off my words as it snarled, thirsty for my blood.

And my nightmare slipped back into my thoughts like a veiled assassin, a wraith hoping to hold me still for the monster to eat. I froze, unable to move. Twin sticks of power abruptly erupted into being in my clenched fists, but my fear swamped me with that stupid nightmare, the sticks held at my side, useless to save me.

Right before the beast's claws reached me, it grunted as something batted it from the air, sending it flying sideways. It struck a tree with another grunt and an angry whine of pain.

I fell to my knees right into a puddle, arms shaking, breathing fast.

My sticks crackled in the rain like live cattle prods, except their entire length was the electrical section — at least to anyone other than me. I could hold them without pain.

Magic was a part of me, coursing through my veins whether I wanted it or not, and Roland had spent many years teaching me how to master it. But I had never been able to fully master the nightmare inside me, and in moments of fear, it always won, overriding my training.

The fact that I had resorted to weapons — like the ones he had trained me with — rather than a burst of flame, was startling. It was good in the fact that my body's reflexes knew enough to call up a defense even without my direct command, but bad in the fact that it was the worst form of defense for the situation presented. I could have very easily done as Roland did, and hurt it from a distance. But I hadn't. Because of my stupid block.

Roland placed a calloused palm on my shoulder, and I flinched. "Easy, see? I am here." But he did frown at my choice of weapons, the reprimand silent but loud in my mind. I let out a shaky breath, forcing my fear back down. It was all in my head, but still, it wasn't easy. Fear could be like that.

I focused on Roland's implied lesson. Close combat weapons — even magically-powered ones — were for last resorts. I averted my eyes in very real shame. I knew these things. He didn't even need to tell me them. But when that damned nightmare caught hold of me, all my training went out the window. It haunted me like a shadow, waiting for moments just like this, as if trying to kill me. A form of psychological suicide? But it was why I constantly refused to join Roland on his hunts. He knew about it. And although he was trying to help me overcome that fear, he never pressed too hard.

Rain continued to sizzle as it struck my batons. I didn't let them go, using them as a totem to build my confidence back up. I slowly lifted my eyes to nod at him as I climbed back to my feet.

That's when I saw the second set of eyes in the shadows, right before they flew out of the darkness towards Roland's back. I threw one of my batons and missed, but that pretty much let Roland know that an unfriendly was behind him. Either that or I had just failed to murder my mentor at point-blank range. He whirled to confront the monster, expecting another aerial assault as he unleashed a ball of fire that splashed over the tree at chest height, washing the trunk in blue flames. But this monster was tricky. It hadn't planned on tackling Roland, but had merely jumped out of the darkness to get closer, no doubt learning from its fallen comrade, who still lay unmoving against the tree behind me.

His coat shone like midnight clouds with hints of lightning flashing in the depths of thick, wiry fur. The coat of dew dotting his fur reflected the moonlight, giving him a faint sheen as if covered in fresh oil. He was tall, easily hip height at the shoulder, and barrel chested, his rump much leaner than the rest of his body. He — I assumed male from the long, thick mane around his neck — had a very long snout, much longer and wider than any werewolf I had ever seen. Amazingly, and beyond my control, I realized he was beautiful.

But most of the natural world's lethal hunters were beautiful.

He landed in a wet puddle a pace in front of Roland, juked to the right, and then to the left, racing past the big man, biting into his hamstrings on his way by.

A wash of anger rolled over me at seeing my mentor injured, dousing my fear, and I swung my baton down as hard as I could. It struck the beast in the rump as it tried to dart back to cover — a typical wolf tactic. My blow singed his hair and shattered bone. The creature collapsed into a puddle of mud with a yelp, instinctively snapping his jaws over his shoulder to bite whatever had hit him.

I let him. But mostly out of dumb luck as I heard Roland hiss in pain, falling to the ground.

The monster's jaws clamped around my baton, and there was an immediate explosion of teeth and blood that sent him flying several feet away into the tall brush, yipping, screaming, and staggering. Before he slipped out of sight, I noticed that his lower jaw was simply *gone*, from the contact of his saliva on my electrified magical batons. Then he managed to limp into the woods with more pitiful yowls, but I had no mind to chase him. Roland — that titan of a man, my mentor — was hurt. I could smell copper in the air, and knew we had to get out of here. Fast. Because we had anticipated only one of the monsters. But there had been two of them, and they hadn't been the run-of-the-mill werewolves we had been warned about. If there were two, perhaps there were more. And they were evidently the prehistoric cousin of any werewolf I had ever seen or read about.

Roland hissed again as he stared down at his leg, growling with both pain and anger. My eyes darted back to the first monster, wary of another attack. It *almost* looked like a werewolf, but bigger. Much bigger. He didn't move, but I saw he was breathing. He had a notch in his right ear and a jagged scar on his long snout. Part of me wanted to go over to him and torture him. Slowly. Use his pain to finally drown my nightmare, my fear. The fear that had caused Roland's injury. My lack of inner-strength had not only put me in danger, but had hurt my mentor, my friend.

I shivered, forcing the thought away. That was *cold*. Not me. Sure, I was no stranger to fighting, but that had always been in a ring. Practicing. Sparring. Never life or death.

But I suddenly realized something very dark about myself in the chill, rainy night. Although I was terrified, I felt a deep ocean of anger manifest inside me, wanting only to dispense justice as I saw fit. To use that rage to battle my own demons. As if feeding one would starve the other, reminding me of the Cherokee Indian Legend Roland had once told me.

An old Cherokee man was teaching his grandson about life. "A fight is going on inside me," he told the boy. "It is a terrible fight between two wolves. One is evil — he is anger, envy, sorrow, regret, greed, arrogance, self-pity, guilt, resentment, inferiority, lies, false pride, superiority, and ego." After a few moments to make sure he had the boy's undivided attention, he continued.

"The other wolf is good — he is joy, peace, love, hope, serenity, humility, kindness, benevolence, empathy, generosity, truth, compassion, and faith. The same fight is going on inside of you, boy, and inside of every other person, too."

The grandson thought about this for a few minutes before replying. "Which wolf will win?"

The old Cherokee man simply said, "The one you feed, boy. The one you feed..."

And I felt like feeding one of my wolves today, by killing this one...

Get the full book ONLINE! http://www.shaynesilvers.com/l/38952

MAKE A DIFFERENCE

Reviews are the most powerful tools in our arsenal when it comes to getting attention for our books. Much as we'd like to, we don't have the financial muscle of a New York publisher.

But we do have something much more powerful and effective than that, and it's something that those publishers would kill to get their hands on.

A committed and loyal bunch of readers.

Honest reviews of our books help bring them to the attention of other readers.

If you've enjoyed this book, we would be very grateful if you could spend just five minutes leaving a review on our book's Amazon page.

Thank you very much in advance.

ACKNOWLEDGMENTS

From Cameron:

I'd like to thank Shayne, for paving the way in style. Kori, for an introduction that would change my life. My three wonderful sisters, for showing me what a strong, independent woman looks and sounds like. And, above all, my parents, for—literally—everything.

From Shayne:

Team Temple and the Den of Freaks on Facebook have become family to me. I couldn't do it without die-hard readers like them.

I would also like to thank you, the reader. I hope you enjoyed reading *COSMOPOLITAN* as much as we enjoyed writing it. Be sure to check out the two crossover series in the TempleVerse: **The Nate Temple Series** and the **Feathers and Fire Series**.

And last, but definitely not least, I thank my wife, Lexy. Without your support, none of this would have been possible.

ABOUT CAMERON O'CONNELL

Cameron O'Connell is a Jack-of-All-Trades and Master of Some.

He writes The Phantom Queen Diaries, a series in The TempleVerse, about Quinn MacKenna, a mouthy black magic arms dealer trading favors in Boston. All she wants? A round-trip ticket to the Fae realm...and maybe a drink on the house.

A former member of the United States military, a professional model, and English teacher, Cameron finds time to write in the mornings after his first cup of coffee...and in the evenings after his thirty-seventh. Follow him, and the TempleVerse founder, Shayne Silvers, online for all sorts of insider tips, giveaways, and new release updates!

Get Down with Cameron Online

facebook.com/Cameron-OConnell-788806397985289
amazon.com/author/cameronoconnell
bookbub.com/authors/cameron-o-connell
twitter.com/thecamoconnell
instagram.com/camoconnellauthor
goodreads.com/cameronoconnell

ABOUT SHAYNE SILVERS

Shayne is a man of mystery and power, whose power is exceeded only by his mystery...

He currently writes the Amazon Bestselling **Nate Temple** Series, which features a foul-mouthed wizard from St. Louis. He rides a bloodthirsty unicorn, drinks with Achilles, and is pals with the Four Horsemen.

He also writes the Amazon Bestselling **Feathers and Fire** Series—a second series in the TempleVerse. The story follows a rookie spell-slinger named Callie Penrose who works for the Vatican in Kansas City. Her problem? Hell seems to know more about her past than she does.

He coauthors **The Phantom Queen Diaries**—a third series set in The TempleVerse—with Cameron O'Connell. The story follows Quinn MacKenna, a mouthy black magic arms dealer in Boston. All she wants? A round-trip ticket to the Fae realm...and maybe a drink on the house.

He also writes the **Shade of Devil Series**, which tells the story of Sorin Ambrogio—the world's FIRST vampire. He was put into a magical slumber by a Native American Medicine Man when the Americas were first discovered by Europeans. Sorin wakes up after five-hundred years to learn that his protege, Dracula, stole his reputation and that no one has ever even heard of Sorin Ambrogio. The streets of New York City will run with blood as Sorin reclaims his legend.

Shayne holds two high-ranking black belts, and can be found writing in a coffee shop, cackling madly into his computer screen while pounding shots of espresso. He's hard at work on the newest books in the TempleVerse—You can find updates on new releases or chronological reading order on the next page, his website, or any of his social media accounts. **Follow him online for all sorts of groovy goodies, giveaways, and new release updates:**

Get Down with Shayne Online
www.shaynesilvers.com
info@shaynesilvers.com

facebook.com/shaynesilversfanpage
amazon.com/author/shaynesilvers
bookbub.com/profile/shayne-silvers
instagram.com/shaynesilversofficial
twitter.com/shaynesilvers
goodreads.com/ShayneSilvers

BOOKS BY THE AUTHORS

CHRONOLOGY: All stories in the TempleVerse are shown in chronological order on the following page

PHANTOM QUEEN DIARIES

(Set in the TempleVerse)

by Cameron O'Connell & Shayne Silvers

COLLINS (Prequel novella #0 in the 'LAST CALL' anthology)

WHISKEY GINGER

COSMOPOLITAN

OLD FASHIONED

MOTHERLUCKER (Novella #3.5 in the 'LAST CALL' anthology)

DARK AND STORMY

MOSCOW MULE

WITCHES BREW

SALTY DOG

SEA BREEZE

HURRICANE

NATE TEMPLE SERIES

(Main series in the TempleVerse)

by Shayne Silvers

FAIRY TALE - FREE prequel novella #0 for my subscribers

OBSIDIAN SON

BLOOD DEBTS

GRIMM

SILVER TONGUE

BEAST MASTER

BEERLYMPIAN (Novella #5.5 in the 'LAST CALL' anthology)

TINY GODS

DADDY DUTY (Novella #6.5)

WILD SIDE

WAR HAMMER

NINE SOULS

HORSEMAN

LEGEND

KNIGHTMARE

ASCENSION

FEATHERS AND FIRE SERIES

(Also set in the TempleVerse)

by Shayne Silvers

UNCHAINED

RAGE

WHISPERS

ANGEL'S ROAR

MOTHERLUCKER (Novella #4.5 in the 'LAST CALL' anthology)

SINNER

BLACK SHEEP

GODLESS

CHRONOLOGICAL ORDER: TEMPLEVERSE

FAIRY TALE (TEMPLE PREQUEL)

OBSIDIAN SON (TEMPLE 1)

BLOOD DEBTS (TEMPLE 2)

GRIMM (TEMPLE 3)

SILVER TONGUE (TEMPLE 4)

BEAST MASTER (TEMPLE 5)

BEERLYMPIAN (TEMPLE 5.5)

TINY GODS (TEMPLE 6)

DADDY DUTY (TEMPLE NOVELLA 6.5)

UNCHAINED (FEATHERS... 1)

RAGE (FEATHERS... 2)

WILD SIDE (TEMPLE 7)

WAR HAMMER (TEMPLE 8)

WHISPERS (FEATHERS... 3)

COLLINS (PHANTOM 0)

WHISKEY GINGER (PHANTOM... 1)

NINE SOULS (TEMPLE 9)

COSMOPOLITAN (PHANTOM... 2)

ANGEL'S ROAR (FEATHERS... 4)

MOTHERLUCKER (FEATHERS 4.5, PHANTOM 3.5)

OLD FASHIONED (PHANTOM...3)

HORSEMAN (TEMPLE 10)

DARK AND STORMY (PHANTOM... 4)

MOSCOW MULE (PHANTOM...5)

SINNER (FEATHERS...5)

WITCHES BREW (PHANTOM...6)

LEGEND (TEMPLE...11)

SALTY DOG (PHANTOM...7)

BLACK SHEEP (FEATHERS...6)

GODLESS (FEATHERS...7)

KNIGHTMARE (TEMPLE 12)

ASCENSION (TEMPLE 13)

SEA BREEZE (PHANTOM...8)

HURRICANE (PHANTOM...9)

SHADE OF DEVIL SERIES

(Not part of the TempleVerse)

by Shayne Silvers

DEVIL'S DREAM

DEVIL'S CRY
DEVIL'S BLOOD

Made in the USA
Middletown, DE
04 August 2020